Faces in the Fire

Also by T. L. Hines

The Unseen

Waking Lazarus

The Dead Whisper On

Faces in the Fire

T.L. Hines

THOMAS NELSON
Since 1798

NASHVILLE   DALLAS   MEXICO CITY   RIO DE JANEIRO   BEIJING

Published in Nashville, Tennessee, by Thomas Nelson. Thomas Nelson is a registered trademark of Thomas Nelson, Inc.

Thomas Nelson titles may be purchased in bulk for educational, business, fund-raising, or sales promotional use. For information, please e-mail SpecialMarkets@ThomasNelson.com.

Published in association with the literary agency of Alive Communications, Inc., 7680 Goddard Street, Suite 200, Colorado Springs, CO 80920. www.alivecommunications.com.

Publisher's Note: This novel is a work of fiction. Names, characters, places, and incidents are either products of the author's imagination or used fictitiously. All characters are fictional, and any similarity to people living or dead is purely coincidental.

Library of Congress Cataloging-in-Publication Data

Hines, T. L.
    Faces in the fire / T.L. Hines.
        p. cm.
    ISBN 978-1-59554-453-7 (softcover)
    1. Psychics—Fiction. 2. Montana—Fiction. I. Title.
PS3608.I5726F33 2009
813'.6—dc22   2009012368

Printed in the United States of America

09 10 11 12 13 RRD 5 4 3 2 1

For anyone who has ever had to
face the fire

First Stanza

Cloth Ghost

The dead man's shoes spoke to Kurt long before he wore them.

He expected the shoes to say something, of course; Kurt had hundreds of articles of clothing from the dearly departed, a wardrobe of wearable ghosts that fueled his existence. It wasn't unusual, when browsing estate sales, to find a jacket whispering of adulterous affairs, a pair of slacks sobbing uncontrollably about financial ruin. While searching through the piles of belongings at these sales, Kurt heard the constant babble of past lies and past lives rising from the tables where the clothing lay neatly folded.

So he wasn't surprised to find shoes with something to say. But while most of the clothing spoke to him in words, in plaintive voices tinged with desperation, these shoes spoke a single, simple image: a catfish.

It started as a white dot on the horizon, floating in a vast expanse of orange. But the dot moved, coming closer and closer, until at last the dot took its fish form, its continual back-and-forth sweeps of the tail coming into focus. Finally, as the catfish filled the entire slate of his mind, Kurt absently set down the light-tan sweater he'd been holding and turned his attention to the shoes.

The sweater had been quiet. Or maybe it hadn't been. But if it said anything, its voice was drowned out by the image the shoes pushed his way.

A catfish. What did that mean?

The scene began to loop again, and Kurt moved to touch the shoes. When he did, the image in his mind became a bit more vibrant, a bit more dimensional.

"Good stuff, huh?"

Kurt swiveled his head in the direction of the voice, the catfish momentarily dissolving as his concentration broke. A short man stood next to him, riffling through the folded clothes of lot 159; a scruffy beard concealed most of his face.

"Sorry," Kurt said, trying to force a smile into his voice. "I didn't catch that."

The bearded guy picked up the tan sweater Kurt had just been holding, examined it a few moments, began refolding it. He finally looked at Kurt. "Good stuff here. Guy left lots of stuff."

"Oh," Kurt said, feeling as if his mind were in a slower gear than usual. "Yeah. Sure."

And even as he tried to sift through the rest of lot 159, an assortment of clothing left by a dead man to scavengers at an estate sale, one item continued to speak to him.

The shoes.

Sending him the flickering scenes of the catfish, swimming against the murky current of his mind.

THIR**39**. NINE

That evening, after paying just fifty dollars for the entire lot (the bearded guy, for all his talk about the quality of lot 159, didn't offer a single bid), Kurt unlocked the rolling doors of his workshop.

He'd already sealed all the clothing from lot 159—shoes, shirts, slacks—in a plastic storage container, and now he carried the container to another door on the back wall of his workshop. He paused to unlock this door as well, then pushed it open and flipped the light switch that illuminated a single overhead bulb.

Cold storage. That's what he called this room. It was the size of a single garage stall—had once been a garage stall, in fact—but it held no vehicles. Instead, giant storage bins just like the one that now held lot 159 filled the entire room, stacked floor to ceiling.

The room remained unheated because there was no reason to heat it. Quite the opposite, really, because cold—especially the frosty autumn and winter nights here in western Montana—fueled the fears, the ghosts, that spoke to him. The fears and ghosts that fed his work.

After all, not every piece of clothing was haunted by the ghost of the person who wore it. Far from it. Perhaps only one out of every twenty pieces had something to say. Putting the clothing in cold storage, keeping it in isolation, tended to amplify the voices caught inside the folds of denim or cotton or silk or wool.

Kurt paused at the door, glancing up at the noticeable flicker in the bulb overhead. It swung slightly on its bare, corroded cord, rocked by a gentle breeze that wasn't there.

From inside the plastic storage containers stacked around him, Kurt heard murmurs. Whispers. Chatters. Even a few screams. No more than a dozen distinct voices in all, out of the hundreds of articles of clothing neatly tucked away into this space. And even now, not amplified by cold storage or isolation, the shoes were projecting images of the catfish in his mind, a movie to accompany the cacophonous sound-track of the voices.

He shuddered.

Kurt didn't *want* to confine ghosts of the dead in cold storage. He didn't want to hear them scream or suffer. He didn't want any of this.

And yet he knew this was what he had to do. It was his task, to listen to these ghosts of the present, because he could never hear the ghosts of his past—the past that stretched beyond truck driving school, beyond his therapy sessions with Todd almost eight years ago.

The invisible past that haunted him more than any of the ghosts ever could.

15.

Kurt sat, nervously tapping his foot against the floor as he waited to meet the therapist for the first time.

He'd graduate from the High Road Truck Driving School soon. Then he could apply to trucking firms all over the country, firms always searching for new drivers. He could go anywhere and start his career. Maybe eventually buy a rig of his own.

Eventually.

But right now, he was here because . . . well, he'd let the therapist decide that. That's what therapists did, didn't they? They listened to your secrets, nodded their heads appreciatively, and told you what was wrong with you. End of story.

So that's why he was here. Not really for the end of the story but for the beginning of it. That was the Great Secret he was going to have to admit to the therapist, something he'd not mentioned to any of the other students at the driving school, something he'd not mentioned to any of the trucking firms trying to recruit him.

In fact, the only person who knew was Marcus, the one instructor who had become something of a friend. One night, after a few beers with Marcus, Kurt had blurted his secret confession. Slowly, hesitantly at first, but then in a torrent as Marcus listened.

After he'd finished his story, Marcus had taken the last swig of his draft, nodded, looked at him, and given him the names of two people. One a private detective and the other a therapist.

So he'd called the therapist. Later, he might be able to call the private detective. But not yet.

Kurt smiled, thinking of the incongruity of Marcus, a stereotypically big, beefy guy with a shaved head and a pointed Vandyke beard, telling him about a therapist. Swigging that last drink of beer? Yeah, Marcus looked natural doing that. But Marcus would look decidedly out of place sitting here, in this room, surrounded by soft flute music and burning incense, waiting to talk to a therapist about his past.

The way Kurt was waiting now.

The door at the back of the waiting room opened, and a pink-faced woman walked in. She stopped a moment, stared at Kurt intently, then moved quickly through the waiting room and to the door to the outside, her arms wrapped tightly against her.

"Mr. Marlowe?"

Kurt turned his attention back to the doorway the woman had emerged from, now filled by a tall, lanky man with dirty-blond, shoulder-length hair.

Kurt stood. "Yeah."

"You ready?"

"Okay. Yeah, sure." Kurt walked across the waiting room. The lanky man waited for him to approach and held out his hand. "I'm Todd Michael Greene," he said. "Just call me Todd."

Kurt stood awkwardly for a moment, then shook hands. "I'm Kurt."

Todd backed into the darkened room, swept his arm as an invitation to enter. "Have a seat."

Kurt looked at the small couch. "Just sit?" he asked.

Todd smiled. "Lie down, if you like. I get that a lot."

Kurt moved to the sofa, sat, started tapping his foot on the floor again.

Todd moved to a small desk in the corner, opened a folder, and looked through it a few moments. While he read, Kurt scanned the office. Nothing expensive; not what he'd imagined. He'd expected heavy furnishings of burled walnut in dark tones. Instead, he saw particle-board shelving units holding several books. At least the books had the kinds of titles he'd expect, tomes about relationships and couples and depression. A couple thick books that seemed to be drug references.

Todd's desk was clean and neat, almost bare. A framed photo, turned away from Kurt, faced the office chair where Todd sat. Still reading.

"So Marcus recommended you?" Todd finally asked, keeping the folder at his desk open and looking at Kurt.

Kurt cast his eyes toward the floor. "Yeah."

"I've known Marcus for a long time. He's a good man."

"Yeah."

Todd smiled, pushed his way back from the desk, rolling on the chair's wheels. "We're off to a strong start."

Kurt looked up again. "Yeah." He returned the smile.

"Okay, you mind if I call you Kurt?"

"No. I mean, sure. Call me Kurt."

"You want a drink?" He rolled the chair over to a dorm-sized refrigerator on the floor. "Afraid I don't have anything harder than your basic Pepsi."

"Diet?" Kurt asked.

"Sure."

Todd retrieved a Diet Pepsi from the refrigerator, rolled back with it. "Ice?"

"No, no, that's good."

Todd rolled back a few feet without retreating behind the desk, and watched while Kurt took his first drink.

"Thanks," Kurt mumbled. He noticed his foot was tapping the hardwood floor a little too loudly and made himself stop.

"Nice gloves," Todd began.

Kurt looked at the driving gloves on his hands. "Yeah."

"Care to elaborate?"

"Driving gloves. Good for . . . um . . . driving."

Todd smiled. "But you're not driving right now."

"I guess not."

"You wear them all the time?"

"Pretty much."

"Why's that?"

Kurt shrugged again. "They make me feel better."

Todd nodded again. "Nothing wrong with that at all." He paused. "Tell me why you're here, Kurt."

"Well, like you said, because Marcus gave me your name."

"Okay. But more than that. You're here to talk, obviously. Maybe find some answers?"

"Yeah."

"So before we find the answers, we have to look at the questions."

"Okay." Kurt took a deep breath, raised the can of soda to his lips and drank again, then exhaled. "I . . . uh . . . don't know who I am."

Todd said nothing, so Kurt rushed to fill the silence. "I mean, beyond the last six months. I'm . . . I guess you could say I have amnesia."

Todd nodded thoughtfully, pushed himself up, and wrapped one leg under him. A casual pose in his OfficeMax chair. "Well, we'll just start by exploring that. Six months, you say?"

"Roughly. About the time I came to California, really."

"And where were you before?"

Kurt smiled grimly. "You tell me."

"So you have no memories before . . ."

"Before truck driving school."

"What about your childhood? Where you grew up, went to school, that kind of thing?"

"Nothing."

"But you're able to form new memories."

"What do you mean?"

"Well, during your trucking school, for instance. You remember what you learned there without any problems, who you met."

"Oh. Sure."

Todd seemed to be considering a deep question.

"I know it's crazy," Kurt said. "But that's why I'm here, huh?" He nervously took another sip of his Diet Pepsi. "Because I'm crazy."

"I'd like to send you to a friend—an MD—for some scans and other tests to start with, Kurt. But the answer to your question is: it's not crazy at all." He cleared his throat. "Most people have no idea who they are."

40.

Bright and early in the morning, Kurt opened his workshop. He'd been plagued by dreams during the night, dreams of his old sessions with Todd. Not nightmares, really, because the sessions with Todd had never been nightmarish.

But uncomfortable. Thoughts of those sessions still made something inside him twist in fear, even after seven or eight years.

He shook off the dust of his dreams, concentrated instead on the locked door at the back of his workshop. Instantly the shoes began transmitting the catfish bathed in orange, but Kurt ignored the image. The shoes hadn't been properly amplified yet, hadn't been kept in storage to distill their message.

Instead he focused on a woman's thin wail emanating from a storage container on the bottom level. He slid away the four containers stacked on top of it, then removed the lid. The smell of mothballs assaulted his nostrils. Not uncommon with clothing picked up at estate sales; often the clothes were packed away in steamer trunks, sprinkled with ancient mothballs.

The wail sounded louder, unfiltered now. Kurt paused, as if gathering his energy, then began to dig through the carefully folded clothing, eventually coming to the silk dress he knew was the source of the wail.

He pulled the dress from the container, placed it carefully on a wall hook, took his time replacing the clothing in the receptacle, resealing it, and restacking the other containers on top.

All the while, the dress continued its lament, even as he gingerly picked it up, brought it into his main workshop, and set it down on a small folding table.

"Find my sister," the dress whispered inside his mind between sobs. "Just find her and let her know . . . I'm . . ." The voice haunting the silk dissolved into a series of sobs again and finally went quiet for a few moments.

This whispered pleading was what he typically heard from ghost clothing: voices in search of lost loves, families longing to be reunited.

Kurt didn't respond. Instead he closed his eyes, letting this heartache, this sorrow, fuel his new project. He was picturing an arm rising from the ground, bony fingers outstretched as it reached for a face.

Yes, that seemed to capture something of the sorrow inside this dress.

He'd been working on this image in his mind since first touching the dress, getting a sense of the loss inhabiting it, examining it from every angle.

Kurt kneeled to the concrete floor, took stock of the plates of iron stacked there, running his fingers along the rough-cut edges. He selected one large, flat piece and carried it to his workbench, then placed it in the vise and tightened the arm to hold it steady.

Satisfied, he retrieved his welding hood from a shelf above the workbench and fitted the band around his forehead, keeping the black mask tipped away from his face for now.

He turned to his left, opened the valve on the acetylene tank, heard the gas hiss as it raced through the tubing to the cutting tip. He picked up the igniter, held it to the torch, and sparked it. Immediately, blue flame leaped to life with a dull roar.

The dress, as if disturbed by the blue flame and black smoke erupting from his cutting torch, began its sobbing once again from behind him.

Kurt closed his eyes for a few seconds, gave his head a quick jerk to let the welder's hood drop over his face, and opened his eyes.

Somewhere inside his stack, a large piece of iron would become that outstretched arm. This particular piece, he felt, contained the face. He would cut the iron, reveal the true face inside, just as the screams behind him were cutting him.

Revealing his own true face inside.

16.

"You said it to me the first time you came here, Kurt. You're an amnesiac."

Kurt looked at the floor, wishing for a Diet Pepsi from Todd's fridge. Probably not the best time to ask for it. "Yeah," he said, sensing that Todd was waiting for an answer of some kind.

At his desk, Todd picked up his file folder, now thick with papers and reports from their several sessions together.

"At first I would have said hysterical amnesia, but now I don't think so. You ever hear that term?"

"No."

"It's what we call people who have been through an overwhelming emotional trauma of some kind—something that's made them block out their past because they're afraid to confront it. There's no physical explanation for their amnesia, but there's a very real emotional explanation."

Kurt tapped his foot on the hard surface of the floor a few times. "But you said I'm not that."

Todd looked at him. "No. In fact, you have . . . well, you have a ton of physical trauma. You're an organic case. Your MRI scans show a considerable amount of brain damage, to be blunt. So I have to say you have traumatic retrograde amnesia—you've forgotten your past because of very real, physical damage to the brain."

Kurt swallowed, unsure how to respond.

"Not just brain trauma, though. Your whole body. It looks like you've had several broken bones—a couple ribs, an arm, both of your femurs." Todd cleared his throat, leaned back. "You know how painful, how serious, a broken femur is, Kurt?"

Kurt fidgeted, felt his foot tapping on the floor. "No."

Todd smiled. "That's just it. You *do* know. You obviously do. You just don't remember it. I've discussed your case with more than one physician, and they're frankly amazed you're alive. Amazed anyone was even able to put you back together, because it looks as if all your injuries happened at the same time. Except—"

"Except what?"

"Well, when someone has major injuries a cracked skull, a fractured femur—you would find an indication of repair. Surgical scars, titanium screws in the leg, that kind of thing."

Kurt nodded slowly. "I don't have any of those things." And he didn't. So far as he knew, he didn't have a single scar anywhere on his body.

"You don't," Todd confirmed. "Further complicated by the fact that we don't have access to your medical records. One doctor said he'd seen injuries similar to yours before, a rather miraculous case herself—except, of course, she recovered with the help of many surgeries, lots of physical therapy."

"What kind of accident?" Kurt heard himself ask quietly.

"A skydiving accident. Her chute failed." Todd leaned across his desk, smiling. "So what do you think, Kurt? Maybe you just dropped out of the sky."

43. THREE

A dull ringing brought Kurt out of his trancelike state. He blinked his eyes behind the welding hood, obviously for the first time in a while; they were dry, cakey.

The ring again. His cell phone in his pocket, he realized. Kurt was old school when it came to phones; he still preferred a plain old ring to any song or tune or ringtone. Phones in his childhood rang; phones should always ring.

He spun the valve on the cutting torch closed, pulled off his gloves, tipped up his mask, and dug into his pocket. He managed to pull the phone out and answer it midring.

"Hello?" he said, his voice thick and scratchy. He swallowed, trying to moisten his throat; like his eyes, it was dry and parched.

"Kurt, Kurt," a woman's voice said. "How are you?"

Macy. His agent. His business manager. His whatever. The person who worked with the outside world so he didn't have to. He swallowed again, cleared his throat.

"Macy. I'm good." He didn't return the pleasantries.

"Listen, I bet you're working right now, so I'm sorry to interrupt you."

"Yeah," he said, sniffing, taking in the acrid, sharp tang of the acetylene inside his shop. He hadn't turned on his fans, but at least he'd left open the front overhead doors to ventilate the area.

(A catfish in a pool of orange)

He closed his eyes, pushed the thought from his mind with some effort. Odd, to have that image working its way into his mind while he was in the midst of this project with the silk dress. The hands and face.

"Listen," Macy said. "How many complete pieces do you have on hand right now?"

He looked around his workshop, taking stock of the various welded sculptures. Some looked like trees, some like multilegged creatures, some like giant stalks of plants. Most—okay, maybe all—had a melting face of some kind hidden inside the iron leaves or branches or legs. It was what Macy liked to call his "overriding theme."

He cleared his throat, tasting the bitter smoke of the welding torch. "I don't know," he said. "Maybe eight or so right now. Working on another."

"Eight? Hmmm. We'll need more."

He paused, waiting for her to continue, but she obviously required an acknowledgment. She was excited, he could tell; she always liked to play this kind of cat-and-mouse game when she had some kind of big news to share.

"We'll need more for what?" he asked, playing along. It was the easiest, quickest way to get back to his work.

"For a show. A gallery show."

"A gallery show?" he asked, hoping his tone sounded interested, knowing it didn't.

"Yeah. No more sending lackeys around on the arts-and-crafts circuit, selling your work for a thousand bucks. We're gonna get you in with people who will spend ten times that much. Just need—oh, I don't know—a dozen pieces anyway. And something big. Something grand, to serve as a centerpiece. A big wow, you know? Do you have something that might work for that?"

Kurt took stock of the sculptures again. None of those. Not really. Maybe the new piece with the arm. He turned to look at the giant plate of iron he'd been cutting, felt his breath stop for a few moments.

"You there, Kurt?" Macy asked. She laughed, mistaking his silence for surprise. Not a bad thing, really. "I know, this is big. I mean really *big*. But don't get caught up on the main piece right now. You'll come up with something, and we have a couple months."

Kurt continued to stare at the image he'd been cutting from the piece of iron. "Yeah," he said, his throat clicking, drier than ever. "I think maybe I can come up with something."

"I just wanted to call, let you know, so you can start thinking about it."

"Sure, sure. Thanks, Macy," he said, continuing to stare.

"Oh, thank *you*, Kurt," she said before hanging up.

Kurt let his arm drop, still clutching the phone. In front of him, he knew, instinctively, what he'd been wrestling from the thick plate of iron with his cutting torch. And it wasn't one of his "overriding theme" melting faces.

It was a triangular pattern with an irregular back side on it. A dorsal fin.

A dorsal fin for a catfish.

Behind him, the ghost in the silk dress sniffled, then went quiet again. Maybe sensing it wasn't connecting with him. Not right now, anyway.

The phone rang again. Evidently Macy had forgotten to tell him something.

He hit the talk button and placed the receiver to his ear again.

"Kurt?" a man's voice asked. Not Macy at all. It was John Cross from Cross Trucking.

"John. How are you doing?" Kurt continued to stare at the dorsal fin he'd been cutting out of the iron.

"Well, not so good," John answered. "I'm running short right now. Hoping you could maybe deadhead it out to Seattle for me, pull back a load to Chicago."

John Cross called once a month or so, asking him to do some OTR trucking. Kurt had driven for Cross Trucking for a few years until he'd stumbled into his iron art. Truth was, the art was doing well—upcoming gallery show or not—and he didn't need to do anything else for money.

But he still liked to get out on the road every now and then. Think about upcoming projects. Bring along a few items from his wardrobe of wearable ghosts, listen to the stories they told.

Kurt thought of the dead man's shoes from lot 159 and smiled. "Sure, John," he said. "I think I can make a quick trip for you."

17.

After several sessions with Todd, Kurt decided to call the other name Marcus had given him. Jenny Lewis, the private detective.

He didn't really want to. But not knowing was like an infection, and if you ignored an infection, it created more problems. Maybe even killed you, eventually. So he dialed her number, set up a meeting, gave her what little information he had about his own past, and waited.

Now here she was, at the bar where they'd agreed to meet, looking nervous. She sat, ordered a Diet Coke, and shook Kurt's hand. They waited quietly for the barmaid to bring her drink before they got around to the business of discussing what she'd found.

The detective nodded to the barmaid when she returned. She took a sip, looked at Kurt, seemed unsure how to start the conversation.

Kurt offered a smile. "I see you drink the hard stuff," he said, nodding at her glass.

"Diet Coke. Breakfast, lunch, and dinner of champions. You?"

He smiled. "Same. More of a Diet Pepsi guy, but I suppose it isn't my bar."

She seemed to relax. "We shoulda met at a soda fountain. The barmaid's in the back snickering at us."

"No such thing as a soda fountain anymore."

Jenny looked thoughtful. "No, I don't suppose there is." Another sip.

Her obvious discomfort was making him nervous. Maybe he shouldn't have called her after all, but . . . well, Marcus had given him her name. After listening to Kurt's full confession, Marcus had written Todd's and Jenny's names and phone numbers on a piece of paper.

"Call them," he had said. "Todd will dig into your head, Jenny into everything else—and they'll both be quiet about it."

Out of a sense of duty to Marcus (and he'd love to hear what Todd might say about *that*), he'd called her. And now here they were, in a bar, drinking diet sodas.

"So," she said, "on with it, I guess."

Kurt didn't like this. When he'd first met her, he'd been reassured. She seemed unflappable, someone who could keep her cool. Now she seemed . . . scared.

She opened a thin file. "There's not much to go on, as you know." She paused. "I ran a check on your New Jersey driver's license. It's a fake. No such registered driver."

He waited. "Okay," he said.

"Thing is," she said, "as fakes go, this one's good. Real good—has the holographic image on it and everything, which is something your typical guy-with-a-printer-in-his-basement operation can't do. So, you had to have some resources to get this."

Kurt shifted uncomfortably, thinking of the ten thousand dollars in cash he'd found stuffed into a nylon money belt and strapped to his chest after . . . after the fire. He hadn't told Jenny about that. Or Todd. No need to.

"Now," she continued, "I did a check of Social Security numbers registered to Kurt Marlowes with your birth date. Wanna guess how many hits I got?"

He itched at his cheek, and she continued without waiting for an answer. "Nada," she said. "I did a criminal background search on the name, first in Jersey, then across the country. Some hits, but nothing that seemed like you."

She handed him a computer printout, but he didn't stop to read it, so she continued.

"Missing persons, wanted persons, tax liens, traffic tickets, unclaimed property . . . I threw everything I had at it, and you weren't a blip on anything, Kurt." She picked up her drink and took a long draw, grimacing at the carbonation. "So basically," she said, her eyes searching his face, "you don't exist. At least not on paper."

He sat quietly for a few moments, sighed. "Can't say this is a big surprise," he said.

Her eyes narrowed. "I don't get that impression, either. But I have some advice for you, if you'll take it."

"What's that?"

"Stop."

His throat was dry and scratchy, so he took a drink of his own. "Stop," he repeated.

"You—or someone close to you—took great pains to conceal your identity," she said. "Someone who has a lot of resources. That's two possibilities: government spooks of some kind, or the Mafia. Either way, it's bad news. You ever consider your amnesia might not be accidental?"

He shook his head.

"I think there might be a very good reason why you don't remember anything: because you're not supposed to. And I think the only reason you might be alive is because you're a clean slate. Long as you stay a clean slate, you're safe. You start digging into your past too much, you might show up on someone's radar. They might opt for some other way to keep you quiet." She took another sip. "A more permanent way."

Kurt thought of his recent conversations with Todd, the discussions of brain damage and broken bones. He—and Todd—had assumed he'd been through some kind of tragic accident. But what if he'd been through something much worse? What if someone had beaten and broken him, wiped him clean, put him on the ground in California with cash and a few pieces of paper? For what reason? He shuddered as he thought about it.

Jenny closed the folder on the table in front of her and pushed the rest of it toward him. "Thing is, if you're gonna do anything from here on out, you need a legit footprint."

"A footprint?" He opened the folder and started to page through the papers inside: Social Security paperwork, bank statements, employment records.

"Like I said, you're a ghost right now. You graduate from that trucking school, apply for a job somewhere, what are you gonna do when they ask for a Social Security number?" She nodded at the folder. "Now, you have one to give them—a Social Security account with a full history of contributions, an employment record, a credit score. It's all in there. A full history for Kurt Marlowe."

He looked at her. "How'd you do this?"

She gave him a disgusted look. "What do you think this is, amateur hour? Told you I checked the unclaimed property databases. You know there's billions of dollars that go uncollected each year in unclaimed property, estates with no heirs?"

"No."

"Well, just call that investment capital for the kinds of things I do."

He stared at her, dumbfounded, for a few moments. "But . . . why are you doing this? You don't even know me."

"I know Marcus, though. Known him a long time, since before—well, since before his trucking days."

"What days were those?"

"Prison days."

Kurt narrowed his eyes. "You met Marcus in prison."

She shook her head, evidently unimpressed by his wit.

"No, I met Marcus long before he went to prison, when we were both on a traveling sales crew."

"So what'd he go to prison for?"

She smiled, a bit wistfully. "For a couple years. Let's just say he got out of traveling sales the hard way. And after that he helped me get out of it. I think Marcus may be the only person ever truly rehabilitated by the United States penal system. In any case, I owe Marcus. And I think you do too."

"More than you know."

She nodded. "You showed up with that acceptance letter in your hand; Marcus knew it was a forge. But he knew it was a good forge, and he also knew it wasn't yours. He's been watching out for you since."

Kurt stayed silent, unsure how to react. If not for Marcus, and Jenny, and Todd, he'd probably be dead by now.

"Then I guess all I can say is thanks."

"And all I can say is you're welcome."

"But there's one thing bothering me," he said.

"Shoot."

"If it *was* the government, or the Mafia, or whoever wiped me clean . . . wouldn't *they* fix me?"

She gave a grim smile. "Oh, I'd say you're in a fix."

He shook his head. "No, what I mean is . . . Todd talked about some extensive injuries, but no signs they were treated. No pins or surgeries or anything. And then, if they *didn't* want to kill me . . . wouldn't they just give me a new identity?

Brainwash me, make me think I'm someone else? Give me that legit footprint you're talking about?"

She bit her lip. "That's what worries me," she said. "I think there's something about you that's wrong. Dead wrong. Something happened. Something didn't go according to plan, and you fell between the cracks." She finished the last of her drink, smiled humorlessly. "And if whoever did this starts seeing some of those cracks, we're both drinking the wrong thing."

58. FIFTY-EIGHT

Kurt downshifted the big Peterbilt and hit the Jake Brake as he followed his headlights down Fourth of July Pass between Spokane and Coeur d'Alene. Few places he could hit the Jake Brake anymore—most city ordinances restricted their use—and he loved to hear the throaty roar of the diesel's engine holding back thirty tons of weight. Just one of the reasons why he often said yes whenever John called him in a bind.

He'd picked up a forty-foot storage container, fresh off the docks in Seattle, and now he was bound for Chicago. Not a bad route, really; he could make it in three days if he pushed it, then deadhead it back to Montana.

On his feet he wore the dead man's shoes. Not typically

the kind of shoes he would wear, to be sure—he preferred lug-soled work boots, and these were somewhat dressy slip-ons—but what of it? The shoes felt right. More than that, they felt electric. Something about them made long-dormant parts inside light up, crackle with anticipation.

He even liked the tags on the inside of the shoes. They displayed a large symbol that looked like a reversed numeral 3, with other strange writing beneath the symbol. He'd seen that kind of writing on old Soviet Union propaganda post-ers, vodka advertisements, that kind of thing, so he guessed the writing was Russian.

Best of all, fueled by the ghost inside the shoes, his mind, as he drove the long miles following the white line of Interstate 90, was filled with constant images of the com-forting catfish swimming in a pool of orange, unfettered by constraints.

Like Kurt himself on the open road.

So when he first heard the voice on the CB, he almost missed it. He wasn't listening, wasn't paying attention; only the mention of his name pierced his consciousness.

"Give her a ride, Kurt."

Kurt looked at his citizens band radio. Yes, he was sure it came through the CB; he'd heard the hiss of static and squelch just before the voice spoke.

Like most truckers, Kurt still used the citizens band radio. And like most truckers, he could only stomach it in small doses; far removed from the good-buddy days of C. W. McCall's "Convoy," it was now a wasteland of mindless egos and arguments. So he really only turned it on when he was near major truck stops or metro areas. Sometimes good for local weather or traffic or speed trap information, but mostly interesting in the way reality crime shows were interesting.

Kurt thought of all this as he stared at his CB radio, because the unit was turned off.

Which meant the voice had to be coming from his wardrobe of wearable ghosts. And the only problem with that was: he'd only brought along one item of haunted clothing.

Well, two, to be precise. The shoes on his feet.

He peered at the floor of the cab, trying to get a good look at the shoes in the darkness.

Odd. The shoes hadn't spoken to him the way the other haunted clothing always did. They had filled his mind with the image of the catfish, yes, but not with words. That's what made them special. What made them interesting.

If they were speaking now—and speaking in a static-filled voice—what did that mean?

Give her a ride, Kurt.

Well. That was the other bothersome part of the voice. No ghost had ever—ever—called him by name. The ghosts, in an odd way, were blind. Maybe *blind* wasn't quite the right word, but . . . *unaware.* They couldn't see him; he was sure of that. He'd come to think of it as a door between their world and his. The ghosts stood outside his door, knocking, knowing someone was inside but never able to see or hear who it was.

For his part, Kurt always stood inside the door, listening to them—listening as they cried out for help and contact—but never answering.

Kurt could never answer them, because . . . well, those ghosts had to be from his past, didn't they? His past, filled with broken femurs and fractured skulls and forged identities and very real spooks (not ghosts but spooks) who would undoubtedly break him into even smaller pieces if he ever unlocked that door to the past and stared into their terrifying faces.

So Kurt kept that door closed. Still, he knew he needed to atone for something, needed to give the ghosts a voice. And that's what his welded art became. He channeled the plaintive whispers of the ghosts into twisted pieces of scrap metal, producing the melted faces that spoke of sorrow and despair and longing and loss.

What would good old Todd have to say about that? Would he call it Kurt's *coping mechanism*, his *manifestation of guilt*? Probably something like that; Kurt himself knew these things to be true. But this wasn't just a simple case of obsessive-compulsive disorder, a need to count things or bring manufactured order to the world around him. It was a pressure valve; if he didn't give the ghosts a voice of some kind, didn't open that door the tiniest crack to let bits of them seep through into the physical world, their pain and sorrow would eventually shatter the door, and maybe him along with it.

Coping mechanism? Maybe. But also mere survival. Without the art, he would be consumed. He could feel that urgent desperation when he looked at one of his welded sculptures. And evidently, others could too.

But now. Now, the ghost—the wonderfully different ghost inside the shoes he was wearing—had not simply spoken to him. It had called him by name. The door wasn't just opened a crack; the door itself had a crack in it.

Which might mean all of them, the hundreds of ghosts that had crowded that massive door, might be finding some way through. Some way to sense him. Some way to reach him.

Some way to touch him.

Kurt felt his skin rippling with gooseflesh. He rubbed his face, opened the console next to his seat, took out a bottle of water, gulped down a few drinks. Had to be highway hypnosis. Every trucker knew if you were on the road long enough, the white line had a way of lulling you into a kind of trance, an almost hallucinatory state that signaled you were getting too tired.

(or brain damage)

He pushed the thought of brain damage away. Nothing to indicate that. Nothing at all. Well, yes, he did have brain damage; Todd had said as much. Todd's doctors had said as much, insisted they should see him and take his case so they could poke him and prod him and solve the mysteries of his past.

But like the ghosts, he'd never wanted the doctors to touch him. Never wanted anyone to touch him.

He calculated quickly. He was in Idaho's panhandle; Kellogg and Wallace weren't far away, and there was at least one rest stop where he could pull over and get eight hours in the sleeper berth, enough to reset his log book and give him eleven hours of straight driving in the morning. He could still make Chicago day after tomorrow, and he'd have to stop in the next two hours anyway.

Yeah, some time in the sleeper berth. That's what he needed.

59. NINE

Something woke him.

Static.

He sat up in his sleeper, pausing and listening. A few moments later, a brief burst of static filled the cabin again, followed by the forlorn voice he'd heard earlier.

"Give her a ride, Kurt."

Then the image of the catfish appeared in his mind, oddly comforting after the terror inspired by the voice speaking his name.

Kurt sat still, waiting, listening. It had to be late, really late, right now. He fumbled, hit the illumination dial on his watch, which displayed 3:23 in soft blue.

He pushed himself out of bed, crawled out of the sleeper, worked his way into the cab of his truck. Outside, the sky above glowed with a million pinpricks of light from distant stars. Out here, in the deep forests of the Pacific Northwest, far from the lights of cities, the stars multiplied in the dark fabric of the sky.

He opened the door of his cab quietly, listening. No footsteps or scuffling outside; only the chirr of a few crickets and the overbearing stillness of the forest canopy above. This rest area near the eastern edge of the Idaho panhandle was one of his favorite stops. Very little traffic, and a thick cove of trees surrounding it, making it seem like a hidden fortress.

He peered into the parking area around him. He was all alone at this time of morning. Most truckers preferred the big stops and plazas scattered along I-90, and at least two of them were within thirty miles of where he now sat. Other motorists who stopped at rest areas invariably passed this one by, as if afraid of the deep woods. Held-over fears from bedtime stories of Hansel and Gretel, perhaps.

He stared around the cab of his truck, now illuminated by the interior lights. Nothing out of the ordinary. He shut the door, enveloping himself in darkness once again.

60.

Early that morning, Kurt settled in for a long haul.

He decided not to wear the dead man's shoes as he'd done the day before.

They stayed in the sleeper.

The voice, speaking his name, had been too close a connection. A connection he needed to break. That door between his world and the world of the ghosts inside the clothing needed to stay comfortably closed.

He could get close to Fargo before he had to pull over and log another break tonight. From there, he'd be within an eleven-hour drive of Chicago. Yeah, he could still make it in three days, even though he'd had a slow start out of Seattle yesterday.

He shifted and relaxed, finally reaching an easier stretch of road that ribboned out from the base of the Rocky Mountains in western Montana. The miles began to fly by, and Kurt retreated to that empty place inside, a place filled with nothingness.

A favorite place.

When things were just right, he could move his mind to this place, a neutral, blank landscape devoid of any thoughts at all. Nothing to do but stare at that long strip of white line, streaming down the road for miles. Part of why he still said yes whenever he was offered a quick OTR route.

Yes, he was there, so there.

Until the static broke the silence inside the cab.

And then, after a few moments of static, the familiar voice returned. "Give her a ride, Kurt."

Then the catfish, swimming in orange, penetrating his mind. Even from behind him, the dead man's shoes continued to pump out their message.

He decided he didn't want to hear that message anymore. It was time for the shoes to go.

He slowed his rig, pulling it to the side of the road with a hiss of the air brakes. He threw on the flashers, sat staring at the road for a moment.

Then he scrambled into the sleeper cab, digging under his bunk to find the shoes. When he touched them, he felt energy radiating from them. The catfish swam inside his mind, even as he fought to push it away.

Yes, the shoes had to go. The catfish, comforting as it was, had now spawned a different kind of fear that didn't just swim in his mind, but in his very veins.

He returned to the cab, opened the passenger door, slid to the ground. Outside, the scent of pine wafted by on a soft breeze. The concrete surface of the interstate stretched away from him in both directions with no visible traffic.

He held the shoes away from him, looked at them, then heaved them as hard as he could down the steep embankment just off the highway. Several feet below him, the shoes bounced a few times off gravel riprap rock lining the slope, tumbling slowly away and out of sight. Maybe, eventually, they would make it all the way to the bottom of this canyon, where the Clark Fork River flowed.

Kurt caught himself holding his breath, waiting for . . . he wasn't sure what. He'd half expected the dead man's shoes to protest or something, to latch onto his wrist with jagged teeth, to pierce his brain with a dull, overbearing stab of pain.

That was ridiculous, of course. But he'd never experienced clothing with such a strong vibe. He needed to get rid of the shoes before they did something bad. He knew this, felt this, deep in his bones.

Kurt turned back toward his rig, just a few steps behind him, and noticed something about the trailer for the first time. When he'd picked it up, it hadn't seemed at all unusual: a large shipping container on a flatbed trailer. Something he'd hauled many times.

But now, for the first time, he noticed markings on the side of the trailer.

Radiation symbols, along with DANGEROUS CARGO warnings painted in garish yellow paint.

He was hauling radioactive cargo.

That was impossible, of course. If the shipping container *did* contain something like that, he'd have government vehicles accompanying him and a mountain of forms and extra paperwork at every weigh station.

Not that he knew this firsthand. He'd never hauled radioactive materials before; he just assumed there would be . . . regulations. Extra hoops. There had to be. The government wouldn't just let dangerous materials out on the road.

He swallowed, trying to replay the images of yesterday in his mind. Okay. Think. What was different about this trip? He rewound, recalling the freight pickup the previous day. Down on the docks in Seattle, nothing out of the ordinary. He'd hooked up the trailer, pulled out of the loading zone, and hit the interstate within half an hour.

So what about the bill of lading? He tried to picture it but couldn't quite remember. Truth be told, he'd barely glanced at it; he'd been too intent on the dead man's shoes, on the catfish image, on the sculpture that he'd started in his workshop. This whole trip he had planned to let those images coalesce in his own mind, give him a fully formed idea of where to take his beginning efforts on a giant catfish sculpture.

Kurt returned to his rig, climbed through the open passenger door, pulled the paperwork out of the console between the seats.

He was at once surprised and not surprised to discover that the company listed on the paperwork was called Catfish Industries.

When he read this, the image of the catfish bathed in orange returned to his mind. Even from their current location at the bottom of that deep canyon, it seemed, the dead man's shoes were still able to send signals.

So what did that say about this particular load? After all, hauling for a company called Catfish Industries seemed a bit too coincidental to be . . . well, coincidental.

The question was: what, exactly, was he hauling? Could it be something radioactive? Was that why the catfish swam in orange?

(brain damage)

There. He'd let himself think it again. The most obvious explanation for all this. Of course he had brain damage; he knew this from long ago, from his first therapy sessions with Todd. The brain damage had somehow awakened an unused part of his brain—the part that received messages from ghosts on the other side of the door.

What waited behind that door had terrified him at first, yes, but had soon become normal. Almost comforting, in a way. Without the moans and screams and wails of the dead, he would be utterly alone in his small cabin and large shop. But hearing them, knowing they were there, meant someone needed him. It let him feel, however briefly, he wasn't utterly alone, cut off from his own past or anyone else's future.

So now, this image of the catfish projected by the shoes . . . well, that had to be part of the brain damage. Maybe his injured gray matter had continued to map new pathways, rerouting signals even after making contact with the clothing ghosts. And now those newer pathways were firing, illuminating portions of the brain long dormant. Maybe forever dormant.

Brain damage. Yes.

But then, none of that had any bearing on what might be inside the shipping container on his flatbed trailer right now. Brain damage or not, he needed to see what was inside. If nothing else, he needed to prove his mind was getting away from him, because he knew it would just be box after box of canned peaches bound for grocery shelves in Michigan or pallets of toys ready for excited children in Iowa or something else innocuous.

Just go look, get it over with, and move on.

He climbed back to the cab and once again opened the storage compartment in the console. He retrieved a flashlight and a safety tool that helped open shipping containers, a bent piece of metal called "the persuader." As a bonus, the persuader could act as a weapon, if need be.

He climbed down to the road again. On the horizon, waves of heat radiated from the surface of the road, even though the overnight chill still hadn't totally left the air. Diesel fumes from his clattering rig filled his nostrils. Nothing out of the ordinary here, just he and his rig on a lonely stretch of Montana highway.

He swallowed, felt his dry throat clicking. Why did he feel such an overwhelming sense of dread?

Kurt walked to the end of the trailer, past the high metal sides, until he came to the large steel doors at the back.

He stared at the container for several seconds, trying to decide what he should do. Eventually he reached for the back door, touching the warm metal, and ran his finger over the yellow-and-black radiation symbol. The paint almost seemed wet, as if it were nothing more than some hastily scrawled gang graffiti. Maybe that's what it was: a joke, some kids who thought it would be great fun to see trailers traveling America's highways with radiation symbols painted on the sides.

But it didn't feel like a joke. And . . . well, if brain damage wasn't causing the hallucinations, surely a bit of radiation would do it, wouldn't it? There it was: another perfectly logical explanation. He was being poisoned by radioactive cargo that had somehow slipped in beneath the rules and regulations.

Which made opening the container, exposing himself to the possible radiation inside, a ludicrous thought. Yeah, he was definitely brain injured to be thinking this was in any way a good idea. Kurt took a deep breath, slipped the persuader inside the container door, and pushed. The door held for a few moments, then came open with a long shudder. Kurt put down the persuader on the flatbed trailer's deck, thumbed the flashlight's power switch.

Maybe he hadn't been exposed to the radiation at all yet. Maybe he'd been perfectly safe until he cracked open the container. Maybe the container was lined with lead, and he was going to kill himself by—

Kurt huffed, pushing the jumbled thoughts from his mind as he swept the beam of the flashlight across the container's contents.

As he'd expected, he saw hundreds of boxes inside, stacked floor to ceiling. The sides of the boxes were printed with the words *Catfish Industries*, as well as Chinese characters he didn't recognize. Or maybe they were Japanese. For a moment he half expected to see a reversed numeral 3 in the mass of markings, a clear tie to the ghost shoes he'd just discarded, but he let himself exhale slowly when he found nothing of the kind.

Okay, so he was hauling boxes. That made him feel a little better. If he were truly hauling something dangerous, it would be in something else. What, he didn't know. Giant cylinders, maybe. Or sealed barrels. Something. He didn't really know what radioactive containers looked like, and that thought was more troublesome than he cared to admit.

The boxes were wrapped tightly in cellophane to prevent them from shifting during shipping. Standard. Kurt retrieved his persuader once more and used the edge of it to hack into the thick plastic coating, cutting a crude gash into the packing material. He reached above him, squeezed his fingers around the edge of a box, slid it out a bit to test the weight. Something inside shifted.

The box wasn't extra heavy, maybe twenty pounds, so he pulled it down from the stack. *Black Tar*, a simple label said on the box's packing slip, inside a clear plastic envelope. He stared a few moments, bent down to pick up the persuader again, and used its edge to cut through the packing tape that sealed the box.

Inside, covered by Styrofoam packing material, were several bottles of dark black liquid, each bottle plainly marked with the words *Black Tar*. Just like the outside of the box. He pulled out a bottle and held it up, shining the flashlight on its surface. The liquid inside swallowed the flashlight's beam. He tilted the bottle; the liquid started to move slowly, like . . . well, like tar. But within a few seconds its viscosity seemed to change, become lighter, and the liquid easily sloshed inside the bottle.

Kurt shrugged, returned the bottle back into the box. He slid the box back into its place, then scanned the other boxes stacked before him. Did they all hold the same thing? He doubted it; no two boxes were the same.

He picked another box from the top of the stack and pulled it down, cut the tape to open the lid. Inside he found bottles that looked like vitamin pills. AMAZING CATFISH CURE! the plain label announced. Inside were tablets, lozenges of some kind. He shook a bottle of the pills and put it back before sliding the large box back into its place.

Okay. He'd opened this storage container, expecting radiation sickness or a laser beam or some other far-fetched, deadly calamity. Instead, he'd found boxes filled with bottles of soy sauce and aspirin, shipped from somewhere in China.

Not exactly the deadly cargo his mind had been painting for him.

He supposed he could sit here another half hour, breaking regulations and privacy laws by opening each and every box in the storage container to reveal what was inside. But he doubted he'd find anything terrifying.

Brain damage, indeed. Maybe he'd obliterated the part of his brain that stored any kind of common sense. Certainly wasn't the first time he wondered such a thing.

Kurt jumped off the flatbed and pushed the door to the storage container closed again, shaking his head as the DANGEROUS CARGO markings came into view once more.

He'd wasted enough time. He needed to hit the highway, something he was more eager than ever to do now that the dead man's shoes were at the bottom of the canyon.

He walked back to the cab, released the brakes, shifted, and pulled back onto the interstate.

61a.

Twenty minutes later, he saw a hitchhiker trying to catch a ride.

Hitchhiking, of course, was illegal on the interstates. But that didn't prevent people from doing it. Kurt bit his lip as he considered. Normally, he didn't want other people around. At all. But right now, another voice—a real one—would be welcome.

Kurt looked at the hitchhiker as he came into clearer focus. A bit bohemian, with wild hair barely contained by a blue bandanna, a large nylon pack on his back. A sign that said MISSOULA in large, markered letters. College student, probably, trying to thumb it back to UM after a long weekend in Seattle. According to corporate regulations for Cross Company, Kurt was never allowed to pick up hitchhikers because of liability issues.

But Kurt was in no mood to follow the rules just now. He'd already broken more than a few by opening the storage container and the boxes inside it.

He slowed to a stop just past the hitcher, watching in the side mirrors as the kid ran up to the cab. In a few moments, the blue bandanna popped into view as the kid opened the door, wearing a big grin on his face. "Thanks, man."

"No problem."

The kid unshouldered the backpack, put it on the floor, scrambled into the passenger seat. "I'm Jonas," he said, thrusting a hand Kurt's direction.

"Kurt," he said, shaking the kid's hand. He threw the Peterbilt into gear and steered back onto the roadway.

Jonas fumbled with some things on his backpack, dug through his pockets, adjusted his bandanna, finally gave a big sigh and seemed to settle in. "How far you going?" he asked.

"Chicago. Trying to get there the day after next."

The kid nodded, as if he'd made the trip before.

"I'm headed back to the U from Spokane."

"You're from Spokane?"

"From all over. Just visiting a friend in Spokane."

"What's your friend do?"

Jonas smiled. "Sells drugs, mostly."

Kurt glanced at the backpack on the floor. "And I suppose that's just dirty laundry you're bringing back."

"Nah. It's all clean. Some books too—gotta get a degree, you know, so I don't end up one of those 'You want fries with that?' people. Fate worse than death, if you ask my parents."

"I'm hoping you're not going to say your parents deal drugs."

"Nope. Solid blue-collar folks down in Colorado. Security guard and an assistant at a title company."

Kurt nodded. "So you're gonna be the great college-educated savior of the family."

Jonas returned the nod. "You get the picture."

"And what are you studying?"

"Pharmacy."

Kurt laughed. "Why am I not surprised?"

Jonas turned. "Hey, I told you my friend sells drugs—and she does. She's a pharmacist. On the job about six months now, after graduating last year. Just getting some big-picture stuff from her." He smiled. "Gotcha."

Kurt laughed, relaxing. "Yeah, you're a clever one. No wonder Mom and Dad wanted to ship you off to college."

They watched the mile markers tick by for a few minutes. No voice since the kid had been in the cab with him, and that was good. And being a pharmacist . . .

"I got a question for you," he said to Jonas.

"No, I can't get you free drugs."

Kurt smiled. "Uh, not really what I was going for. But it is about drugs. Maybe. Kind of."

"Okay."

"I . . . uh . . . say I have a friend who's had some brain damage."

"What part of the brain?"

Kurt smiled, thought of his many sessions with Todd, thought of the few scans and tests he'd agreed to, thought of the doctors who would have loved to sink their hooks deeper into his case if he'd let them. "Temporal lobe."

"Right or left?"

"Um . . . both."

The kid looked at him, doing a bit of a double take. "Is your friend a vegetable?"

Kurt smiled, shrugged. "That's the thing: he's supposed to be. But he's a walking, talking miracle. And he's been fine with this brain damage for years now. No real problems. But after that time . . . could he start having . . . hallucinations?"

Jonas turned and stared at him a few moments. "I'm not a doctor, you know. Not even a pharmacist yet."

"But you have to study brain function, right? Effects of different drugs, that kind of thing."

Jonas scratched at his chin. "Brain's a funny thing. You start messing with it, you don't know what's gonna happen. So, yeah, I'd say it's possible; might be the brain finishing its remapping, establishing new connections."

The same kind of thing Kurt had told himself. Maybe even Todd had said something to that effect, long ago. "Even after all that time?"

Jonas shrugged. "Like I said, the brain's a funny thing. So yeah, even after all that time there could be some healing. You read about cases of people coming out of comas after years." He paused. "Your friend should see a doctor, though, especially if he needs to do, um, do a lot of driving. There are drugs, choline acetylase inhibitors and others, that can offset some of those symptoms."

"Okay. I'll do that. I mean, I'll let him know."

A few minutes later, the blue bandanna turned his way again. "My feet are killing me. You mind if I slip off my shoes?"

Kurt kept his eyes on the road, shrugged. "Go ahead."

Jonas sighed as he bent to remove his shoes. "Okay," he said. "True confession time."

Kurt looked at the kid, noticing something was . . . odd . . . about his passenger's skin. It was flecked, black and white, and a bit out-of-focus. As if he were an image on a television screen with poor reception.

"My dad wasn't really a security guard. He was a Russian gangster. Own brother tried to kill him. Long story."

"Okay," Kurt said, unsure where this was going.

"And I'm not really a pharmacy student anymore," Jonas said. Kurt noticed the kid's voice was a bit more distant, more tinny. More static-filled. "I'm dead."

Kurt tried to laugh, but it caught somewhere in his throat.

Static filled the cab of the truck, and Kurt aimed for the side of the road, hitting the brakes as much as he could without jackknifing his trailer.

"Give her a ride, Kurt," Jonas said before he faded from view with a final burst of static and white noise.

Finally at a full stop, the air brakes hissing, Kurt stared at the empty passenger seat beside him. No Jonas, no backpack, no nothing.

He reached out, tried a tentative touch of the seat. Empty. Just as it looked. Then, as he pulled away his hand, something on the floor caught his eye.

Shoes.

Shoes that looked very much like the ones he'd bought in lot 159. Shoes that had a large, reversed numeral 3 on the inside of the tongue. Shoes that had been thrown down a steep canyon miles ago.

Shoes that had been left inside his truck by a ghost named Jonas.

Kurt stared at the shoes as if they themselves were radioactive, wondering what to do with them. He couldn't let them stay—they'd already come back to haunt him once, and they'd cracked open the door to the dead even farther. The ghost who occupied the shoes had actually been in his rig, right here. So yes, the shoes had to go, had to be destroyed, because they were obviously a beacon of some sort. A magnet for the ghosts that had before only spoken to him.

A knock came on the passenger door, followed by the muffled voice of a woman. "Everything okay?"

Kurt sprang back from the noise in surprise, painfully jamming his elbow on the steering wheel. He rubbed at his arm for a moment as he looked at the passenger door.

"Hello?" the voice asked again, hesitantly.

Not sure what else he could do, Kurt leaned across the cab and popped the door release, then pushed it open. On the ground, just beside the door, stood a thin woman with pale, milky skin. Her brows furrowed when she saw his face, and he realized he was sweating, panicky.

She turned toward the back of the truck, pointed down the road behind them. "I . . . I saw you go by me just down the road back there, and you were . . . um . . . looked like your truck was having problems."

Kurt stared at her a few moments. "Problems," he echoed.

She itched at her cheek a moment. Kurt noticed she was wearing a short-sleeved shirt only, no jacket of any kind on this chilly Montana morning. She carried a baglike purse with her but that was all. Looked like she hadn't showered or combed her hair for a few days. Probably a junkie of some kind, coming down off a high. Different kind of pharmacist, ha-ha.

"Yeah," she said. "I mean, I thought you were having some kind of problem with the truck at first, the steering or something. But when you got it pulled to the side here . . . " She let the sentence trail off, looked up at him again for a few seconds.

"You thought maybe I was the one having problems, rather than the truck," he said.

She nodded.

"I'm fine," he said, getting his bearings again. He tried to ignore the dead man's shoes and concentrate on the woman. "Just dropped something on the floor, tried to get it. Stupid, I know." He tried a smile.

She didn't return the smile, and he knew she didn't buy the story at all.

"Okay," she said. "I just, uh . . ." She seemed at a loss for words. "I'll let you get back to it." She backed away, as if willing him to close the door again.

The words returned to him again. *Give her a ride, Kurt.*

Yeah, well, that might be a trick. He guessed the last thing on her list of things to do right now was crawl into the cab of a diesel that had come to a shuddering, uneasy stop with a sweaty, manic-looking driver behind the wheel.

But: *Give her a ride, Kurt.* What if he didn't? What might

happen then? Would that itself be the bit of pressure that busted open the ever-weakening door between his reality and the ghosts' reality?

"You need a ride?" he asked, surprised when his voice didn't crack.

To her credit, the terror in her eyes flared only briefly. "I . . . uh . . ."

"Look, there's a truck plaza down the road about ten miles. Me, I think I probably need to pull off for a quick break. I'll buy you breakfast."

Her hand returned to her cheek again, and Kurt felt the blood draining from his face when he noticed the tattoo peeking out from beneath the sleeve of her right arm.

"Your arm," he said, studying the tattoo.

She looked at it, as if unaware it was there, then back at him. Almost unconsciously, she folded her arms, trying to hide the tattoo. "What about it?"

"It's a catfish," he said.

"Long story," she said.

"What do the numbers mean?" he asked.

She wrinkled her eyebrows. "Numbers?"

"Numbers, kind of hidden inside the tattoo—right at the snout of the fish." He pointed, realizing it wasn't doing any good—he was in the cab of the truck, and she was on the ground—but he still pointed. "See? Starts with a one—"

The woman gasped. "1595544534," she said, looking

at her arm and reading the numbers. Suddenly, any trace of fear disappeared from her eyes. She climbed into the cab and shut the door behind her. "I guess I will take that breakfast."

62b.

"Hash browns and gravy," she said to the waitress.

"Hash browns and gravy," the waitress repeated. "Got it. What about you, honey?" she said, glancing at Kurt.

"Coffee, to start with," he said. "And I'll do steak and eggs, over medium, wheat toast."

"Hungry?" the tattooed woman said to him after the waitress left.

"Always." Plus, Kurt was . . . waiting. He'd given the woman a ride, as the ghost in the shoes had asked him to do quite clearly. Now that he'd done that, he was waiting for something else to happen.

Dreading it, yes, but waiting.

The woman spoke again. "I'm Corrine," she said. "I suppose we should get that out of the way."

He nodded. "Nice to meet you, Corrine. I'm Kurt."

"And what's your story, Kurt?"

He smiled. "Still working on it."

"Guess that's as much as I'm gonna get right now, huh?"

"Trust me, you really don't want to know."

She smiled. "You think I'm worried about you escaping from a prerelease program?"

The waitress brought his coffee; he watched Corrine across the table as the hot, dark liquid sloshed into his white ceramic cup. Well, what was the harm in telling her? Maybe that's what the ghost wanted.

When the waitress left, he spoke, avoiding her eyes while he did so. If he looked into her eyes, the whole thing would dissolve like sugar.

"I had a brain injury several years ago. Since then, I . . . well, I can hear ghosts. Ghosts in the clothing of dead people."

Her jaw tensed for a moment. "And what do the ghosts say?"

He shrugged. "They ask me for help. Finding relatives, giving messages to others, that kind of thing."

"And you like doing that?"

"I don't."

"Why don't you like it?"

"No, I mean I don't do it. I . . . ignore them."

She sipped from her glass of water. "You don't do it."

"I go to estate sales, auctions, buy all the clothing that belongs to dead people so I can listen to the ghosts inside," he said. "But I don't talk to them. I don't answer them. I don't help them."

She leaned back in the leather booth, shifting her weight to get more comfortable. Kurt waited, listening to the sounds of metal utensils clanking on plates all around them. The comfortable sounds of dining.

"Well," she finally said, "it would seem you're one sick puppy." She raised her glass of water to him in a toast, smiled, and took a drink. "Welcome to the club. I'm the president."

"What qualifies you to be the president?" he said.

"Cancer, for one," she said. "But that's not the half of it. You got an e-mail account?" she asked.

Odd question, but they were in odd territory. "Yeah."

"Get spam?"

"Who doesn't?"

"Well," she said, "you can thank me for that. You're about to have breakfast with a woman who sends out a million e-mails every week for fake degrees, online prescriptions, and—what's a delicate way to say this?—male enhancement. Bon appetit."

He waited for a few minutes, and was about to ask her about the tattoo when she looked at it herself, as if reading his intentions.

"Those numbers on my arm. I didn't even know they were there, but—they're kind of what brought me here."

"Well, if you don't mind going a bit deeper into the twilight zone," he said, "one of the ghosts told me I was supposed to give you a ride. Just before you showed up. So—no offense—I'm a little worried this is all some kind of hallucination. The brain injury I told you about."

She shook her head. "Oh, I'm real, Kurt. I'm so real it hurts."

The waitress brought their food. Kurt took a bite of steak, picked up his ceramic mug, drank from the hot, dark liquid. It looked like black tar, he thought. Like the boxes in the shipping container. Maybe he was hauling nothing more than some strange Chinese coffee. He closed his eyes, exhaled loudly.

"So about the numbers . . ." he said, opening his eyes and focusing on her once more.

"I don't know much about them." She forked a bite of hash browns into her mouth. Part of the gravy dribbled down her chin, and she dabbed at it with her napkin, looking embarrassed.

"You don't know? So why'd you get them?"

"I didn't ask for them. I didn't even know they were there until you saw them."

"But they mean something to you, don't they?"

She paused for a long time. "Yeah, they mean something."

"They . . . they mean something to me, too," he said. "I just can't put my finger on it now." He continued staring at the tattoo, as if searching it for more hidden answers.

He found none.

The waitress brought the check, and he paid the tab. As

he put away his wallet, Corrine dug in her bag for a few minutes, then quickly pushed her way out of the booth.

"Be right back. I'm going to the restroom."

He watched her walk away. He had no illusions about her really coming back. Not after what he'd just told her. He'd be lucky if she didn't sneak away somewhere and dial 911.

Actually, that might be good.

He stood, noticed something on her side of the booth; she must have dropped it when she got up to leave. He bent over and picked it up: inside a plastic sandwich bag, a napkin with the numbers 1595544534 scrawled on it. The same numbers hidden inside her tattoo. He caressed it between his thumb and forefinger, lost in thought. What was so special about this napkin, these numbers, the catfish connection?

(brain damage)

"So where you headed?"

He spun around, slipping the plastic bag and the napkin into his front pocket as he did. "Huh?" he asked, flustered by her sudden return. "Oh, Chicago."

Was she actually hoping to catch a ride with him? Bad idea. Bad, bad idea.

He smiled, instantly feeling a cathartic clarity in his thoughts for the first time that morning. He started to walk toward the doors, and she followed.

"How about you? Where you going?"

"No clue," she said. "Just trying to outrun my past."

"It's a vicious circle," he agreed.

She stopped walking suddenly, and he turned to see what had stopped her. For a moment, he thought she'd been shocked, or maybe she'd bitten her lip.

"What did you say?" she whispered.

"A vicious circle," he repeated.

She stared off into the horizon, a smile creasing her face. "Yes, it is," she said, almost dreamily.

Her next question was even more of a surprise.

"Do they . . . ah, have a computer I could use in here?"

Odd question. But then, he'd hit the jackpot on odd this morning, hadn't he?

"Truckers' lounge upstairs. Wireless Internet, a computer workstation you can use. Nothing special."

"I don't need anything special."

"I think . . ." he started, then shook his head. "I need to get going."

They were standing at the glass doors, looking at the parking lot. He wasn't the person who ever offered to shake hands, who ever offered to touch anyone else at all, but for some reason, it seemed right this time. He extended his hand, waiting for her to shake it. He wished he was still wearing gloves, but that was one habit Todd had managed to help him break several years before. He didn't have to wear gloves anymore, but he secretly yearned for them. Once an alcoholic, always an alcoholic; once a glove addict, always a glove addict, he supposed.

She looked at his hand a moment before she stepped close, hugged him, and kissed his cheek. It felt awkward, but on a deeper level it also felt right. He was a bit disappointed when she stepped away again.

"You take care of yourself," she said.

He nodded numbly and felt his body turning toward the doors, his legs carrying him to the clear air outside, leaving her behind the double-paned glass.

As he walked toward his rig, he turned to glance back, and she was still standing there, watching him walk. When he turned a second time, she was gone.

Kurt opened the door to the cab, climbed inside, fired up the diesel, sat, and listened to the clattering of the exhaust for a few moments. On the floor of the passenger side the dead man's shoes seemed to glow with a dark, oily sheen, pushing the image of the catfish into his mind once more.

He waited for the static to break in again, but it didn't. Only the catfish, implanted in his brain.

Instead of static, he heard the sound of hydraulics nearby. He turned and noticed a large garbage truck emptying giant bins of trash into its belly, compacting the trash into tight folds.

Kurt smiled.

He grabbed the shoes, crawled out of the cab of his truck, and walked over to the garbage truck. He hailed the driver, held up the shoes, and pointed to the rear of the truck. The driver gave him a thumbs-up, so Kurt walked to the rear of the truck to throw the shoes into the gaping maw.

The driver emptied another bin of trash before he hit the hydraulics again. Iron jaws clamped down on the garbage, and a large plate of metal pushed it to the front of the truck's payload. Kurt caught a glimpse of one shoe, pinched against the side of the compartment for a moment before the iron compactor shredded it with the rest of humanity's discarded past.

18.

"So, Kurt, tell me about yourself," Todd said, sitting in his chair.

He hadn't yet adjusted, folding one leg up in the chair and staring at him thoughtfully. But Kurt knew he would soon. Todd always did in these sessions.

"Like, what do you want to know?"

"What kind of person are you?"

Kurt shrugged. "Working on being a trucker, you know. That's about it."

"A trucker, yes. Why do you think that is? What is it about your past that makes you want to be a trucker?"

Kurt bit his tongue, literally and figuratively, as he thought about the only thing he knew of his past. Because when he'd awakened, in the fire, the only items he had were a driver's license with his name, an acceptance letter from High Road Truck Driving School, and about ten thousand dollars in cash.

The cash thing had always troubled him, but he'd never told Todd about it. Or the fire. Not yet. Maybe not ever.

"What I mean," Todd continued, "is just this: you were going to become a trucker before your blank slate, right? You'd already applied to the school, been accepted. So that's a link to your past. Something to explore. But more than that, I think it says a bit about you."

"Like how?"

"What's appealing about trucking?"

Kurt had to admit the whole thing did appeal to him; he'd done well in the school and felt perfectly matched to trucking. "Well . . . I suppose the open road."

"And where does the open road lead to?"

"I don't know. Anywhere, I suppose. Forward."

"Forward. Interesting."

"Why?"

Todd folded his left leg beneath him, shifted, and settled in the chair again. Kurt smiled; he knew it had to happen sometime. It was something solid, something that marked their time together.

"It's not like I've done a personality inventory or anything, Kurt, but I'm guessing a lot of truckers like the lifestyle because it's solitary. Not much contact with other people, lots of time on the road alone, being the captain of your own ship, as it were."

"I suppose. I mean, that sounds good to me."

"Being on the road means never staying in one place for long. In your case, it may mean you're running from something in your past—running from something even before you lost your memory."

Kurt hesitated, thinking of his recent conversation with Jenny Lewis, the detective. If she was right, he had a lot to run from. "Maybe."

Todd leaned back in his chair. "But when I asked you why you wanted to be on the open road, you said because it meant you would always be moving forward."

"Yeah."

Todd unfolded his legs again and pushed his chair away from the desk, out onto the open floor so he was facing Kurt. "You know much about sharks, Kurt?"

Kurt shrugged.

"I guess I don't either. But I heard a story once, and it's always stuck with me. Sharks, you see, are one of the few animals that can't move backward. Incapable. Other fish, other animals of just about any kind—even amoebas—can reverse their direction. But a shark always has to move forward to stay alive."

"Okay." Kurt wasn't sure where this was going.

"So that says to me it's sometimes healthy to move backward, to see your past. That's something you've been unable to do, even after our several sessions together, but it's something you *have* to do. We need something to help you move backward before you can really start to move forward again. You're human, Kurt. You're not a shark."

Kurt thought about the fire, thought about the heavy stash of bills strapped to his midsection, thought about the pain in his body starting to fade as he walked away from the scene of destruction.

"Don't be so sure," he whispered to Todd.

64.

Ten miles down the road, Kurt was feeling better. Like the sky above, his head was clear. Sharp. Fresh. He could hold on to that sharpness, lose himself in the blur of miles streaking by, clear his life of everything that had happened in the last day.

After dropping this load in Chicago, he'd deadhead it back here—at this very moment, he was within an hour of the small town where he normally hid—and get to work on new projects for Macy. For the show she'd lined up for him.

There would be no catfish sculpture, of course. He'd have to abandon that. In some odd way, the catfish (shark?) was what had opened up the door between his world and the ghost world. He was sure of it. And now that the shoes were gone—not just gone, but destroyed—he could return to the life he'd had before, such as it was. When he made it home, he was going to pull out that silk dress, start working on the hands reaching for a face. That was the kind of thing Macy would want, anyway.

But those thoughts were instantly pushed away by a terrifyingly familiar image. The catfish, bathed in orange, filled every corner of his mind with equal parts brilliance and violence.

Shocked, Kurt tried to push the image away, but it would not leave. Even more terrifying, he heard a burst of static, followed by the voice of the ghost inside the shoes.

"You can't hide anymore, Kurt."

The voice was loud, painful, felt as if it were inside his head.

"You have to see. To understand."

"To see what?" He tried to concentrate on the voice. Was it Jonas again? It didn't sound like that voice, but it was familiar nonetheless. Eerily familiar.

"To see everything. Look in your mirrors."

Kurt did as instructed, and saw the headlights of another rig—another Peterbilt like the one he was driving—coming up fast. Terror raked his stomach with dull claws.

Jonas again? Had to be. Okay, so Jonas wasn't in the truck with him this time. He was in a truck behind him, intent on . . . something. That was impossible.

Okay, so *impossible* was something of a relative term in the world of Kurt Marlowe, Amazing Amnesia Boy. After all, following his head injury, he'd been able to communicate with the ghosts trapped in the clothing of dead people. He'd even spoken to one sitting in his front seat not so very long ago this morning. But this was even breaking all the rules of that world. The shoes had been destroyed in the garbage truck several miles behind.

He bit his lip. Had he really thought that would work? Deep down he had known it wouldn't. He'd thrown the shoes down a canyon just a few hours earlier, and Jonas, wearing the very same shoes, had reappeared inside the cab of his truck shortly after. Why would such shoes let a little thing like shredding keep them away? He knew they had to be in the truck directly behind him, waiting to be delivered by Jonas or whatever other ghost was driving his twin Peterbilt.

He pushed the pedal to the floor, knowing it would do him no good. All of Cross Trucking's rigs had governors installed, preventing them from traveling above seventy-five miles per hour. He was maxed out.

Kurt glanced in the rearview mirrors again. The truck behind him was gaining; evidently, it had no such governor slowing it down.

Ahead, on the right, a highway sign announced a turn-out for a chain-up area. He smiled. Yes, of course. He was about to go over Lookout Pass on the Montana/Idaho border. It would slow him to a crawl, but it would also slow the truck behind him. That would give him time to think of something.

He hit the beginning of the pass as fast as he could, using the inertia of the moving load to propel him, keeping the accelerator floored until he had to downshift once, then twice.

He glanced at his rearview mirrors and was unsurprised to see the form of the other truck behind him, hovering in the waves of heat radiating off the highway's surface. He still had a few minutes of lead time; if he could get over this pass, maybe even somehow get rid of the trailer . . . well, no, that wasn't an option. He'd need a few minutes to pull the king-pin and unhook the pig's tail that held the trailer, then jack it up off the fifth wheel.

Kurt downshifted again, slowing to a crawl. Behind him the other diesel slowed as it began to climb the pass, and Kurt felt a sense of relief. A sense of hope. He'd half expected the other truck to keep accelerating, to keep gaining on him as he tried to outrun it.

Maybe he could just cut the trailer loose. Really, all he needed to do was pull the release lever to unlatch it. Something inside told him he needed to avoid whoever—or whatever—waited in the truck behind him. If he could get to the top of this pass, cut his load loose, he could get down the opposite side, get away somehow. The other truck would still be climbing while he freewheeled it. And the other truck would still be hauling its own load, slowing it down.

After one more corner he was at the top of the pass; the road flattened for a quarter mile or so, offering a pullout. Without thinking, Kurt wheeled into the pullout and brought the Peterbilt to a halt with a hiss of air brakes. The entire rig shuddered as he hit the parking brakes and spilled out onto the pavement. He stumbled on the concrete surface, turning to look for the diesel he knew was behind him. He couldn't see it, but he heard it, and he saw the chug of black exhaust a couple turns behind him. He had a few minutes, at most.

Kurt scrambled to the front of the trailer, unlatched the safety chain from the pintle hook, and pulled the release lever; inside, he heard the safety jaws holding the trailer's kingpin retract, and the trailer shifted just a bit. For a moment, Kurt thought the trailer might start to roll away, but it stayed put.

He heard the other diesel, so very close now, even saw the twin smokestacks coming into view around the last corner approaching the top of the pass. He ran back to the cab and climbed inside once more.

He'd forgotten to release the electrical and air lines connecting the trailer, but that didn't matter now. They would simply snap off. Nothing mattered now, except outrunning the demon, the phantom, the ghost that pursued him.

Kurt put the rig into gear; it chattered as he tried to

move it too quickly. The tires began turning slowly, ever so slowly, and within a few seconds, he felt his truck moving. Sparks danced from the road's surface as the trailer's hitch snapped away from his truck and fell to the concrete. Now much lighter, he topped the rise at the top of the pass and began moving downhill; the big red Peterbilt—almost an exact double of his own, filled the rearview mirrors. His lead was now only a few hundred feet.

Odd; his pursuer wasn't pulling a load. Kurt could have sworn, when he'd watched the truck in the rearview mirrors before, that the truck was hauling a shipping container on a flatbed. But now, it was just the truck itself, like his own. If he hadn't ditched his trailer at the top of the pass, he would have been doomed for sure.

He felt gravity beginning to work with him rather than against him. He gained speed, moving around one turn and then another. Behind him, the other truck kept pace. He wasn't sure how the driver was managing, but he had a couple miles of downgrade on the Montana side of the pass to increase his lead.

Kurt peeled his eyes away from the rearviews and concentrated on the road ahead.

Forward, always forward. Like a shark. Todd had said that. Yes, like a shark. Not a catfish.

Kurt saw the next corner, felt the incline of the road becoming steeper, checked his speedometer. He was pushing fifty now, and he wasn't going to make the corner. He spun the wheel into the turn, struggling against the big rig as the tires beneath him chattered.

His truck rocked, and for a moment Kurt was sure he was going to tip; he tilted at the precipice for a moment, and then the wheels on the left side slammed to the ground again, bottoming out the suspension. A deep, mechanical burning smell began to waft through the cab; maybe he'd snapped something in the suspension.

Immediately, another corner came, this one curving to the right, and Kurt turned into it.

Somehow, his rig righted itself once more. Then, a few yards ahead, Kurt spotted a runaway truck ramp, a giant turnout filled with deep gravel for trucks that had burned out their brakes on giant passes like this one.

Maybe he could hit that ramp at that last second, surprise the truck behind him. If he managed to catch the ramp, and if the other truck went by, it would most likely tumble off the steep cliffs beyond. Kurt was almost doing that right now.

He looked into his rearview mirror and felt a giant shudder; his neck snapped backward, and he realized the other truck had bumped him. Impossibly, it had kept pace, even caught him.

Now or never, he thought, and he wrenched the wheel to the right as hard as he could, guiding his Peterbilt onto the long surface of the runaway ramp. As he hit the gravel, his truck sank immediately, and Kurt felt his whole body being thrown forward.

Even as this happened, another shudder pushed his whole truck forward, and Kurt knew the other Peterbilt had somehow, inexplicably, followed him onto the ramp and rammed him from behind.

A long, slow metallic shriek froze the world around him, but Kurt felt his body lifted out of the seat and through the windshield—through the windshield as if it were nothing more than paper—across the giant hood into the gravel beyond. He tumbled forever, spinning until he came to a stop facedown in the thick, heavy gravel. He smelled diesel, and that odd mechanical burning now stronger than ever, but beneath all that, the comforting smell he loved so much: pine trees. At least there was that. As he lay dying, he would be able to take with him the memories of fresh pine.

But his body wouldn't cooperate with his mind's wish to die. He felt it trying to stand, against his will, even though his legs wouldn't work. Nothing in his body would work. Maybe a broken femur or two. This thought struck him as funny, and he opened his mouth to laugh; instead, he felt liquid coming from his mouth. Blood, he realized. That meant a punctured lung or another internal injury.

After a few moments, though, his breath came back, and Kurt felt his legs, almost as if working on their own, bunching beneath him and forcing him to stand.

He turned and looked at the giant heap of twisted metal behind him. A thick, twisted column of bitter smoke erupted from the wreckage as angry orange flames rose toward the sky.

Amazingly, another man emerged from the wreckage.

Kurt stepped back, felt his right leg give out, and he went down again. The man, now free of the burning heap, moved toward him with a pronounced limp. One of the man's arms hung uselessly at his side.

Kurt struggled to his feet again. It wasn't Jonas, as he'd expected. And yet it was someone he recognized, someone from long ago.

(Stan. Stan _____.)

Stan something. His mind wouldn't give him the name of that kid . . .

(Stan Hawkins)

. . . from his childhood, that kid who had accidentally killed their gym teacher.

The man came to a stop in front of him, swaying. He spoke, and Kurt suddenly knew: it was the voice that had been speaking to him through the radio.

"It's not the ghosts outside haunting you," the looming form said. "It's the ghosts inside."

Kurt recognized the voice, still filled with broken static. But as the static filtered the voice, everything else suddenly cleared.

Looking into those eyes, Kurt remembered his past. And his future.

The man held out his hand, so Kurt—

65.

"Hello?" a voice said.

He opened his eyes a crack, closed them again as the light assaulted them in bright, rusty daggers of pain.

"His eyes moved," the voice from above said. "He's coming awake."

He tried to shake his head, but it felt weak.

"Just relax, Mr. Marlowe," the voice said. "Take it slow."

He tried to open his eyes again, and this time it was better. Colors began to resolve and come into focus. After a few seconds he made out two faces bent over him.

"You've been in an accident, Mr. Marlowe," the nearer face said to him. A man's face, unshaven. The face abruptly spoke to the other one, a woman. "Go get Dr. Chambers," it said, and he heard the squeak of shoes on a hard surface as the other face disappeared.

He opened his mouth to speak, but only a squawk came out.

"Like I said, Mr. Marlowe, you'll need to take it easy. You probably won't get your voice for a day or two. We just took you off the ventilator a few days ago."

Ventilator? Okay, so he'd been in an accident. Immediately, images flooded his mind. A column of smoke. Fire. Looking out on the destruction. All of it came back to him.

And . . . images of before. As if a new door had opened. Not just a ghost door, but a much bigger door.

He looked at the unshaven face still hovering above him. "How long?" he managed to rasp. The guy was right; his vocal cords felt like shredded cheese.

A puzzled expression crossed the unshaven face, and it came closer. "What was that?" the face asked, a little too loudly and slowly.

"How long?" he asked again.

The face seemed surprised, backed away. "Um, maybe you should talk to Dr. Chambers. Just relax."

He closed his eyes. Fine. He'd wait for Dr. Chambers. He felt warmth spreading throughout the rest of his body, and he moved his right hand.

"You moved your hand, Mr. Marlowe. That's very good."

He kept his eyes closed, smiled. The Amazing Amnesia Boy had a new trick: moving his hand.

New footsteps squeaked on the floor, and the voice from above spoke again. "This is Dr. Chambers, Mr. Marlowe."

He opened his eyes, looked at the face of Dr. Chambers. She had thick, curly hair and a warm, reassuring smile.

"You've been in an accident, Mr. Marlowe," she said.

So he'd heard.

"You may feel weak for a time, because . . . ah, there's no way to put this gently: you've been in a coma."

A coma. Well, that wasn't a surprise, was it?

"How long?" he tried to say again, but his vocal cords still wouldn't work. He wasn't sure if Dr. Chambers had understood his mouthed words, but she answered him anyway.

"You've been in a coma for almost a month. A long time, I know, but the good news is: you started coming out of it a week ago." She smiled. "We've been expecting you."

He wanted to ask more, but it was evidently impossible at the moment.

"I don't know what to say about your case," she continued. "When they brought you in, we expected you to be shattered. Broken bones everywhere. But no major injuries at all—some old injuries, extensive injuries—but . . . I don't know, it's like you bounced. Sometimes we see that with drunk drivers. They're so loose, they get through their crashes without a scratch." She cleared her throat.

He felt his brow furrow, and Dr. Chambers must have understood his confusion.

"You should just rest right now, Mr. Marlowe," she said. "Take this slow. Your major injuries were to the brain, but, ah—" She paused.

(brain damage)

She was going to tell him he had major brain damage. Big surprise.

"Ah—" she continued. Her voice dropped. "Well, to be perfectly honest, Mr. Marlowe, there's so much we don't understand about the brain. You had major swelling, which put you into the coma. But the brain is so much more resilient than we can even understand. Your MRIs have been steadily improving as you've been waking up, and I have to say, I think you're going to make a full recovery."

He smiled, closed his eyes again. And then, he slept.

66.

Doctors expected him to take several weeks, maybe even months, to recover. They told him to expect some grueling physical rehabilitation as he retaught his brain how to control his body. There had to be extensive damage, they told him, lingering effects. But then they did MRIs, CT scans, EEGs, a whole alphabet soup of tests and scans, and went quiet as all the results came back normal.

As everything showed a perfectly functioning brain.

When he surprised them by walking out of the hospital a week later, they were even quieter. Only Dr. Chambers spoke. She asked if he'd be willing to participate in a study, help her understand what had led to his recovery.

He smiled when she asked, said he'd be happy to.

After all, he knew, deep inside, that he'd fully recovered—from so much more than she would ever know.

His conversations with Todd had returned to him as he lay in the hospital bed that week. How sometimes, as humans, we need to move backward before we can move forward. That was what had done it. Moving backward.

That was what had brought him through the fire.

As he was checking out of the hospital, the woman behind the counter handed him a large plastic bag.

"What's this?" he asked, holding the bag up to examine it.

"Personal belongings. Mostly, um, the clothing you were wearing."

She was printing some paperwork, so he opened the bag and sifted through it. It smelled like smoke, dark and dangerous; scorch marks and bloodstains tattered the shirt and jeans. Evidently his hospital bill wasn't going to include laundry charges.

In the back pocket of the jeans he found a wallet with some credit cards, his commercial driver's license, and fifty dollars in cash.

He smiled. No, not ten thousand dollars in cash.

He transferred the wallet to the back pocket of the new jeans he was wearing, then dug through the front pockets of the scorched jeans. His fingers brushed plastic, and he grasped it and pulled it out.

It was a plastic bag holding a napkin with a number written on it: 1595544534. The number from Corrine. Surely, that part hadn't been physically real, had it? In many ways, that seemed the most disjointed of all.

And yet, here he was, holding the napkin. And now, as he looked at the number, he realized what it was. A ten-digit phone number.

He put the napkin into his pocket and began to sign the discharge paperwork the nurse was stacking in front of him.

He wasn't ready to touch the last two items in the bag yet. The shoes would have to wait.

67.

The shoes fit amazingly well. He had to admit that.

He still didn't understand the reversed 3 or the other writing, but he knew these leather shoes that had walked a thousand strange miles were now, somehow, his alone.

So he wore them. And he welcomed the image of the catfish (not a shark, but a catfish), which he now recognized was not simply swimming in a sea of orange. It was swimming in a sea of fire.

As he himself had done. As he himself would continue to do.

He returned to his home, opened his workshop, returned to the cold storage at the back of the shop. Inside, he heard the plaintive voices of the ghosts, begging for his help. He found the silk dress, pulled it out, listened as the ghost in the dress asked him to help find her sister.

He smiled, holding the dress lightly in his hands. "Tell me the name of your sister," he said.

And he listened to the ghost inside the dress, no longer

afraid of what it might say. No longer afraid of what the ghost inside his own clothing might say.

68.

Later that night, he took a break from the catfish sculpture. Yes, he would finish it. Yes, it would be the centerpiece of his exhibit. Macy had been able to reschedule the show, and was excited because his accident had created some buzz around the event.

He took the napkin, shielded inside the plastic bag, out of his pocket. He studied the number for a few moments, not sure if he really wanted to dial it or not.

In the end, he forced himself not to think about it too much, and he dialed.

It rang once, twice, and then a voice answered on the other end: "Hello?"

He recognized the voice immediately; the tears began to stream from his face. An odd sensation, really. Crying. When had he last wept?

For the first time in years, he spoke to his mother.

Moving forward, moving backward.

Human.

Second Stanza
Bottom-Feeder

20.

It was hell to watch the needle pierce her skin.

She should be used to it, of course. And thankfully this wasn't a chemo session; the R-CHOP kicked her to the ground every time, making her puke.

Or worse.

This was just a CT scan, and the IV would only be in her arm for a few minutes. Then it would all be over, and she would head back to her apartment and send out a fresh batch of e-mails while she waited for the next round of chemo in another ten days.

"Okay, you'll feel a rush," the radiation tech said to her.

Corrine nodded, as if this were all news to her. As if this radiation tech had never seen her before. As if she didn't know the radioactive solution would spread a wave of warmth from the top of her head to the tips of her toes, leaving the taste of old pencils in her mouth.

As if this whole cancer thing were nothing more than a minor inconvenience.

She closed her eyes, listened to the tech leave the room, listened to the hum of the scanner cycling just above her head.

After a few seconds the scanner cycled at higher RPMs, and the tech's voice came over a tinny speaker: "Take a deep breath and hold."

She did as instructed, keeping her eyes closed as she felt the table beneath her moving, carrying her through the giant doughnut-shaped machine. She wasn't a diver, but that's what she imagined it to be like; you took a deep breath, held, sank beneath the surface, lost all sensation. It sounded comforting, really, to be in a place where she couldn't feel anything. It would be a nice break from what she'd been in the midst of, which was the exact opposite: feeling everything.

The table beneath her stopped moving, and the radiation tech's voice came over the speaker again: "Breathe."

Yeah. Breathe. A good command, one she'd told herself after Dr. Swain gave her the news. It hadn't been the way she'd seen it in places like the Lifetime channel, with a doctor who placed a comforting hand on her leg while speaking with a tremulous tear in his eye: "I'm sorry, but you have cancer."

Instead, Swain had been looking at a folder of notes, black-and-white X-ray images on the screen next to him as he spat out a big mouthful: "It looks like you have diffuse large B-cell non-Hodgkins lymphoma."

Not even a "sorry" worked in there.

The table beneath her came back to its starting position, and the disembodied voice told her to take another breath and hold it.

Diffuse large B-cell non-Hodgkins lymphoma. Swain

had said it without looking up from his notes—the pathology report from the biopsy, she knew—and she half wondered if he was reading it to make sure he said it properly.

She'd been holding her breath ever since sitting down on the bench in his office, waiting for him to flip a page of the report and give her the news. So she'd been given the news, and she knew there was no reason to keep holding her breath, but the problem was: she couldn't breathe.

Nothing in, nothing out. She just sat there, dumbfounded, not really taking in anything he'd said except that last word. Lymphoma.

The doctor had looked up then. "You okay?" he asked.

Well, that had been a stupid question, hadn't it? She'd just been told she had some gobbledygook kind of lymphoma, and he wanted to know if she was okay. Still, she was thankful he'd asked, because it's what broke the paralysis of her lungs.

She'd laughed. Actually laughed. *Are you okay?*

The CT scanner finished its second cycle, and she heard the voice tell her to breathe again.

Yeah. Breathe.

22.

An hour later, back in front of her computer screen, waiting for a mass e-mail to relay through several fake IP addresses, she heard her cell phone ring. She recognized Dr. Swain's office number; since being diagnosed three months ago, she'd dialed it many times.

Could be bad news. Of course it could be bad news. But then, it could just be a reminder to give blood; she always had to give samples a week before each round of chemo to make sure her counts were holding up. Probably that, now that she'd thought of it; she faintly remembered being told to give blood on the day of her CT scan, but she'd forgotten until just now.

"Hello?"

"Corrine. Dr. Swain."

She smiled grimly. "Hi."

"You had your latest CT scan today."

"Yeah."

Surely he wasn't calling just to tell her this; she had, after all, been present at the scan, so this wasn't exactly news to her.

"I just talked to the radiologist, and he's still doing a report, but I wanted to talk to you about it right away."

"Oh." Just oh. That was the only word her mouth would form.

He paused, and when he did, she knew it was bad. Good old Dr. Swain wasn't a pauser; this was the guy, after all, who had casually blurted out her cancer diagnosis while he scanned pages of a report.

"I'm afraid," he said, "we're not seeing much of a response to the R-CHOP. Your chemo regimen."

And there it was again. That holding of the breath, that paralysis of the lungs, that inability to speak or think.

Breathe. Breathe normally.

"Okay."

"I think we need to look at other options."

Options. That was a good word, wasn't it? She held on to it.

"Which are?"

"You can come in and we'll talk about it, but I think you should consider a bone marrow transplant."

Transplant. That wasn't such a good word.

Dr. Swain was on a roll now, able to talk about the kinds of technical things that gave him comfort.

"We'll look at the donor registry, hope for a match. If I recall, you don't have any siblings."

"No."

"Related donor is the best, but if we can find a good match . . ."

She waited, but Dr. Swain evidently felt he'd uttered a complete sentence.

"But I can't have a transplant until we get rid of the lymphoma."

"We'll switch chemo regimens. High-intensity, myeloablative."

Myeloablative. Score that one on a Scrabble board.

"And that means?"

"That means, essentially, a very high dose. Higher than what you've been getting. Kills off the lymphoma cells, but also kills healthy cells—in your bloodstream, in your bone marrow. Then you receive new donor cells to bring back your blood counts."

Blood. From someone else. How Count Dracula.

"And?"

"And, if all goes well, you're cured."

"That's what you said about the R-CHOP."

Another pause. Actually, he hadn't said that, exactly. What he had said, not long after the old "You've been diagnosed with . . ." line, was "This is a highly curable form of cancer—85 percent or more. It's a good one to get, if you get cancer."

She had laughed at that line, too, because really, what else could she do? That Dr. Swain was a real comedian. *Are you okay?* after dropping the lymphoma bomb, followed quickly by *This is a good cancer to get.* Swain would kill—*kill*—at the Improv.

"Hello?"

She shook her head, trying to wrap her mind around this latest news. "Yeah. I'm here."

But for how much longer?

She pushed the question from her mind.

"As I said," Swain continued, "we need to search the registry. Several thousand names, lots of people on it. There's a college football team, even, that signs up for the registry during spring drills—kind of a tribute to their coach."

Wow. Now they were talking about college football.

"What . . ." Her tongue felt thick. "I mean, this transplant thing . . . is it dangerous?" Okay, that was a stupid question, but she figured old Swain could give her a break. Especially after some of his one-liners.

"It's a complicated process. You'll be in the hospital a minimum of a month. There's a treatment-related mortality rate of . . . well, perhaps 10 to 15 percent. And afterwards, GVHD—Graft-versus-host Disease—but a little bit of that is actually helpful. Let's just take the first step with the registry."

"Okay."

But that Swain-speak euphemism was sticking in her mind: treatment-related mortality. Really just another way of saying *death*. So 10 to 15 percent of people died just going through the transplant.

"I'll call you Monday. We'll talk more then, and I should have some news on the registry."

"Okay." She hung up the cell phone, glanced briefly at her computer screen to make sure her e-mails were still spooling.

Breathe. Breathe normally.

25.

Most people would never be able to become bottom-feeders. Corrine knew that. Their sense of self-worth prevented them from doing so, along with their sense of order and hierarchy. For the vast majority—and this included people everywhere, not just in the good old US of A—the true comfort zone was a basement in their souls. No matter what they did for a living, there were always people in their own personal basement who were farther down the chain of misery. Prostitutes and druggies lived in that basement, sure. Hicks from the sticks or down in the holler. Welfare moms in the projects. Used-car salesmen. Tobacco executives.

That basement was there so people could say, no matter their lot in life: *At least I'm not that guy on the corner with a WILL WORK FOR FOOD cardboard sign. At least I'm not that woman living in a tin shack without air-conditioning, waiting until the first of the month so I can get more food stamps. At least I'm not that firebug I keep reading about in the papers and seeing on the TV news, a guy who gets his kicks by burning down buildings.*

Corrine understood this. But she also understood that, in reality, most people were too weak to be part of the basement. That was the contradiction of it all. The bottom-feeders, the basement people, were the ones who were *real* because they didn't constantly stuff their egos with talk about how they were doing just fine.

Corrine understood this because she'd been a bottom-feeder since age fifteen. First as part of a traveling sales crew, carted from city to city and door-to-door trying to sell people overpriced magazine subscriptions so she could "fund her education" or "stay off the streets and out of trouble." Those were carefully rehearsed lines drilled into the heads of any kid on a traveling sales team, designed to appeal to that fear inside the people answering their doors.

See me? I've sunk so far that I'm going door-to-door hawking magazines, and I'm only fifteen or sixteen years old. By buying a magazine subscription from me, you'll be able to feel better about yourself because you'll believe it's improving my lot in life—if I win, I get a college scholarship—and because you'll be able to reinforce the disembodied voice that speaks to you from the basement of your own soul. The voice that says well, at least I'm not stuck going door-to-door like this poor kid.

But even for the kids on the traveling sales crews, there was a certain hierarchy. At the bottom were the door-to-door sales robots, repeating lines they'd learned by rote and hoping to appeal to the pity of homeowners. And then above them were the crew heads, like Marcus. And at the top were the ringleaders, the people who owned and financed the sales crews.

Of course, that ladder was reversed for the kids who were actually part of the crews: they placed themselves at the top, followed by the crew heads, followed by the owners. Time and again, she'd heard other kids on the crew talk about how the job sucked, but at least they hadn't sold their souls and become someone like Marcus.

Of course, Marcus ended up paying for his time in the basement in a big way.

Corrine didn't resent Marcus or his presence in her life, didn't point to her time with him as the great Traumatic Event that let her forever be a victim.

She was no victim.

Maybe Marcus was even out of the pen now, running another crew or two, or bankrolling a few if he'd come into some cash. Marcus was a bottom-feeder, and once you were a bottom-feeder, you never became anything else. Corrine knew this too well.

She sighed, pushed her chair closer to the computer keyboard, started typing another e-mail message promising an instant degree from Heritage Springs University. Even now, more than a decade after getting out of the traveling sales crew game, she was still selling the same elusive dream.

Better yourself, keep yourself out of the basement.

She'd graduated, long ago, from a traveling salesperson to an e-mail spammer. A phishing artist. A site scammer.

Still a bottom-feeder, though.

Most people could never picture themselves doing any such thing. In many ways, it was even worse than the prostitutes and the druggies who were often the lowest dregs.

But then, for someone like Corrine, who was strong enough to stand here in the basement without any qualms about her self-image, it was just a part of existence.

In an odd way she was proud of what she'd been able to accomplish; she was on InterNIC's list of the ten biggest spammers and always one step ahead of efforts to block her work. One step ahead of most of the other spammers out there, even; she'd developed techniques others had incorporated. So that made her something of a Bottom-Feeder Leader.

She smiled, started spooling the latest e-mail message into her database of more than ten million harvest addresses. Desperate as some people might think she was, there were always people on this list of addresses—roughly half a percent, day in and day out—who would respond to the e-mail and make her some money. Add in the account numbers from phishing scams, the ad revenue from ghost sites for search engine keywords, the comment spams from blogs linking to yet more ghost sites . . . well, as bottom-feeders went, she ate well.

Still, she had to admit, even though she scoffed at the people who felt they were somehow better off than the others around them, she wasn't immune to the behavior herself.

She realized this shortly after being diagnosed with

lymphoma. How easily, before, she'd been able to see stories of people on the Internet who were paralyzed in car accidents, who tremored with Parkinson's disease, who sank into vegetative comas, and think: *At least I'm not there.*

But now, she was there. Had been there for four months, one week, two days, and sixteen hours. A cancer patient.

Luckily, because her only real contact with the outside came through e-mail and the Web, she hadn't been subjected to the pity of those around her. Yet another benefit of being a bottom-feeder.

But these things did gnaw at her when she went to see Dr. Swain, when she showed up for blood draws or chemo sessions. She saw the pity in the eyes of the staff and the nurses, and that, almost more than anything, killed her.

The first time she'd been sent to see Dr. Swain was the worst. Just before her biopsy, just before her diagnosis, just before the whole nightmare began springing to life around her. She checked in at the desk, filled out forms with her address and financial information, then turned them in.

The woman at the receptionist's desk had looked over the forms as she pulled out an electronic tablet and handed it to her.

"What's this?"

"It's a survey."

"A survey for what?"

The receptionist had looked at her and offered a well-practiced smile. "All of our cancer patients here fill out the survey every few weeks or so, to help us get an idea of how they're feeling."

Corrine stared, then slowly took the electronic tablet. The receptionist had said "cancer patient." She was here for a *consult* with Dr. Swain. She didn't know that she, in fact, had cancer. Neither did Dr. Swain. No one did, least of all this woman wearing a too-tight blouse and handing her an electronic tablet. That's why she would need a biopsy, follow-up blood work, and scans.

Coming in for a *consult* did not automatically make her a cancer patient.

Fuming, Corrine retreated to a chair in the corner and pressed the power button on the tablet. The screen told her this was a five-minute survey to help her medical team offer the best possible care, and that the answers would not be shared with anyone else. Fine. She touched the Continue button with the stylus.

She answered a few demographic questions about her age, health history, family history. Then the questions took a turn. During the last two weeks, had she felt depressed?

Well, yes. Being told you may have cancer (emphasis on *may*) does that.

The questions continued, all of them very concerned about what had happened to her in the last two weeks. Had she cried uncontrollably? Had she vomited after chemotherapy? Had she entertained suicidal thoughts? Had she noticed bleeding gums or skin ulcers?

She wanted to scream at the tablet, tell it what she hadn't told the woman in the tight shirt: I'M NOT EVEN A CANCER PATIENT YET. I'M JUST HERE FOR A CONSULT. But of course, that wasn't an option on the touch screen; only Yes or No buttons to be pressed.

She started by answering No to these kinds of questions, but after a few minutes she changed tactics and clicked Yes every time. Put that into their statistical models. Bloody stool? Yes. Tingling in her hands and feet? Of course. Hair loss? Oh, yes. They wanted her to act like a poor, pitiful cancer victim, she'd give it to them.

At the end of the survey, she was given an option of connecting wirelessly to an Internet support forum that would help answer more of her questions about cancer.

She smiled. Some light at last.

She pressed Yes, indicating that she did want to get information, and gave one of her many e-mail addresses to log in.

Later that night, after her first visit with Dr. Swain (who even then, that first time, felt most comfortable explaining everything to her while referring to his notes), she replied to the cancer subscription e-mail in her in-box. She stripped the header information from the e-mail, tracked down the fixed IP address where it originated, pinpointed the server that hosted the forums. A couple hours later, she'd hacked all the e-mail addresses from the forums and planted a robot script that would harvest additional e-mails from member address books whenever they logged in.

After that, she'd managed to break into the network and software that controlled the electronic tablets in Dr. Swain's office. She left a little something in the system for them. Call it a welcoming gift from their newest *cancer patient*: a self-replicating virus that would paralyze their whole network.

Two weeks later, after a couple more appointments with Dr. Swain, she'd told the receptionist it had been two weeks since her last survey, and it was time to take another.

The receptionist, wearing another shirt that was just as tight, seemed a bit perturbed at her cheerfulness, as if such emotion had no place in a facility that treated cancer.

"We're having some troubles with our survey system right now," she said.

"That's too bad," Corrine had replied with a straight face. "It was really comforting and informative for me." She knew the woman would love those words.

The receptionist had unexpectedly reached across the desk and patted her hand. "Do you want to talk with one of our social workers?"

"Social workers?"

"Sure. Just to talk. Many patients say it helps."

"Do the social workers have electronic access to my medical records?"

"Of course."

"And can I keep in touch with them by e-mail? I mean, do they have access to the Internet with their computers?"

"Yes."

Corrine had smiled. Ah, new back doors into the system. How wonderful.

"Yes, I think that would be very helpful. Even more comforting and informative."

She offered a perfect pity-inducing smile, a smile she'd been able to perfect after knocking on the doors of thousands of people and telling them she needed their help to stay off the streets, to stay out of trouble.

31.

Over the weekend, she netted three thousand dollars just from click-throughs and ad revenue at her several shell sites. Not bad, not bad at all. And that didn't even count the value of the fifty names and credit card numbers she'd captured in phishing scams; on the black market, she could get several hundred dollars for each one. Or keep them for herself, if she wanted to do some shopping.

She rarely did that, though. No need to leave a trail. Let the others get caught for the identity thefts; she was happy to be the middleman. Middlewoman. Whatever.

She logged in to one of her Chinese servers, scanned the list of available IP addresses she'd reserved. Thousands of them, hosted by a fake company she'd set up with a couple other SpamLords. That's what they actually liked to call themselves, she found out after her first tentative contact with them some years ago. SpamLords. Evidently, everyone had to rule over a kingdom of one's own, no matter how small.

So she'd become a SpamLord too. And quietly, over the last two years, several of them had been building up their own backbone in mainland China, hosting their own sites and scams, even attracting some legitimate business. All of it housed on servers at a giant warehouse in northern China's Heilongjiang province.

China. The true final frontier, with apologies to Gene Roddenberry.

She'd seen photos of her warehouse, even done some quick translations of words, signage, and characters she'd seen in the photos. She quickly found out that Heilongjiang, the name of the province, literally meant "Black Dragon River." She liked that. Black dragons.

The warehouse where her servers were stored had a simple sign on its chain-link fence, consisting of two Chinese characters. One character roughly translated as "cat," the other translated as "fish." It made absolutely no sense to her, but what of it? For all she knew, it had some specific meaning in Chinese culture; certainly, dragons and catfish were revered in the country, from what little she'd been able to glean online. And she was immediately drawn to the image of a catfish, anyway. The perfect bottom-feeder. Much like herself. So in her mind, she always called the warehouse the Catfish Compound.

The Catfish Compound, and the server farm it housed, helped her send millions of e-mail messages through the Internet, relaying them back and forth among dozens of active IP addresses and legitimate servers in other countries. Invariably, legitimate service providers tracked the originating IP addresses and blacklisted them. But she always had more. Always.

She selected a ten-digit IP address and began setting up a relay script when her cell phone rang.

She looked at the caller ID, again recognizing Swain's number. Monday. Right. He had promised to call back today. Lost in her work, she'd forgotten the *cancer* word for a while.

She sighed. But never for long; cancer was never out of her mind for long.

She picked up the phone, answering with a quick "Hello?"

"Corrine," Swain's voice said. "Dr. Swain."

"Hi."

"I said I'd call you about the donor registry," he said.

"Yeah."

"Maybe you could come in, and we can talk about it."

Oh, so here was Swain, trying to pretend he had a bit of human warmth. Wanting to deliver bad news—and it had to be bad news—in person.

"I'm a big girl, Dr. Swain. Just tell me what's going on."

"Well," he said, "we're not finding a good match."

She pursed her lips. "A donor match, you mean."

"Yes."

"So no go on the transplant."

"Well, right now . . . that's right. No good match for a transplant."

She smiled. As if continuing to repeat "no good match for a transplant" somehow sounded better than a simple *no*.

"Okay."

"I . . . well, I would like you to come in so we can talk about some different options."

"Such as?"

"A clinical trial, maybe."

"We already did that."

"Well, yes. We looked at Phase II and above. But I think there might be some Phase I trials we can look at."

Translation: time to start grasping at straws. Phase II through IV trials were designed to fine-tune treatments already proven in Phase I trials. They experimented with dosage, timing, routes of administration, that kind of thing. Phase I trials were always one step away from lab mice, rolls of the medical dice. Important, yes, but often the last hope.

"How about if I transfer you to the front desk, and they'll schedule you for an appointment this week?" Swain sounded desperate to end their conversation.

She stared at the IP addresses glowing on her screen. "Yeah. Sure."

She waited, and he put her on hold. When she heard the soft tinkling of the hold music, she hung up the phone.

36.

Late that afternoon she sat staring at her screen, a jumble of information cramming her mind. She'd spent the intervening time looking up lymphoma information on the Internet, had visited at least two dozen sites, followed several rabbit trails for treatment.

She'd already been to most of the sites before, right after her diagnosis. But now she had a renewed sense of urgency. She'd moved from "highly curable" lymphoma to "investigational treatment" in the span of three rounds of chemo. Four months. And one head of hair.

She looked at the white Styrofoam heads in the corner. Three of them, each holding a different wig. One auburn red, one dusty blonde, one coal black. Her mix-and-match headgear.

She stared at the wigs, realizing for the first time that it was unlikely she would regrow her own natural hair, a nice chestnut brown. Not now. Not ever.

She would die before it happened, because she would most likely be on chemotherapy of some kind for the rest of her short life. Sure, maybe she'd participate in one of the Phase I clinical trials Swain had talked about. But then, if those did nothing in a couple of months, Swain would move on to "palliative care"—yet another medical euphemism for *dying*.

And because anything she did from here on out would probably involve heavy chemotherapy of some kind, maybe even some experimental new kinds of chemotherapy (hello, Phase I clinical trials!), her hair would never be back.

Tears began to flow, and within seconds, Corrine was sobbing uncontrollably.

41a.

The next morning, Corrine caught a cab to the address for GraceSpace, the tattoo shop she'd picked out of the dozens she'd found and researched on the Web.

After her crying jag, she had decided to do what she'd pledged to do at the beginning of the ordeal. To be more impulsive. Like Lance Armstrong.

She had seen a documentary on TV just a few weeks

after she'd first heard the *lymphoma* word, a puff piece about Lance Armstrong, the most famous man to have cancer.

During the interview Armstrong had said, "Cancer's the best thing that ever happened to me," and Corrine had laughed. That Lance Armstrong, he was almost as funny as good old Dr. Swain. Most people laughed when they heard things that were truly humorous; Corrine, on the other hand, laughed at anything absurd. Or painful. Or, truth be told, frightening. Laughing gave her so much more control than the alternative.

But after watching all of Lance Armstrong's interview, after absorbing everything he had said, she hadn't laughed. In an odd way, what he'd said made sense. A little bit. After all, this whole cancer could be a chance to change her life, reprioritize, get back in touch with people she hadn't talked to forever, explore the things she'd always wanted to do someday.

But she hadn't done that. Two weeks after diagnosis, a round of chemotherapy under her belt, she had told herself she was going to be more impulsive, do some different things the next week. Just as soon as she'd recovered from the chemo a bit, which had exhausted her.

Two weeks after that, well, she was just a week out from her next chemo, and she didn't want to do anything that would interfere with it. Her blood counts needed to stay high, and if she went anywhere, caught a cold, she could jeopardize it all.

Two weeks after that, she'd been in the middle of a new

project, and the second round of chemo hadn't been that bad at all, and another two weeks after that—

Well, that's what brought her here now. With incurable lymphoma, it turned out.

When it all started, she had a *highly curable form of cancer.* That had seemed somehow comforting. That made it a test, a thing to be conquered, a challenge that could be referred to in the future as *the best thing that ever happened to me.* That's what Lance Armstrong had said, and that's what she had believed.

So she went through the motions, believing all along that she would have time to make all those healthy changes, do all those impulsive, life-celebrating things. She was already ahead of most people, ahead of people who never faced any kind of scary diagnosis like cancer. It was a wake-up call, but she could press the snooze button and go back to those changes at some point down the road. After all, she had a *highly curable form of cancer.*

But now she realized she'd done nothing with the wake-up call. Instead, she'd slipped into that dark zone where you never woke up. She'd been told, in a lot more words, that this cancer was going to kill her. It wasn't a challenge, or an obstacle, or a chance to reprioritize. It was death.

Maybe it was the best thing to ever happen to Lance Armstrong, but it would be the last thing to ever happen to her.

And so, it really was time to be impulsive. She'd always

wanted a tattoo. What better time to get one? What better time just to drop everything and do something unexpected?

Two weeks ago she might have told herself it was dangerous to get a tattoo at this time, with her immune system impaired by chemo and the risk of infection or complications or any of a thousand other things going wrong. Swain would have a coronary if he saw her doing this.

But really, what was the worst that could happen? She would die? Cancer was already taking care of that; might as well enjoy the ride on the way down.

The cabbie pulled to the curb, pressed the button for the final fare, turned, and looked at her. "Fifteen-sixty," he said, announcing the fare.

She pulled out a fifty, shoved it at him. "Keep the change," she said.

He paused. "Fifteen, not fifty," he said, pointing at the fare.

"Yeah, I know," she said, smiling. Her wig—the dark, dark one—itched her scalp, but she ignored the sensation. She wanted to concentrate on Spreading a Little Love to others, and she'd start by giving a cab driver a giant tip.

The cabbie held the bill up to the light, inspecting it.

"You think I'm passing you a counterfeit fifty?" she said, a bit incredulous and insulted.

He shrugged.

"How about, 'Wow, lady, thanks for the big tip,' something along those lines?"

"Wow, lady, thanks for the big tip," he deadpanned, stuffing the bill into his pocket and looking out into traffic, waiting for her to get out of the car.

She slid out the door, turned to speak to the cabbie again. "You know, I have terminal cancer, so I'm trying to spread a little goodwill. You're not helping."

He flipped on his left turn signal without turning. "I got hemorrhoids, lady. I keep 'em to myself."

She closed the door, and he zoomed out into traffic. So much for that good deed.

She was in the heart of Fremont, the Seattle neighborhood generally acknowledged as the artsiest, quirkiest, funkiest, everythingiest. With a troll under the Aurora Street Bridge and a Lenin statue on its most famous street corner, the neighborhood embraced the odd, and Corrine had always liked that. In Fremont, she could find Fellow Travelers, people who weren't afraid to let their bottom-feeder flags fly.

She liked the tattoo shop. Tattoo parlor. Whatever you wanted to call it. It was sandwiched between a taco shop and a place billing itself as a "bohemian outfitter," one of the small street-front spaces in a converted warehouse of some kind. She'd been drawn to the name immediately when she'd done her Web search the night before: GraceSpace. Sounded like a place for a fresh start, a renewal.

A giant chained gate covered the storefront, and a round, hand-painted iron sign was bolted to the brick above her. GRACESPACE, the iron sign said, intricate black cursive letters on a lemon yellow background, with ivy adornments. Artsy. She liked it.

She was drawn out of her reverie by a woman unlocking the chain gate in front of the storefront. The woman didn't look like a tattoo artist, but what did Corrine know? She'd never gotten a tattoo.

Maybe she'd expected some Goth girl with powdered makeup and pierced, bloodred lips; instead, she was staring at a middle-aged woman with shoulder-length hair, un-assuming slacks, and a long-sleeved print blouse. Corrine stepped in and helped her raise the gate.

The woman turned, thanked her. Corrine noticed dark, sunken eyes. Clammy skin. Almost as if she were a chemo patient herself. It added a bit to the Goth vibe, but still, she seemed more Soccer Mom than Tattoo Chick.

"I want a tattoo," Corrine said, watching the woman now unlock the door behind the gate and feeling like a five-year-old asking for candy. She followed the woman inside, offered her hand when she turned around again. "I'm Corrine," she said.

"Grace," the woman answered, shaking her hand.

Grace. That would explain the name. GraceSpace. Grace's Space. Corrine decided she liked that, too, this woman who was unafraid to claim her own bit of land. Like some kind of intrepid explorer at the North Pole.

A soft beep was coming from the phone's digital answering

system, and she could see the woman—Grace—glance in the phone's direction nervously. Obviously, she didn't want to check messages with a potential customer here.

"Better check your messages," Corrine said, trying a smile. It felt grotesque. The wig itched her scalp.

"You sure you don't mind?"

"No, no. Not at all." Corrine sat in one of the wooden chairs in the main reception area. Nice and cozy inside, almost a Beaux Arts feel. A little help from the "bohemian outfitter" next door, maybe. She waved her hand at the woman, a motion that said go ahead.

The headset on the woman's phone was way too loud, and Corrine heard every message. She tried not to listen, but attention to detail had been pounded into her since her days on the traveling sales crew. Standing at someone's door, you always looked for clues to help you make the sale; harvesting e-mails from the Web, you always looked for clues that would tell you what kinds of messages people might respond to. Details.

Every message the woman listened to revolved, in one way or another, around something called Black Tar. Tattoo slang, obviously.

Eventually, the woman hung up the phone.

"What's black tar?" Corrine asked, and Grace spun to look at her, seemed to lose her composure for a moment. "Sorry," Corrine said, filling in the awkward silence. "Your headset—I couldn't help but hear it."

The woman nodded. "Black Tar is a new ink I'm using. Good coverage, darkest black you'll ever see."

Corrine felt a bitter smile on her face. *You want to see true darkness, try looking at the blood that drips out of your vein after they finish a six-hour chemo session. Try sitting in Swain's office while he stares at his reports, stumbling his way through a complete sentence. Try looking at your bald reflection in a mirror after you've been told a transplant is a no-go.*

This woman had no idea what the darkest black looked like.

"I've seen some pretty black stuff," Corrine said, but she could tell the woman was just giving her a polite smile.

Still, Corrine liked her. She felt . . . comfortable with this woman. Grace. Especially after being stuck in rooms with nurses and radiation techs and Swain, people who stuck needles into her skin and prodded her while barely acknowledging her presence.

It would be nice to have needles in her skin by choice for a change.

"Let's do it," she said too cheerfully. "Let's use some Black Tar."

The woman offered another polite smile. "Okay, well, I usually do a consult on a design—give me an idea what kind of tattoo you're looking for, where it's going, that kind of thing. Then we schedule a time."

Corrine nodded, feeling oddly lightheaded and chipper.

"Here's the thing," she said. "I made an oath to myself a couple months ago to be more impulsive. Only I haven't been. Until now. Until last night, actually. I decided I wanted a tattoo, so today I'm getting a tattoo."

The woman seemed serious for a moment. "Well, that's part of why I do the consult. Make sure you're *not* doing it on just an impulse, make sure you're comfortable with something that could last the rest of your life."

For once Corrine controlled the impulse to laugh. It was her natural reaction to bad news and stress, true. But now would be a bad time. Still, that was a good one—right up there with some of Swain's zingers. And Lance Armstrong's. A tattoo from a box of old Cracker Jacks might last the rest of her life, as far as she knew.

She took a deep breath, looked at Grace. Time to play the cancer card.

"I, uh . . . I was diagnosed with incurable cancer a couple months ago. That's when I decided to be more impulsive, like I said. And . . . I guess I'm running out of time to be impulsive."

So she'd fibbed a bit on that; she'd actually been diagnosed with a *highly curable* form of cancer, but . . . well, that had been a fib told to her, now, hadn't it?

Grace stared for a few moments before she nodded. At least the woman didn't spout off about being sorry, her voice going syrupy-sweet as if she were talking to a three-year-old.

It had happened to her before. More than once. Often in the chemo room at the oncology center. Or at the front desk. Ms. Tight Blouse.

"What were you thinking of doing?" Grace asked her.

"I don't know. Impulsive, like I said. Call me a blank canvas."

The woman sat in thought, then abruptly stood. "Okay, then," she said. "Let's do it."

Corrine followed her to a small room at the back of the shop. Dark. No windows. Grace crossed the room, turned on a light clamped to a small table covered by white paper. Next to it was another table, this one sans paper on its gleaming chrome surface, and a large dentist's chair.

"Have a seat," Grace said, sitting down on a wheeled stool and pulling on surgical gloves.

Corrine hesitated. Maybe this was a bad idea. It looked a little too much like . . . a little too much like a chemo session. Comfy chair, designed to make you think this really wasn't a Big Deal at all, this poison getting injected into your bloodstream. Low light to keep you quiet and still. Sharp instruments on a clean worktable, ready to Make Everything Better. Grace was even fastening a surgical mask to her face, of all things, and she turned to peer through the darkness at Corrine.

"Time to be impulsive," she heard Grace's voice say, but it was disconcerting being unable to see her lips.

Be impulsive. Who had said that? Oh, yeah. She had.

Corrine walked across the floor, settled into the chair,

tried to relax. She wanted to check her hair, make sure she hadn't jarred the wig when she sat down, but she didn't want to draw attention by messing with it now. At least it had stopped itching.

Grace had her back to her, messing with stuff on the table. Preparing. After a couple of minutes, she turned again, holding an instrument that looked somewhat like a bad kitchen implement.

"This is the tattoo gun," Grace said, obviously picking up on the questions in Corrine's eyes. "I attach the needle here, draw ink into the tube up here. Just relax."

Relax. Sure, she could relax. *Breathe. Breathe normally.*

"Okay," Grace continued. "Any more thoughts on what you want? Where you want it?"

"My arm," she said. "Something big. Something strong."

Grace nodded, adjusted the task light so it was focused on her arm. "Maybe slip this arm out of your shirt," she said. "So we don't stain it."

Corrine did as instructed.

"Now," Grace continued, "like I said before: just try to relax."

Corrine heard a whirring sound—also something like a bad kitchen implement—and immediately felt a ripple of pinpricks on her arm, followed by a few seconds of silence. She watched as Grace wiped away some ink, then triggered the gun again with another whirr. This time, the pinpricks didn't feel quite so bad, and her eyelids seemed heavy.

She closed her eyes, listening to the tattoo gun grind, the wheels on Grace's chair squeak with subtle movements, the lightbulb in the work lamp hum, and within seconds, she felt nothing.

3.

The appeal of being on a traveling sales crew had faded faster than a cheap T-shirt.

Corrine had answered an ad in her local newspaper just a few months earlier, a small ad filled with exclamation marks and promises: *Earn $100+ Every Day! Exciting Travel Opportunities! Full Training!* The ad had said nothing about traipsing from door to door, aiming to look like a poor, starved soul doing your best to stay off the streets and stay out of trouble or, depending on the person who answered the door, to earn scholarship money for college. After a few months on the road, Corrine had begun to write the ad that lured her in her own style: *Earn $100 Every Day for Your Crew Leader! Exciting Travel Opportunities for Anyone Who Loves Riding a Thousand Miles with Six People Stuffed into a Junky Van! Full Training, Complete with Hotel Lockdowns and Beatings!!*

Corrine had figured out in her second week that she'd signed up for something like a forced labor camp. Marcus, their crew leader, kept them locked away—all six of them in one room—when they weren't on the streets selling. He pitted them against each other, making them compete to get the most sales. Sometimes, if you didn't meet your quota, he handcuffed you to the bed in the dive hotel room, kept a gag over your mouth.

Yes, the wonderful world of traveling sales was certainly *Exciting!* Still, Corrine had figured out the most effective way to deal with it was to roll with the changes, keep your eyes forward, don't stand out by being at either the top of the ladder or the bottom.

But not everyone in her crew was like that. One of the girls, Jenny, seemed to have this odd fascination with Marcus, a hero-worship thing. Something like the dog that gets beaten by its owner, yet always runs to lick the owner's hand when he holds it out. Jenny, you had to be careful of; if you said anything in the hotel room at night, she would run and tell Marcus the next morning.

At the opposite end, a round-faced kid from Iowa named Terrance often seemed to thrive on the abuse. He tested Marcus at every turn, almost willing him to beat him or take away his money or lock him away for the day. Terrance, it seemed, thrived on being the whipping boy. And after he'd been on the crew just two weeks (he'd joined about a month after Corrine, at another of the endless stops across the Midwest), she saw the pressure building between Marcus and Terrance. She understood that pressure would naturally find its release in an explosion, and she also understood she would very likely be standing at ground zero when it happened.

So it came as no surprise to be here, at this very moment, stuck in the third seat of the minivan next to Terrance somewhere in the middle of Oklahoma, as Marcus screamed at him from the driver's seat. Corrine watched casually as Marcus's hateful gaze darted to the rearview mirror every few seconds, fixing on Terrance in the backseat beside her. Terrance, for his part, simply smiled beatifically every time he saw Marcus glance at him in the mirror, which in turn caused fresh waves of anger to radiate away from the front seat.

It had been like this the whole hour they'd been on the road this morning, and they had about another nine hours to get to Sioux Falls, their next destination.

Terrance, she thought idly, might actually be energized by nine more hours of listening to Marcus losing his self-control. What little self-control he had. The rest of them in the car winced every time Marcus screamed—especially Jenny, who seemed to take every uttered expletive with a painful jolt.

Of course, Corrine could stop it. She could step into the middle of it, be the peacemaker, calm Marcus's frustrations, distract Terrance with some idle chatter. Terrance had a thing for her, anyway. She could tell.

But that would go against her personal code. She needed to stay invisible, in the middle of the pack. Just ride the waves and get through it. That code had brought her through her first couple months, and it would bring her through a couple more. Until she figured out her next steps. Until she figured a way out of this white van with the taped-on bumper and the red passenger door retrieved from a junkyard.

Just before the accident, Marcus had said something she knew would stick with her forever, a bit of Confucius-inspired wisdom that would change her life even though Marcus had meant it as just another of his many insults.

Marcus looked into the rearview mirror, beads of sweat on his angry red forehead. "You're just a bottom-feeder, Terrance," he said. "You're all just bottom-feeders, and that's all you'll ever be."

Yes, there was something that rang true about that in Corrine's mind. She liked the image of herself as a bottom-feeder; it was comforting.

But the image didn't have long to give her comfort, because Marcus had kept his eyes away from the road for too long, staring at Terrance, who dumbly smiled and nodded. Jenny had time to get out a single "Marcus!" (and even in her panic, Jenny had managed to inject his name with a reverent tone) before the van slipped off the small shoulder and into the ditch running beside the highway.

At roughly seventy miles per hour, the van had cartwheeled, going end over end once, twice, three times. Corrine knew this because the whole event had slowed down, happened in slow motion for her.

Both she and Terrance, in tandem, had slid forward in their third-row seat. She had clipped the back headrest of Jenny, just in front of her. But Terrance had somehow become more airborne than she, as if he were lighter, and he actually slid over the top of Brad, the freckle-faced kid sitting just ahead of him.

At the next revolution, Terrance had disappeared, sliding out of the van somewhere—one of the windows? the windshield?—and Corrine had time to think that this was what it must feel like inside a clothes dryer. She tumbled, her face hitting the ceiling of the van and then her shoulder being painfully wrenched away, and then it all stopped.

It was only then she realized that all of this had happened in utter silence; amazing as it was, she'd never heard a scream, or a shudder of metal, or a screech of brakes, during the whole accident. It was only after they'd come to a stop, the van slowly rocking back and forth on its collapsed roof, that sound returned.

Jenny, of course, was wailing. Outside, something sounded like rain coming down on the van, even though Corrine knew the sky above had been blue. After a moment, she realized it was dirt, kicked up by the rolling van, coming back down in a fine mist on the van itself.

"Shut up, Jenny," she said, and amazingly, Jenny did. The fine spray of dirt ended, and Corrine pushed herself away from the ceiling of the van; next to Jenny, the window was literally gone.

"Crawl out the window," she said to Jenny.

The girl sniffed a few times, muttered something under her breath, and managed to slide out the window.

Corrine shifted position, feeling a deep twinge in her shoulder, and slid forward, then out the window behind Jenny.

Now there was a new sound surrounding them. A ticking sound, punctuated by a slow hiss. Steam from the radiator, maybe?

"Help me get them out," she said to Jenny, deciding she needed to go back into the van. She went in and pulled out Brad, dragging him across the ceiling and onto the dewed grass of the field where the van now lay on its back like a helpless bug.

Jenny remained outside, rocking back and forth with her knees pulled up toward her chest. Corrine started to say something, then decided it really didn't matter.

Now she smelled smoke, and when she slid back inside the van, she saw a thick black cloud starting to spew from under the dash. Or rather, above the dash, since the van was upside down. Terrance had slipped out of the van somehow, and so had Dianna, who had been sitting in the front seat beside Marcus. Marcus was the only one left.

Corrine slid outside once more, noticed the driver's door beside Marcus was wedged open just a few inches, tried to push at it. It was stuck. She stepped back, kicked at it a few times, finally got it open another foot or so.

Black smoke now filled the interior of the van, making her cough.

"Leave him."

Corrine spun around, and Jenny said it again.

Still sitting on the grass, still pulling her knees in toward her chest, still rocking. She stared at nothing in particular and repeated her command: "Just leave him."

Odd words coming from the one person who seemed to care anything about Marcus, but Corrine had no intention of leaving him. She didn't know why, and now was no time to start wondering.

She slid into the door, grabbed hold of Marcus's purple button-up shirt, and pulled. His body came easily, as if he were nothing more than a bag of flour or something, and she continued to pull at him until he was free of the van. Grass now stained his purple shirt.

Corrine stared back at Jenny, sitting on the grass next to Brad, who still hadn't stirred. "You better get away from the van," she said to Jenny as orange flames joined the black smoke.

Then, out on the lonesome secondary highway, which seemed an impossibly long way off, she saw a blue pickup pull to the side of the road. Evidently, it was the first vehicle to pass since the accident.

An older man in a straw cowboy hat popped out of the door, yelled something she couldn't understand, then disappeared into the ditch for a second and began running in her direction. She walked toward him, making it fifty feet or so before Cowboy Hat met her and clutched at her arms a little too tightly; her shoulder rumbled in pain.

"Are you all right?" he asked, and she thought it an odd question.

She'd just been in a huge car wreck—how could she be all right? She laughed, realizing it was an inappropriate reaction but knowing she couldn't control it. Laughing was her natural reaction.

She started to point back toward the van, then pulled her arm back when the shoulder protested. "Can you check on them?" she asked, and Cowboy Hat nodded before continuing toward the van, eager for his chance to be a hero.

Corrine ran toward the blue pickup, stumbling down into the ditch and crawling up the other side. The pickup was still running, idling at the side of the highway, where dark chunks of dirt marked the path of the van.

Without looking back, she crawled into the pickup, shifted it into first, and sped out onto the highway.

Toward her future.

42b.

Corrine awoke, shuddering as she shook off the effects of the bad dream. She'd dreamed about that morning on the

Oklahoma prairie so many times. But not in the last few years.

She opened her eyes, peered into hazy darkness, felt someone rubbing at her tingling arm.

Oh yeah. Be impulsive. She was in a tattoo shop. Parlor. Whatever.

She turned to look at her arm, to see what Grace had chosen to do, and for a moment she stared breathlessly.

She'd heard people call tattoos body art, and now she fully understood why. Her upper arm had been transformed into a colorful catfish, sparkling with iridescent blues and greens, the entire image outlined in a heavy, black line.

A catfish. A bottom-feeder. It even tied in with her Catfish Compound in China. Perfect.

"A catfish," she said in wonder.

Grace looked at her, as if shocked to hear her speak. And maybe she *was* shocked to hear Corrine speak, after she had obviously slept through the whole tattoo experience.

"What's that?" Grace asked.

"I said, a catfish. A beautiful catfish."

Grace stared at the tattoo, as if seeing it for the first time. "I was thinking more like a dragon," she said.

Corrine smiled. "Same thing, really, in Chinese culture." She thought about the Heilongjiang Province, the Black Dragon River province, home to her Catfish Compound. "To the Chinese, the catfish is a dragon, a fighter, a symbol of strength," she said. "That makes it perfect."

Grace was scrubbing her arm, looking intently at the tattoo, so Corrine shut up for a few minutes.

Finally, Grace spoke again. "I . . . uh, need to give you something," she said. She turned, picked up a couple of needles and some other piece off the tattoo gun, transferred them to a plastic sharps container.

"Yeah? What is it?" Corrine asked, staring at the back of Grace's head. At the thick, real hair.

"You're gonna think it's weird, but it's . . . I guess it's a memento of something I've been holding on to for a long time. Call it a good luck charm."

Now Grace crumpled everything into the paper lining the top of the table, threw it into a garbage container somewhere out of Corrine's sight.

Well, it had to happen, didn't it? Everyone felt sorry for the Poor Cancer Victim at some point, decided they needed to offer advice or comfort. Corrine looked at the wonderful fish, a symbol of strength and perseverance, on her arm, and felt a stab of guilt. Accepting Grace's lucky charm would be the least she could do.

She flexed the arm, amazed that it didn't seem sore at all. In fact, it felt stronger. Come to think of it, she felt stronger, better, all over.

"Hang on just a second," Grace said. She left the room and returned a few moments later, clutching a small plastic sandwich bag in her hands.

"What is it?" Corrine asked, taking the bag from her.

Inside, she saw a napkin with a ten-digit number written on it: 1595544534.

"It's a . . . I don't know. I've held on to it for years now, and . . . anyway, I want you to have it. Sometime, after you've beaten this cancer, you'll hand it to someone else who needs a good luck charm."

Corrine smiled. *After you've beaten this cancer.* She liked the sound of that. "It's *Fu*," she said, clutching the plastic bag tightly in her hands.

"*Fu*?"

"Chinese symbol for good luck. So this is your symbol for good luck—your *Fu*."

Grace smiled. "No, it's your *Fu* now."

44. FOUR

Corrine was shocked to discover she'd spent more than four hours inside the tattoo shop, and it had felt like nothing so much as a fifteen-minute catnap.

She decided she was going to avoid cabs for a while, and she didn't feel like riding public transit, so she ambled down the street, enjoying the sunshine.

She thought about Marcus as she walked, wondering, not for the first time, what had happened to him. She'd done a couple Internet searches for his name a year after the whole accident, and found he'd been convicted of man-slaughter for the deaths of Brad Franklin and Terrance Tompkins, but he would only serve a couple of years, thanks to a plea bargain.

Corrine had been surprised at her reaction. She expected she would feel rage or hostility toward Marcus, but instead, she felt . . . nothing. Not exactly nothing; in an odd way, she felt relieved Marcus would only serve limited time. Maybe he would go on and do something useful, actually help other people. He'd said something once about being a truck driver . . . maybe he could go back to that.

In the end, she couldn't feel anything but kinship for Marcus. He was, after all, a bottom-feeder like herself. Had been the one to give her the term *bottom-feeder*, in fact. So in a way, she owed her sense of self to Marcus.

Eventually, old thoughts tired her, and she hailed a cab after all. When it dropped her off at her building, she decided against offering a giant tip. One good deed a day was enough.

Safely cocooned in her apartment, she went back to work on the script for her next e-mail message, filling in blocks of ten-digit IP addresses that would relay it. She felt good, invigorated after the tattoo session; the catfish was a symbol of power, of triumph. She'd hold on to that as long as she could. Already, she felt a sense of calm she hadn't felt for so long. Maybe not ever at all. She was comfortable in her own skin, comfortable in who she was, comfortable in her journey, wherever it may take her. Even if it meant that journey would last only a few more months, dead-ended by cancer.

Grace's *Fu*? Maybe. Maybe it was. She pushed herself away from her computer, away from the next spam mail she was composing, her mind occupied by the gift Grace had given her. She dug through her bag, brought out the plastic baggie, peered at the napkin inside.

1595544534

A ten-digit number. An IP address. Why hadn't she seen that before?

She went back to her screen, hooked to the backbone of the Catfish Compound in China, and did a search on 159.554.45.34. After a few minutes she found it. A server somewhere in New Zealand, it looked like. She did a bit of exploring, testing the security; it looked like an old Unix box running an outdated version of Apache. She knew of several security vulnerabilities that would give her an open door.

She smiled, enjoying herself. Why not embrace the *Fu*? She could use some of Grace's good luck, after all.

Half an hour later she had control of the IP address, rerouting all the traffic to one of her own servers. She sent a message to one of her test accounts, then flipped to her e-mail client to check.

It came through perfectly, followed immediately by another e-mail.

A spam e-mail.

Odd. She'd locked this e-mail address down tight; she never used it for outside correspondence of any kind, to keep it clean. Even as a SpamLord, her accounts weren't immune to other spam; in fact, it was something of a game among the SpamLord group, trying to hack each other's addresses, flood in-boxes.

She used this e-mail address for testing only; she'd never actually sent a message from it, let it relay over the vast connections of the Internet. And yet, she'd received a spam message. *Catfish Cancer Cure!!* the mail's subject line said, stopping her cold. She'd never seen this particular e-mail before, and yet its coincidences with her current condition were . . . well, like other recent events, they didn't seem like coincidences.

She opened the e-mail, letting the message load an image. Like many spams, the entire sales pitch was contained in an image, rather than in text, to help it bypass spam-blocking software.

Amazing cancer cure breakthrough! the image said. *New 1500 milligram tablets, manufactured with GENUINE fatty oils and extracts from catfish—a staple of Eastern medicine for centuries. FIRST ORDER FREE!!!*

Corrine opened the header information, sent a ping to her mail server, and traced the origin of the message. It came from the IP address she'd just activated. Odd; she was the only one controlling that address.

She looked at the napkin, the numbers scribbled on it,

then back at the screen. Instead of clicking on the image to follow the order link, she copied the URL, opened her browser, masked her current IP address, and pasted the destination into a new window.

The browser chugged for a few seconds, bouncing the traffic, then resolved with an order screen.

She stared for a few minutes, wondering who might be behind this. At least five people she could think of, off the top of her head. Maybe one of the other SpamLords had discovered some new back door into her world, which meant she needed to discover the back door herself. She couldn't leave herself vulnerable.

She smiled. *Couldn't leave herself vulnerable.* Her life motto, wasn't it?

After further consideration, Corrine decided the best way to find the back door was to go down this new wormhole; she filled in order information using a fake name and address and billing information from one of the many credit card numbers she had on file. She clicked on the order button, then returned to her e-mail script.

She'd see where the package came from, track the shipping label, see if she could get a handle on who might be in her system. Yes, one of the other SpamLords was trying to mess with her mind.

But she was the smartest SpamLord of all. They would find that out, because she would continue to teach them.

She would not be a victim.

46.

The next morning, as she lay in bed, Corrine heard a solid thump at her door. At first she thought it was a knock, a single rap beckoning her. Then she realized something had actually hit the front door itself.

She waited a few minutes, slipped on some shorts and a T-shirt, and went to the door. A quick look through her peephole didn't show anyone, but she kept the chain secured, opening the door just a crack.

On the floor of the concrete walkway outside her apartment she saw a small square box with a multicolored label. Odd. She never received mail or packages at her real address, always getting shipments sent to fake names at vacant addresses around the greater Seattle area. It was better to do that, because as a SpamLord you might need to pack up and change your whole base of operations with just a few hours' notice. Like the IP addresses that bounced all of her messages, Corrine had to bounce from address to address herself to stay hidden.

She undid the chain lock, opened the door, grabbed the package, and closed the door again.

Inside her apartment, she shook the box. Something shifted inside. She went to the kitchen, retrieved a steak knife from the utensil drawer, cut through the packing tape, ripped off the top of the box. Inside, buried under some packing peanuts, sat a white bottle. CATFISH CANCER CURE! it declared in plain block letters on the label.

No FDA warnings. No manufacturer name. No nothing.

Corrine was puzzled. Yes, she'd ordered this—just yesterday, in fact—but she hadn't given her real name or her real address. And yet, here it was.

Mentally she started cataloging the names of the other SpamLords who might have the means to pull off this level of intrusion. There really were none. She was careful—maybe even a bit paranoid—about sharing any of her information with others. Even so-called friends. Be quiet, keep to yourself, don't stand out. The great lessons she'd learned on the traveling sales crew.

So if this wasn't from one of the other SpamLords, who could it be from? Really, there was no logical explanation.

Fu.

The word came to her, instantly and suddenly. It was *Fu*, it was good luck, it was exactly what Grace had talked about. Hadn't Grace said she'd held on to those numbers for a long time, waiting to share them with someone else who needed them? Hadn't Grace known, deep down, the power of those numbers, the *Fu* they represented?

Corrine was quite sure Grace knew all that.

She opened the top of the bottle, pulled out a plug of cotton, shook out a couple of the tablets. They looked like vitamins. Probably were.

She knew better, of course, than to order anything off spam e-mail. She knew better than to actually *use* any product ordered off spam e-mail.

And yet: *Fu.*

What was the worst that could happen? She'd die? She'd been concerned about the tattoo yesterday—she admired it now, glowing brightly in the morning sun spilling through the window—and that had been a smashing success.

Be impulsive.

She went to the sink, drew a glass of water, and swallowed three of the pills.

48.

Late that morning, her cell phone rang. It was Swain's office—specifically, the woman with the tight blouses—calling to schedule an appointment and tell her to drop by the lab at the hospital for her weekly blood tests. Tight Blouse informed her that Dr. Swain had cleared an hour this afternoon to talk to her about "next steps," and if she went in right away for blood tests, he could look at the results in time for the appointment.

Yeah. Weekly blood tests. At least she could do those. She looked at her clock and headed toward the door. E-mails could wait. E-mails could always wait.

At the hospital she jotted her name on the sign-in sheet and took a chair. She picked up a copy of the morning's *Seattle Times*. The front-page story was yet another article about the firebug roaming the Greater Seattle area. Evidently he'd hit three separate businesses down in Federal Way last night. Over the past few months the firebug had struck at least two dozen buildings, and the police didn't seem to have any leads.

A few minutes later, one of the phlebotomists came out of the room at the back and called her name. Corrine stood and followed the woman to a row of chairs in the back room.

"My name's Leslie, and I'll be drawing some blood today," the woman said, looking at her paperwork.

Swain would be proud; the woman didn't look at Corrine's face once. Leslie had drawn her blood at least three times in the last two months, but she never seemed to recognize Corrine. Modern health care.

"Can you tell me your full name?" Leslie asked.

Corrine gave it to her.

"And your birth date?"

Corrine gave that to her as well.

Leslie nodded, then wrapped a band of rubber around Corrine's left arm. She studied the veins on the inside of Corrine's elbow for a few seconds, poked a needle into a vein, and attached a tube to collect the blood.

At least Leslie was good at what she did. Always got it on the first try. Corrine stared at the dark liquid squirting into the collection tube, absently wondering just how many lymphoma cells were crowding out the red blood cells of her own bloodstream. The lymphoma cells, when you thought about it, were something like the spam of the blood.

The needle suddenly reminded Corrine of Grace's tattoo gun, and she looked at the fresh tattoo on her right arm. The catfish peeked out of the sleeve of her T-shirt, reassuring her. Yes, whatever else might happen now, the catfish would be her constant companion. She was comforted by its presence.

Leslie pulled the full tube of blood from Corrine's arm, put a cotton ball over the point of entry, and asked Corrine to hold the cotton over the wound while she wrote the information on the tube: patient, date and time collected, doctor, tests ordered.

Corrine knew the whole routine, had been curious enough to ask about it the first time. But her interest had faded with each subsequent draw.

A few minutes later, she was on her way, forcing herself to think about her next batch of e-mails. It was her work, after all. It needed to be done.

Twenty minutes later, she was almost home when her cell phone rang again.

She looked at the caller ID, although there really was no reason to; Dr. Swain was practically the only one who ever called her number. By design, yes. Everyone else she knew contacted her through e-mail.

"Yeah?" she said, answering the phone, not really in the mood to talk to Swain.

"Corrine," he said. "You went in for a blood test."

It was a statement, not a question, but she answered anyway. "Yeah. Just a few minutes ago. You wanted to see me this afternoon, so—"

"Yes, yes. That's why I put a rush on the tests."

She felt the familiar Swain pause that always preceded bad news, but this time she wasn't afraid. Not at all. Odd.

"Have you been feeling okay?" Swain eventually asked.

Ha. Yet another hilarious knee-slapper from the comic oncologist. He'd recently told her all hope of a cure had circled the drain, and now he wanted to know if she was feeling okay. A wonderful reprise of his earlier zinger. And yet . . . she *did* feel okay. Better than she had felt since starting treatment. Better than she'd ever felt, in fact.

"Yes," she said. "Why, are—"

"They're normal," Swain said, interrupting her.

She waited for him to say something else, but he didn't. "What, exactly, do you mean by 'normal'? Normal for the stage I'm at, or for the chemo I've been on, or what?"

"No, I mean . . . they're within normal range."

She closed her eyes, not quite ready to believe what he was saying.

"I'd like you to come in for another blood test," Dr. Swain continued, "just to make sure there's been no mistakes. And I've already made some calls. We need another CT scan."

"I just had one last week."

"I know, I know. But if these results are right, I think you've maybe broken through a wall. Maybe the cumulative effects of the chemo are adding up. Maybe we'll want you on another cycle, rather than looking at some of the . . . ah, more investigational clinical trials."

Corrine pictured herself swallowing the catfish pills. Embracing her vulnerability.

"I'm headed back now," she said and hung up.

51. ONE

Late that afternoon, Corrine was in Swain's office, looking at printouts of her two blood tests and the fresh scan.

"Spontaneous regression," Dr. Swain said. He looked at her, his face flushed, his mind obviously unable to wrap itself around the test results and lab reports he normally found so comforting. "That's all I can come up with."

"Spontaneous regression?" she asked.

He shrugged, looking at the scans rather than at her. "Happens in about 15 percent of follicular lymphoma cases— the lymphoma suddenly disappears. Not overnight, of course, which seems to have happened in your case, and it usually returns at some point, but still."

Good old Swain. A cloud in every silver lining.

She ignored the last comment, instead asking, "So how often does spontaneous regression happen with diffuse large B-cell?"

He bit his lip, shook his head. "It doesn't." He backtracked a little then, saying: "I can look at the literature, see what else I can find."

"I'm not that interested," she said.

"I'd like to see you in another three months," he said. He seemed flustered. "No, I . . ."

"How about we repeat blood tests in a couple weeks, see how we're holding out?" she suggested.

Swain nodded, obviously rattled. And Corrine had to admit: more than anything else, that gave her a bit of perverse pleasure.

On the way out, Tight Blouse asked if Corrine would like to schedule her next appointment.

Corrine smiled, sauntering by. "Nope," she said. "Don't need one."

She had to admit that gave her just as much perverse pleasure.

As she made her way home, officially cancer-free for the first time in four months, renewed energy coursed through her body. Swain had told her it was the cumulative effects of the chemo, but she knew better.

She looked at the catfish tattoo on her right arm, swimming just beneath the surface of her shirtsleeve.

She had looked death in the face and said she wasn't afraid. And now, paradoxically, death had loosened its grip on her.

Grace's *Fu* had paid off.

52. Two

When she returned to her computer, another e-mail message had popped into her master account, originating from the same IP address.

Regrow LUXURIANT hair!! the subject line said. Corrine paused, unconsciously put a hand to her temple, feeling the few wisps of hair she had left. She'd automatically removed her wig when she entered her apartment; no need to keep up any pretense.

She paused. There was something wrong about all this, something very wrong. Maybe the Catfish Cure had halted the cancer, but what else had it done? She couldn't know; she had no way of even figuring out what was in the pills. For all she knew, she'd swallowed drain cleaner that was eating away her intestines.

Well, okay, so she knew that wasn't true. Based on her most recent CT scan, all of her intestines were intact, along with all the other normal internal organs.

Plus, the shipment had come to her apartment, not to the fake name at the fake address she'd provided. Shouldn't that be a concern? Shouldn't that tell her something sinister about all of this?

Yes, it should. But she was sitting in front of this computer, cancer free, because she had already been impulsive and ordered something she really shouldn't have.

She went to the Web site for the hair foam, clicked the order button, filled out the form with fake information.

Yes, in her head, she knew all those things should be red flags. But in her heart, a heart that now pumped lymphoma-free blood to the rest of her body, none of it made any difference.

Seconds after she completed the order, she heard another thump at her front door. She moved toward the door, unsure if she'd really heard the sound, checked the peephole, slid off the chain latch, and saw it sitting on the concrete: a square box with a simple multicolored label.

She stepped onto the concrete pad outside her door, peeked toward the other apartments on her level, then finally looked over the iron railing to see if anyone had scrambled down the stairs and left the building.

She saw no one.

She bent over, scooped up the package, brought it inside the apartment. This time she didn't go to the kitchen for a knife to help her open it; she immediately began tearing at the package with her bare hands. The chemo had bruised her hands, softened her fingernails, anyway. And she wasn't concerned about her appearance. What did it matter?

By the time she made it to her small dining table, she had one flap of the box peeled back. She put the box on the tabletop, perforated a bigger gash, then turned the box over and shook.

Packing peanuts spilled out, followed by a small, oval jar of cream. HAIRESTORE, the plain label said in large, brightly-colored letters. Again, nothing on the label told her the ingredients or the origin of the cream.

She twisted off the jar's lid, sniffed at the milky-white paste inside. The immediate smell was minty. But she decided the mint was there to mask another smell: something earthy, fishy. The same odor as the catfish cure pills.

Without hesitating, she dipped her fingers into the cream and began rubbing it into her scalp.

Immediately, she felt exhausted. Maybe that was understandable; the events of the last day had been impossible, and venturing into the impossible had to be a soul-draining experience. Even though it was only dinnertime, and even though she was ravenous, her body told her it needed sleep.

Maybe she was Snow White, she thought as she made her way to the bedroom. Maybe she'd bitten into a poisoned apple.

Now the only thing she could do was fall into a deep sleep.

53. THREE

She awoke, her brain feeling mushy. A quick look at the clock told her she'd only been asleep for a few hours. She didn't remember lying down, didn't really remember too much at all after . . .

The hair cream. Yes, after that. She wanted to put her hands on her head, but she resisted the urge. She would walk to the bathroom, calmly, and look at her reflection in the mirror. She'd done it many times since starting the chemo, revulsed by the liver-colored bruises blooming like flowers beneath her skin, shocked by the sudden appearance of bright-red rashes across her chest, amazed at the sores and abscesses lining her lips and mouth. Yes, chemo made for interesting self-talk at the mirror.

Corrine slid out of bed, careful to avoid swinging her head, careful to avoid anything that would give her an indication of change, and padded softly to her bathroom door.

She opened the door, closed her eyes, and stepped inside the small room. She turned to her right and turned on the light switch, keeping her eyes closed, knowing the mirror was just in front of her.

One. Two. Three. She opened her eyes.

Her reflection stared back at her, her long, shoulder-length mane of hair frizzed and tangled by a few hours of sleep.

She stared for a few minutes, because that's all she could do. How recently she'd mourned the loss of her hair, the odd realization that she would probably never live to see any on her head again.

And now here she stood, looking at her reflection, her hair, her soul, fully restored.

She finally let herself touch the hair. It was soft, as if it had just been washed. She wrapped a strand around her face, breathing in, smelling her new hair. Minty, like the cream. She tugged and primped at it, turning her face just so, smiling.

She pulled out the top drawer in the bureau in front of her, then laughed as she remembered: about six weeks ago she'd thrown away her brush and curling iron, horrified by the sight of clumps of hair sloughing off her head.

But now it was funny. She laughed, then cried, then laughed some more again as she looked at her tangled hair, her wonderful, tangled hair, in front of the mirror.

The hair was clean, but she immediately wanted to wash it, to experience that daily ritual she'd done since her teen years. So she slipped into the shower, soaping and cleaning her body, and then used simple bar soap for her hair— overcome by a fresh bout of laughter when she remembered she'd also thrown out all her shampoo and conditioner.

When she stepped out of the shower, she was as clean as she'd ever been. Reborn, even. A new child in a new world.

She slipped on her robe and walked into the living room of her apartment. Over in the corner, her computer was emitting a steady beeping sound. An alarm she usually set, to tell her when scripts had finished.

She walked to the computer, looked at the screen. Even though she didn't remember doing it before she went to sleep, she'd obviously set up her e-mail harvest bot to search the Web, find e-mail addresses, and add them to her database of names. She scanned the script, noting the sites the bot had indexed; most of them, it seemed, were cancer sites. She'd already set up a section of her database specifically for cancer patients, filling it with names she'd harvested from Swain's hacked electronic survey tablets and the computers of the oncology social workers.

And now, apparently, she'd gone on the Web in search of more names.

She didn't specifically remember doing any of this, but she had to give herself a break. In the last few days, she'd cured herself of cancer and grown back a full head of hair. Her brain deserved a break, a night to recharge.

Still, it was nice to see the bot had found several thousand new names overnight. She smiled, did a quick capture of the collected e-mail addresses, opened her master SQL database on one of her servers in China, and saved the new names to her main file of more than ten million addresses.

It was early evening, she felt great, and she had been given a fresh start. She should start composing new spam messages, she knew, maybe even checking in on some of her ghost sites and other ventures. Maybe she was no longer a cancer patient, but she was still a bottom-feeder. This is what she did; more than that, it was what she was meant to do.

And yet she didn't want to. She simply wanted to celebrate, to take the night off.

A flashing icon on her screen illuminated, telling her she had new e-mail in her secret account.

She clicked on the icon and opened her mail client, revealing a subject line meant to terrify. *Forward this to avoid DISASTER!!* it screamed.

Her mouth dry, Corrine sat in the chair and opened the message. She felt a rivulet of water, left from her shower, running down her forehead from the base of her beautiful new head of hair.

Or maybe it was a rivulet of sweat.

This message will bring GOOD FORTUNE to all who read it and forward it to five friends within twenty-four hours, it began. Then it detailed the circumstances of poor, unfortunate souls who had ignored the message. One woman in Georgia had succumbed to a sudden stroke. A man in Texas lost his family business to bankruptcy. A college student in Ohio had died in a horrific car crash.

Meanwhile, the people who had kept the chain alive by forwarding the message to five friends had experienced wondrous joys. A retiree from California had won the lottery. A poor mother on food stamps had received an inheritance from a long-lost relative.

The e-mail ended with a plea to forward the message to five friends within twenty-four hours or face the dire consequences that would surely befall her for breaking the chain.

Corrine noted the message had been sent at 12:07 the previous morning. Shortly after midnight. Hours before her adventures with catfish cures and hair cream began. She checked her watch: 8:32 p.m. So, would certain *DISASTER!!* befall her three and a half hours from now, twenty-four hours from when the message was sent? Or twenty-four hours from now, when she received it? And why had the message been delayed some twenty hours anyway?

She shook her head. Like any of it mattered. The send time was likely forged, anyway, or set to the server of origination. This mail, in truth, seemed more like a true spam message than either of the first two she'd received. Corrine had seen a thousand—no, a million—just like this one. Maybe she'd even seen this very one. For that matter, maybe she'd even written it, many years ago, and now the endless waves of Internet forwarding had deposited it once again on her beach. These kinds of messages were something of a primitive way of gathering e-mail addresses; they contained a virus that searched computers for vulnerabilities, then retrieved e-mail addresses from people who opened the forwarded message.

Kind of amateur hour, really. Corrine had passed this level of sophistication early in her rise.

So there it was: this message was nothing like the others. She closed it and let her hand hover over the delete button for a few moments.

So if this message was unlike the others, why did she feel a dark pit in her stomach? Why did the catfish on her arm twist and constrict as she read it? This message had come to her secret e-mail address, just like the other two mystical messages; couldn't it be a test, as well?

DISASTER!!

She smirked at the screen. What could be more disastrous than cancer? She'd already beaten that in the last twenty-four hours.

Corrine pressed the delete button and went back to her bedroom. Five minutes later, she was asleep again.

55b.

Late that night, her doorbell awakened her. Someone ringing it seven or eight times in quick succession, then pounding on the door. She sat up and immediately forgot the doorbell.

The strong, earthy odor of smoke floated around her.

(She was dreaming again Marcus it was Marcus inside the van and the smoke was filling the van and she just needed to get Marcus out so she could leave and say good-bye to this life forever)

She sat up in her bed, reached for the lamp on her nightstand. No, she wasn't dreaming. And yes, she could smell smoke. She clicked the switch to turn on the light, but nothing happened.

And now she coughed as the smoke infiltrated her lungs, making them burn.

She fumbled for the flashlight she kept in her nightstand—the power seemed to blink out in this building at least once a month—and thumbed it on. Instantly, the beam illuminated the haze in the air. She coughed again as she ran the flashlight's beam across the bottom of the door.

Bad news; smoke poured into the room from beneath it, which meant fire on the other side. If she opened her bedroom door, she would create a vacuumlike effect that would instantly suck heat and flames into her room and kill her. She knew this from her school days.

Okay, okay. At least she was awake. She knew every fire safety precaution would tell her to get out of the room immediately, but she slipped on jeans, a shirt, and shoes first, then grabbed her bag and opened the window of her bedroom. Every unit in the Villa Apartment building was exactly the same. The apartments were little more than glorified hotel rooms, with the front door and the bedroom window both opening to a concrete slab and black iron stairs on each of the four stories.

144

Corrine easily climbed out of the window and onto the concrete. She scrambled down the stairs, taking her cell phone from her bag and opening it to call 911. Just as she dialed, she heard the scream of sirens approaching. Someone had already called.

People were milling about outside, unsure where to go, what to do. Maybe a couple dozen of them in all, including some weird guy who sat on the grass with a leg wound of some kind; he sat transfixed as he stared at the building, his injury evidently forgotten. She didn't recognize him. Probably one of the guys from the ground floor.

Then the text of the e-mail came back to her. *Forward this to avoid DISASTER!!* it had screamed, begging her to do it within twenty-four hours. She looked at the time on her cell phone. 12:36 a.m. The e-mail had been sent twenty-four hours and twenty-nine minutes ago. Yet another seeming coincidence.

Had she brought this on herself by ignoring a message she should have heeded? Even worse, had she brought it on all the people who lived in her apartment complex?

The catfish on her arm moved in response.

Corrine looked around her. Children crying. Men in pajamas, staring dumbfounded. Mothers holding robes close to them, pulling their kids near. One woman in hysterics, trying to get back into the building as two men held her back.

She didn't know anyone else in her apartment building; she'd always kept to herself, to her computer. And now she understood that was what had made her bottom feeding so easy. She never had to see the faces of the people she targeted. Even back on the sales crew, she only saw people for a few minutes as she stood with them, filling out a magazine order form.

This was different. She'd ignored an important message, failed the latest mystical test, and this was what she had created. She couldn't face them. Couldn't stand there with them and wonder aloud what had happened, pray that the firefighters would get everyone out.

She couldn't do those things, because she *knew* what had happened.

And so she ran. She ran as fast as she could, letting her feet carry her anywhere, anywhere but here.

For the second time in her life she ran from a fire, and she never looked back. Not even once.

FIF**57.**SEVEN.

The next morning Corrine awoke in Gas Works Park, a surreal setting of rusted metal and pipes on Lake Union. Once upon a time it had been a refinery or some such thing; in the nineties it had become a city park, and the original industrial pipes and ductwork still stood, rusted reminders of what had once been.

Corrine sat up on the bench where she'd slept, checked her wig to make sure it hadn't come loose.

Wait. She didn't have a wig anymore; her hair was real.

Unfortunately, the rest of her life was fake. Yes, she'd miraculously been cured of cancer, miraculously grown a full head of hair. But then she'd put the lives of other people in jeopardy by concentrating solely on herself. Stupid stupid stupid.

Even worse, she was terrified of what she might face next, because she had no doubt it was going to get worse. The e-mail said as much in big block letters: *DISASTER!!* And to top it all off, she had no idea what she should have done to answer the latest test. Forward that disaster message to thousands, even millions, of other people? How would that help?

(It might have helped the people in your building)

She sighed, rose to her feet, twisted to stretch her back, and started walking, bag strung over her shoulder. She was traveling light, everything she now owned in the world slung on her arm, but each step felt heavy and awkward.

She knew of an Internet café a few blocks away where she could find coffee.

She tried to clear her mind as she walked, but it didn't work. It didn't help that her clothing smelled like smoke, a constant reminder that she didn't *Forward to Avoid DISASTER!!*

Standing in front of the glass door of the coffee shop,

she wiped at her face, brushed off her clothes, couldn't help but run a hand through her hair as she looked at her ragged reflection. Then she opened the door and walked in.

She ordered a giant latte and a scone, dug into her bag, and started to bring out one of the several unused fake credit cards she carried. But as her fingers closed around the small wallet that held all the fake cards, she felt the catfish move again, and something inside her resisted.

Instead, she reached into the front pocket of her jeans, found a twenty, and handed it to the barista. She received back $12.38, which would have to hold her for . . . she didn't know how long. She had thousands of dollars pigeonholed away in dozens of accounts overseas, most of them in China. But she never used real credit cards or debit cards, anything that could be traced or linked to an identity. She, better than anyone, knew those dangers.

She'd have to get into a bank sometime, have cash wired to her from one of her foreign accounts. But that would take time, and something told her she didn't have much time right now.

She took her coffee and scone to an open Internet work-station tucked in the back corner, sat down, and opened the browser.

She punched in the IP address of her secure mail server in China, then entered her username and password, hesitating just a moment before punching the enter key.

At the top of the in-box sat the *Forward to Avoid*

DISASTER!! message she'd read the day before. Hadn't she deleted it?

Then, as she watched, new unread e-mail messages began to roll into the box: five of them, then ten, and more. She stopped counting when it reached fifty unread messages, even as new messages continued to flood her in-box.

Every message was a carbon copy of the one she'd received the day before.

Every subject line told her to *Forward to Avoid DISASTER!!*

The color drained from her face, and suddenly she didn't feel like eating her scone or drinking her coffee. She wanted only to crawl under the table where she currently sat, curl into a ball, and cry.

And still, the messages in the in-box kept piling up, now more than seventy-five of them. All sent at the exact same time: 12:07 p.m. Just after noon, Pacific time.

She looked at the clock on the computer, surprised to discover it was almost one in the afternoon. Had she really slept that long?

That meant twenty-three hours until more fire and destruction. Or worse. And it would happen seventy-five times over. Or worse.

A thought popped into her mind immediately. She had a database of more than ten million names on her servers in China. That meant ten million addresses she could forward this message to—more than enough addresses to take care of a couple million *DISASTER!!* messages.

It would take just a couple hours to write the script, and she was pretty sure she could spool up to a hundred thousand messages or more in the next fifteen hours.

Her e-mail list could save her. Her bottom feeding could, as ever, be useful.

But she dismissed the thought even as it happened. It was one thing to send mostly harmless e-mail, clog someone's in-box with text or images. Even harvesting e-mails, phishing for identities, stealing from unsuspecting souls, well . . . none of that had killed anyone, and buyer beware. Those scams only snagged the people who were dumb enough to fall for them. If anything, they taught people valuable lessons, made them smarter. She'd always been able to tell herself she was performing a crude public service.

Forwarding this message, however, would create thousands of disasters around the world. Like the fire last night. Or worse. She knew this with absolute certainty. For those poor souls who were stupid enough to forward the message—and Corrine knew all too well there were plenty of those people—the disasters would be magnified among friends and family.

No. It would end with her. She would sacrifice herself to the disaster, whatever it might be, to avoid taking anyone else down with her. At least she could do that.

Better that than to be the person who sacrifices the rest of humanity to try and save herself.

Corrine sighed, feeling a tear threaten the corner of her eye. She was becoming a weaker bottom-feeder all the time.

61b.

The next morning she was somewhere in Idaho. She'd tried to thumb rides all afternoon and evening, headed east on I-90, but she realized, with her unkempt hair, her dirty clothes, that she probably looked more like a desperate addict than a nice young girl on her way to see Mom somewhere back in the Midwest.

Still, she'd managed to make it to the next state, to the wild uninhabited woods, in less than a day. That was progress. A T-shirt for sale inside the last truck stop had read *This ain't the middle of nowhere, but you can see it from here.* That's what she wanted. The middle of nowhere. So whenever *DISASTER!!* came, it would claim her only. No one else would be around, to be swept up in the dark deal she had made with the devil.

And now she was walking down a lonely stretch of the interstate, surrounded on all sides by nothing but giant pine trees. Not a bad place to die, she decided.

Corrine was out of money now, and desperately hungry. Sure, she could have used one of the fake credit cards to buy something at that truck stop, but she was past that. She'd dropped all the cards into a garbage can before blowing out of Seattle.

A breeze moved past her, almost lemon-scented in its freshness, and a quiet seemed to settle over the heavy forest. Corrine stopped walking, forgetting her blistered and swollen feet, forgetting the hunger in her stomach, forgetting everything.

She closed her eyes, noting that the highway had suddenly become abandoned. Granted, this didn't strike her as a section of highway that would ever be packed bumper to bumper, but the sudden stillness only punctuated the emptiness. She couldn't even hear the sound of traffic in the distance, which had been a constant for so very long.

And then the sound returned, suddenly and brutally. Not the sound of traffic, to be exact; as near as she could tell, it was just a truck, its diesel engine laboring, coming around a corner somewhere behind her.

She opened her eyes, looked back down the road. The truck—a large, red behemoth—came barreling around the corner, weaving and changing lanes. Abruptly, she heard a hiss of air as the driver hit the brakes; the vehicle's front end chattered and shuddered, and the large trailer behind it weaved back and forth, threatening to break free.

Corrine backed away into the ditch, not wanting to be

anywhere on the paved surface as the truck went by. It blew past her in a rush of air and a scream of air brakes, the smell of its diesel exhaust obliterating any scent of the fresh forest she'd been enjoying.

A hundred yards or so down the road, the truck finally came to a halt beside the road and sat, idling.

Okay, so what now?

Had the driver seen her and decided to pull over to check her out? No, she knew that wasn't the case; the truck had been weaving all over the road as it came around the corner, before the driver could have seen her.

In all likelihood the driver was in trouble. A heart attack, maybe. A seizure.

She should help. It might not be the safest idea, but actually choosing to help someone else might, in some small way, make up for all the times she'd been so wrapped up inside her own skin. The last time, the only time, she'd helped others had been at the scene of the car wreck. When she'd escaped from the sales crew. She'd pulled Marcus and Jenny to safety. Brad, too, though she had no way of knowing at the time he was already dead.

She probably only had an hour or two to live. The least she could do was help someone else, genuinely and self-lessly, for once.

She ran to the truck, ignoring the pain in her swollen feet, and knocked on the passenger door. "Everything okay?" she asked, then had to stifle another inappropriate laugh.

She'd used one of Dr. Swain's famous one-liners in a rather unseemly situation.

She tried again. "Hello?" she asked, unsure what else to say.

After a few seconds she heard movement inside the truck's cab, and the door above her popped open. A man, sweaty and pale, looked down and tried to smile. *Tried* being the operative word.

She'd heard about truckers, had maybe even seen a documentary at some point that talked about how a lot of them were druggies. That's what this guy had to be. He was on drugs and having a bad trip.

"I . . . I saw you go by me just down the road back there, and you were . . . um . . . looked like you were having problems."

She winced inside, knowing she was stumbling over her words but unsure how to extricate herself. This truck driver scared her, and she just wanted him to leave so she could keep walking. Maybe in an hour or so, she'd just step off the interstate's path and wander into the forest itself, keep herself isolated as she waited for the end.

"Problems," the trucker parroted back to her. She wasn't sure if it was a question or a statement. Or maybe he was mocking her.

"Yeah," she said. "I mean, I thought you were having some kind of problem with the truck at first, the steering or something. But when you got it pulled to the side here . . ."

She wasn't really sure how to finish that sentence, so she didn't. She looked at him, tried to show resolve, let him know she wasn't scared, she wasn't some victim he could pick up and beat in a drug-induced frenzy.

"You thought maybe I was the one having problems, rather than the truck," he said.

Okay, so she'd been ready to say something very much like that, but she'd decided against it. She didn't want to suggest to the driver that he was somehow incompetent. No telling how he'd react. But she found herself nodding anyway.

"I'm fine," he said. "Just dropped something on the floor, tried to get it. Stupid, I know."

Wow, this guy was the world's worst liar.

"Okay," she said. "I just, uh . . ." What could she say? She just wanted him to leave. "I'll let you get back to it."

She stepped back, hoping he'd just close the door and leave her life forever. What little bit of it might remain, that was; *DISASTER!!* lurked just around the corner, after all, a much larger and faster-working adversary than cancer, evidently. Or maybe this guy, this truck, was part of the disaster; she hadn't thought of that. She wanted to check her watch to find out.

Then he said the one thing she was most terrified of hearing. "You need a ride?"

DISASTER!!

"I . . . uh . . ." she said, trying to think of a way out of the situation.

"Look," he continued, "there's a truck plaza down the road about ten miles. Me, I think I probably need to pull off for a quick break. I'll buy you breakfast."

Think, think, think. No, don't think. Just turn and walk away. *Run* away. What was he going to do, scramble out of the cab and chase her? Maybe, but at least she'd have a chance of getting away. Standing here, staring dumbly, wasn't going to do much for her.

Then the druggie truck driver said something that sucked all the air from her lungs: "Your arm."

Instantly, she knew what he was referring to, even before she turned to look at the catfish tattoo peeking out from beneath her sleeve. Not for the first time, she wished she'd grabbed a jacket before leaving her apartment to the flames. She'd grabbed her bag, why not a jacket along with it?

"What about it?" she heard herself ask, terrified of the answer—whatever it might be.

"It's a catfish," he said, and something about his face had changed. He didn't look quite so drug-crazed, quite so scary. He looked . . . harmless.

"Long story." Longer than he could imagine.

"What do the numbers mean?" he asked.

Numbers? What numbers? She turned her head back to the tattoo, heard the truck driver speaking from somewhere in the distance.

"Numbers, kind of hidden inside the tattoo," he was

saying, but she lost the rest of it because the catfish was moving, and there *were* numbers inside the tattoo, something like ripples of water. Even before seeing all the numbers, she knew what they were.

"1595544534," she whispered.

Fu.

She was supposed to accept a ride from this trucker. Maybe it would end in *DISASTER!!* but that was her *Fu*, and she would accept it.

"I guess I will take that breakfast," she said, pulling herself up into the cab.

At least she might die with a full stomach.

62a.

She told the waitress she wanted hash browns and gravy. A greasy, artery-clogging breakfast she'd loved as a teen but hadn't let herself eat in years.

Of course, her arteries were the least of her worries right now.

The trucker ordered coffee, steak, and eggs. "Hungry?" she asked him after the waitress had retreated.

"Always." He smiled as if he knew some private joke he was keeping from her.

Corrine liked that; she, herself, had worked her way

through most of her life by smiling when she was dumb-founded. She'd laughed her way through cancer, thanks to the high jinks of that joker Dr. Swain.

"I'm Corrine," she said. "I suppose we should get that out of the way."

He nodded. "Nice to meet you, Corrine. I'm Kurt."

"And what's your story, Kurt?"

He smiled. "Still working on it."

Well, everyone had to have secrets. Even freaky truckers who took an unnatural interest in tattoos.

"Guess that's as much as I'm gonna get right now, huh?"

"Trust me, you really don't want to know."

But she did want to know; she'd spent the last several hours, several days, several months, worrying about herself and her cancer. She wanted to concentrate on someone else for just a few minutes. Even if that was all she had left.

"You think I'm worried about you escaping from a pre-release program?"

The waitress, her poor timing impeccable, chose that moment to bring Kurt's coffee. Corrine waited patiently while the waitress poured, noticing how Kurt stared at her across the table.

He spoke in a low, monotonous tone after the waitress retreated. "I had a brain injury several years ago," he said. "Since then, I . . . well, I can hear ghosts. Ghosts in the clothing of dead people."

Well. Certainly not the story she'd expected to hear, but

much more interesting. Somehow, it put everything she was going through in context. Kinda like finding out you weren't the only one in solitary confinement when you heard someone scratching on the walls of the cell next to you.

"And what do the ghosts say?" she asked. She hoped she didn't sound flippant, even though she knew she usually did.

"They ask me for help. Finding relatives, giving messages to others, that kind of thing."

"And you like doing that?" Now she did have to suppress a nervous giggle. As if she were asking him about his hobbies and interests: *So, you enjoy talking to ghosts . . . how do you feel about stamp collecting?*

"I don't," he said.

"Why don't you like it?" Seemed like a natural enough next question, something any well-trained therapist might say. Not that she was one of those.

He looked at her, blinked a few times. "No, I mean I don't do it," he said matter-of-factly. As if he'd answered the question thousands of times before. "I ignore them."

Her mouth suddenly felt dry, so she picked up her glass of water and sipped. "You don't do it," she repeated.

"I go to estate sales, auctions, buy all the clothing that belongs to the dead so I can listen to the ghosts inside," he said. "But I don't talk to them. I don't answer them. I don't help them."

He was staring at her now, studying her for a reaction. He'd bared a deep, dark secret, and he was worried about her reaction. It was obvious he felt this was some shameful secret, and if he knew how she really felt about what he was saying—and she believed every word, because after all, she was the woman who had just cured her cancer and grown her hair after ordering strange concoctions off the Internet, which made ghost-talk seem perfectly plausible—he'd probably be appalled.

Because the truth was, she wanted to say *Good for you*. Or *Smart move*. Or *You're a genius*. The ghosts he talked to, they were invitations to disaster, weren't they? By ignoring their calls he stayed grounded in reality—or what counted as everyone else's reality—and he didn't veer off the deep end that was filled with *DISASTER!!*

If she herself had done something else with the last spam (exactly what, she didn't know), she wouldn't be sitting here right now, waiting for the end of the world. Or the end of her world at the very least.

At least she would die cancer-free. After all that, she was ashamed to admit, the thought of being cancer-free still felt fresh and cleansing.

How was that for a deep, dark secret? But she couldn't say any of that, couldn't say anything she really felt. So she relied on her good old crutch: use a little black humor, see if it worked on him.

"Well," she said. "It would seem you're one sick puppy." She raised her glass of water in a mock toast. "Welcome to the club. I'm the president."

He smiled. Good.

"What qualifies you to be the president?"

Well, heck, he'd let his inner freak out to play; why not do the same?

"Cancer, for one," she said. "But that's not the half of it. You got an e-mail account?"

"Yeah."

"Get spam?"

"Who doesn't?"

"Well, you can thank me for that. You're about to have breakfast with a woman who sends out millions of e-mails every week for fake degrees, online prescriptions, and— what's a delicate way to say this?—male enhancement. Bon appetit."

His brow furrowed for a moment, and a trace of a smile stayed on his lips. Probably trying to decide if she was telling the truth. Either way, she hoped that she'd helped him feel a bit better about himself, provided a bit of absolution. Because this Kurt guy, she decided, wasn't really a bottom-feeder. Didn't seem to have the stomach, or the heart, for it.

So he was at least a few rungs up from the basement where she resided.

He wasn't saying anything, so she continued. "Those numbers on my arm. I didn't even know they were there, but—they're kind of what brought me here."

This time he spoke immediately. "Well, if you don't mind going a bit deeper into the twilight zone, one of the ghosts told me I was supposed to give you a ride. Just before you showed up. So—no offense—I'm a little worried this is all some kind of hallucination. The brain injury I told you about."

She smiled bitterly, biting her tongue. If only that were true: her whole life, nothing more than a hallucination, an illusion. So much easier.

"Oh, I'm real, Kurt," she said, almost without realizing she was speaking. "I'm so real it hurts."

The waitress, true to her perfect bad timing, picked that exact moment to set big platters of food in front of them. Or maybe it was good timing in this instance. Corrine was still trying to decide.

After a few minutes, Kurt spoke again. "So about the numbers . . ."

"I don't know much about them," she said, truthfully.

"You don't know? So why'd you get them?"

"I didn't ask for them. I didn't even know they were there until you saw them."

"But they mean something to you, don't they?"

She thought of the numbers, written on a napkin inside a plastic sandwich baggie, still safely held inside her bag. A curse. Grace had passed along a curse to her, told her there would be a time when she would know she should share it with someone else. Something like that. Only at that time, she thought it had been a good thing.

"Yeah, they mean something."

"They . . . they mean something to me too. I just can't put my finger on it right now."

She stared at him. Maybe that was it. All she had to do was pass along the numbers, pass along the curse to someone else. Then she would be free of . . . everything. And this man, sitting in front of her . . . well, it sounded harsh to say it, but he was a little simple wasn't he? She was already thinking of him as Forrest Gump.

She dismissed the thought and suddenly felt a little sick to her stomach. She'd just sat here and thought about killing someone else to save herself. Once again. She'd thought of herself first for . . . forever. No more. Last couple hours of her life weren't exactly an opportune time to make some big moral stand, but that was where she was. No, she wouldn't condemn this man. She wouldn't condemn anyone else. She had been a bottom-feeder, and she would pay whatever price needed to be paid now. Even so, the hash browns sat uneasily in her stomach.

She turned and rummaged through her bag for a few seconds, hoping that doing something else, anything else, would take her mind off the sick feeling inside.

Instead, she felt even worse, knowing she was on the verge of throwing up. She slid out of the booth awkwardly, pulling her bag behind her. "Be right back. I'm going to the restroom."

She moved toward the restroom, bag in hand, made it through the door and into a stall before the hash browns came back up.

Her stomach felt a bit better after that, but her hands started to tremble. After a few dry heaves, she finally gave a deep sigh and opened the stall door.

Another woman was at the counter, ostensibly washing her hands, but obviously staring at the stall Corrine occupied; she dropped her gaze when Corrine left the stall.

Probably thought she was bulimic. Heck, might as well run with it. She moved to the sink beside the woman.

"Well," she said brightly, looking into the mirror, "there's a couple pounds I won't have to work off at the gym."

The woman recoiled, actually sprang back in horror, then grabbed for a paper towel and rushed out the bathroom door.

Corrine laughed, knowing she would at least be immortalized at the woman's next kaffeeklatsch.

She looked at herself in the mirror, and suddenly, inexplicably, she was terrified. In a few hours, it would be—

DISASTER!!

Yes, disaster. By that time, she had to be alone, away from here, away from everyone. Go for a hike in the forest. Maybe get eaten by a bear.

She smiled, looked at her smirk in the bathroom mirror, ran a hand through her hair, secretly thrilled to see it so full, finally wiped at the tears welling in her eyes. Cured of cancer, only to be killed a day later. *I'll take Irony for 100, Alex.*

Deep breath. *You can do this,* she said to her reflection. But her reflection didn't seem to be convinced.

She left the restroom and returned to the table. Kurt was standing with his back to her, studying something.

"So where you headed?" she asked as she walked up behind him.

He turned, surprised, stuffed something into his pocket. A fresh secret. Let him have the secret; she'd just thought of killing him by passing along the cursed numbers. Her stomach did one more uneasy flip, so she did her best to think about anything else.

"Huh?" he said. "Oh, Chicago."

He smiled, and for a moment, she panicked; was he really going to ask her to come with him? Bad idea. Bad, bad idea.

"How about you? Where you going?"

"No clue," she said. "Just trying to outrun my past."

"It's a vicious circle," he agreed.

When he said it, the idea bloomed in her mind instantly. Something she hadn't thought of before, but something that just might be a way out. A way to relieve the curse and a way to redeem herself, all in one. "What did you say?" she whispered, even though she knew exactly what he had said. The words still rang hollowly inside her head.

"A vicious circle," he repeated.

"Yes, it is." Then: "Do they . . . ah, have a computer I could use in here?" she asked.

A clumsy segue, to be sure, but this vicious circle idea was expanding in her mind even as she stood here. She needed to start on it. Now.

He looked at her. "Truckers' lounge upstairs. Wireless Internet, a computer workstation you can use. Nothing special."

She bit her lip. "I don't need anything special." She hoped.

"I think . . ." he started, then shook his head. "I need to get going."

They had stopped at the doors to the truck plaza, the flow of people entering and leaving moving around them like smooth water in a river.

He offered that goofy smile, held out an awkward hand, waiting for her to shake.

Instead, she stepped close, kissed his cheek, hugged him tight. For some kind of human contact, if . . . just if. Maybe some penance for her thoughts. "You take care of yourself," she said.

Corrine stepped back, watched him walk toward his truck, then pulled out her cell phone to check the time. It was 9:43 a.m. That meant 8:43 a.m. Pacific time. Three hours and change before . . . well, before *DISASTER!!* If she could get on a computer upstairs, and if she worked quickly, she might make it.

The "truckers' lounge" was a bit more barren than she'd pictured, and only one person—a guy at a small counter or bar, reading a newspaper—was in it. He glanced at her, nodded, went back to reading. Maybe this time of morning wasn't exactly trucker rush hour. In the corner, a TV sat on a stand, images flickering silently. In front of the TV, two large overstuffed chairs. On the back wall, a couple of wooden desks.

She moved to the desk that held a computer, surprised. It was actually a somewhat newer model, not one of the old gerbil-powered workstations she'd expected.

A few minutes later, she was connected to her e-mail. Her in-box now held more than five hundred e-mail messages promising *DISASTER!!*

She logged in to her communications backbone in China. Well, not hers alone; along with the other SpamLords, she'd bought the equipment, rented the space, developed the bandwidth. In China, no one could take them, and they could route all their own e-mail traffic without fear of getting mails bounced by stateside providers. Blacklists were an entirely different thing, of course, which was why they'd registered literally thousands of individual IP addresses through their Chinese backbone; once an IP address moved to a published blacklist, they could simply switch to another IP address and keep pumping the e-mails through.

It was a solid system, really. One she'd been proud of, in a freakish way. And now, the closed system was going to be her salvation. She hoped.

What triggered the idea was Kurt's comment. *Vicious circle.* When he said it, the entire architecture popped into her head instantly. Block out five hundred IP addresses, assign them to all the servers hooked into her Chinese backbone—currently, about two hundred servers in all. Then create e-mail accounts at each of those IP addresses, and set each account to automatically forward to five addresses on other machines on the backbone.

A vicious circle. The e-mails would keep forwarding, back and forth, until the software or hardware started to melt down. She was sure the system would easily handle at least a hundred million forwards before it bogged down; it was, after all, designed to move a lot of traffic.

And when it did start to melt down, well, what of it? She would be ridding the world of some of the heaviest spammers on the Internet. Including herself.

Her fingers flew, installing software remotely, setting up auto-forwards, configuring IP addresses and databases.

And more than ever, she enjoyed her work.

63.

At 12:15 p.m. Montana time, 11:15 a.m. Seattle time, Corrine decided she had to quit. That only left her forty-five minutes to set everything in motion, then get away from the truck stop, away from everything, in case her scheme didn't work.

And there was no guarantee it would work, was there?

She logged into her secure e-mail account from the Web, selected the five hundred *DISASTER!!* e-mails waiting in the in-box, then forwarded them to the first e-mail address in the vicious circle.

It would either work or it wouldn't. She would either live or she wouldn't.

But she had one last task.

She'd thought of the correct answer to the last test. All the signs had been there: her computer, magically harvesting thousands of e-mails from cancer patients all night. The spam message, begging her to forward to five others. The eye-opening experience of seeing the misery she'd caused at her apartment.

And more than anything, the exhilaration of discovering what had saved her.

It hadn't been the catfish pills that staved off the cancer, hadn't been the cream that restored her hair.

It had been her decision to be impulsive, to actually live rather than simply exist. She had built a wall around herself for so many years, vowing she would never be a victim.

But she'd learned in the last few days that there was a huge difference between being a victim and being vulnerable. By admitting her own frailties, she had opened new avenues of strength she never knew she had. By pulling herself out of the impersonal world of spam mail and phishing scams, she had entered the personal world of pain and joy and sacrifice.

And that world was much more real than anything she'd ever created.

She opened her master SQL database, told it to extract all the contacts tagged with cancer as a keyword; a few minutes later, she had about ten thousand addresses.

She went back to her e-mail and hit the Compose New Message button. The subject line was obvious: 1595544534. Then she moved to the body of the message and paused for a few moments before beginning to type.

> Four months ago I was diagnosed with an aggressive form of lymphoma, and I thought it was the end.
>   I now realize it was the beginning.

Corrine continued to type, pouring out her story until the screen blurred. Only then did she realize she was crying as the words poured out of her.

She would pass along the numbers. She would share what she had learned. She would check this e-mail address every day, responding to every person who wrote, just as long as the vicious circle held. She would share her story, her pain, her frustrations, with anyone else who wanted to share their stories, their pain, their frustrations.

It was her *Fu*, after all. And her *Fu*, she now understood, was not about luck. It was about love.

Even for bottom-feeders.

Third Stanza
Dragon Chaser

19.

You chased the dragon, and it chased you.

Grace knew this, thought about it often as she lit up and inhaled, feeling the lazy tendrils of white smoke wrap around her face. Like dragon tails, yes.

She closed her eyes, losing herself in the embrace, waiting for the dragon to begin its roar inside. Ten minutes, fifteen minutes tops. So much slower, of course, than shooting it, but there was always a trade-off. Shooting gave you an immediate hit, punched you in the gut with instant euphoria. But it was more dangerous.

And it left tracks, that particular dragon. Puckered pink tracks. Not that it mattered much in her case; her arms had been ruined long ago, before she'd even hit her teen years.

She caught herself absently itching at the insides of her forearms, forced herself to stop. The junkie's tattoos. She had many of them. Too many. But what had she known then? It was positively punk rock, this constant companion with exotic names like horse and Harry Jones and smack. Sid's sedative. Cobain's candy.

And so, because she needed to forget, it became her choice. How old-school of her.

She leaned back on her ratty sofa, closing her eyes, trying her best to close all her senses. It would come soon, maybe as soon as five minutes. Not that long at all. A small trade-off, really, to save her skin: a few minutes weren't too long to wait. She could do that. Usually. Plus, smoking staved the real danger of an OD or a bad batch of tar.

Okay, so she wasn't totally off the tar. Once a week, maybe, she brought out the sharps, trying her best to find a gutter on her stomach. Or her thighs. Sometimes, the bottoms of her feet. No sense adding more junkie tattoos on her arms. She did a different kind of tattoo now, didn't she?

How many more minutes? Three? Maybe. Maybe.

Grace opened her eyes, tried to ignore the itch behind her corneas, the itch that simmered when she needed a hit, turning to a steady boil when she was desperate. That itch would be gone soon.

Chasing the dragon worked.

It always worked.

Of course, the dragon always chased you too.

21.

Grace unlocked the gate in front of the shop, rolled up the metal framework, enjoying the feel of the iron sliding into the frame above. A solid sound, a solid feel.

She keyed the front door, opened it, walked inside, set down her bag, and flipped on the lights. She'd named her shop GraceSpace because it fit—fit her and fit the funky Fremont location here in Seattle.

The shop always smelled the same: a bit like soap, a bit like iodine, a bit like . . . well, like ink. They were both here: the antiseptic soap and iodine to wash skin, the ink to fuel the designs.

She looked at the clock. First one in, as usual. Vaughn would be here within the next hour, probably; Zoey sometime after noon. Vaughn and Zoey weren't their real names; they were stage names, concocted personas so adored by some folks in the body-art trade. Affected names aside, she couldn't complain about either of them; they were both going to do just fine when she cut them loose. She'd taken them on as apprentices at roughly the same time a couple years ago. It was how you learned the trade, how she herself had learned it.

She smiled. Here she was, mentally hacking on Vaughn and Zoey for using fake names, and Grace wasn't even her own given name. A bit of "do as I say, not as I do," she supposed. Grace seemed like a perfect persona for her, so she started using it soon after coming to Seattle.

Amend that: soon after coming to Seattle for the second time. But the first time, something of a disaster, didn't count in her mind.

And now she was probably the oldest working tattoo artist in the area. Maybe people should call her Ancient

Grace. She told everyone she was from the Midwest, which was only a slight fib since she'd come from Montana, and that seemed to satisfy them; like her, many of them had left behind so-called normal lives. That was also part of this body-art persona. You lived an invented existence, a world filled with skulls and stars and flames. Really, it was like a real-life comic book sometimes, the only difference being that the pages were human skin.

She looked at the appointment book. Chelsea would be here in fifteen minutes or so, a twenty-something girl who wanted to get twin violin f-holes tattooed on her lower back as a gift to her boyfriend. As if she were a Stradivarius, some instrument to be played.

Grace shook her head, dismissing her thoughts. She wasn't a therapist or a pastor, here to analyze why people did the things they did. And if she were, her own life had rich veins of dysfunction to be mined long before she should ever start drilling in other people's lives. No, she was here to give clients what they wanted, build their own invented existences. Everyone needed that. Even Grace.

She found herself scratching at the insides of her forearms through the thin fabric of her long-sleeved knit shirt. She always wore long sleeves. Always. Yeah, she'd manufactured her own existence on her skin. Not tattoos, but a good bit of needlework over the past few years. The needle tracks created something of a patchwork quilt over the previous scars left by her mother.

(You got the dead blood, child)

Yeah. Well, if there's one thing she didn't need to concentrate on now, it was motherhood in general. Her own mother, in specific. Those memories were best left to the dragon.

Grace put down her bag, went to her room, flipped on the lights, rummaged through the converted dresser she used to house supplies. The ink was easy enough this time: all black. She opened another drawer, admired the prepackaged single-use needles inside.

Was it any wonder she'd been drawn to this trade? Was it any wonder she'd found a natural knack for skin art?

She set down her tools next to the chair just as she heard the bell of the front door opening in the lobby. She wiped at her hands, pulled a set of latex gloves from the box on the small table, turned to head back to the lobby.

"Hey, Grace."

Chelsea was a pretty girl, a little thin, maybe, but that was all the rage these days. Hair colored dark, the color of—

(black tar)

—yes, Mexican Black Tar. Street slang for one of the most potent forms of heroin. The kind you injected. The most potent fire-breathing dragon of them all.

She stifled an urge to itch at her forearm and offered a smile. The itch was at a low simmer this morning, would stay that way all day if she just used a bit of self-control.

"Morning, Chelsea. Looks like you're ready."

"Oh, I'm ready," Chelsea said, excited. "Billy's gonna freak when he sees it."

Grace smiled again. Yeah. Time to help Chelsea get her freak on.

23.

Chase the dragon, chase the dragon, chase the dragon, chase the dragon. Four times a day. Go to sleep. Get up and repeat. All in all, not such a bad thing, considering the alternative. Which was to live in the hell she'd created for herself.

Grace stood, went to her shop's waiting room to get some bottled water from the refrigerator she kept there. Maybe an apple or something for a snack. She was careful to eat organic foods, lots of fresh fruits and veggies. Vitamin supplements.

An odd contradiction for a heroin addict who added poison to her body several times a day, yes. But every life was a contradiction of sorts.

She'd needed some time to herself, so after her session with Chelsea and a couple consults with new clients, she'd sent Vaughn and Zoey home early in the afternoon. Neither had complained.

Standing, drinking the water, she looked out the window,

caught the reflection of her GraceSpace logo—a warm, buttery yellow—in the glass.

GraceSpace. She'd never really considered calling it anything else, because that's what it was: the space where she defined herself, built her own reality. At home, away from GraceSpace, she was a woman who had failed as a human being, abandoned her family, chased the dragon down a deep hellhole. But here, she was in GraceSpace.

Other people were drawn to GraceSpace too. They wanted GraceSpace because they wanted to see Grace, enter her own private Dark Room for a closed-door session. No outside light, just the darkness and her work area—the smooth pink or brown or yellow skin illuminated by a small task light.

Maybe that was part of why she was so popular. She didn't view her work as advertisements for her ability, as so many other artists did, but as expressions of the people wearing them. No two people were alike, and so no two of her tattoos were alike. Nuances of designs changed with every client.

She lingered at the open door of the refrigerator, enjoying the sensation of the cold air on her hands. Her arms stayed warm under her long-sleeved shirt, one of many that lined her closet. In public, she never wore short sleeves. In public, she never let anyone see the real person, the one who had once gone by the name Janet Sohler, and had lived in the small town of Red Lodge, Montana, as the wife of Kenneth and the mother of Tiffany and Joey. The one who had spent her first sixteen years as the daughter of Florence.

If anyone saw that person, they would never want to visit GraceSpace. They would want to lock her away for being so wretched.

She stood at the refrigerator, staring at nothing, thinking of the first time she'd been to Seattle.

The first time she'd tried to run away from her life.

9b.

She was no mother. She knew it. This, despite having a daughter. And she was no wife either. This, despite having a husband.

She curled into a ball on the bed of the small, ratty hotel room, shivering. It was hot outside—a ninety-plus day being something of a rare occurrence in Seattle, she'd been told by the woman at the front desk—but she shivered all the same.

It wasn't that she didn't want to be a mother. A wife. She just couldn't. Something was broken inside her. Missing. She had her own mother to thank for that, in many ways.

So she had left. *For* them, really. For Kenneth, her husband, and for Tiffany. They were better off without her. She knew it. Deep inside, probably they even knew it. Besides, she was here to avoid repeating her earlier mistake; Seattle would have places to take care of that, she knew. It was a city, and cities always had solutions to any problems you might face.

Also, she was better off without them. At least she would be, she knew, once she figured out where she was going, what she was doing. That was the other reason she was here, in Seattle. Wasn't it? She couldn't just go back, after walking out like that. Running out.

A giant thump next door broke her reverie. Something falling. Or someone.

She'd seen the guy in the next room a few times, out in the lobby, that kind of thing. He'd been in the hotel even longer than she had, and she'd been here four days now. She'd listened to him talking on the phone a few times, fascinated by his accent. Russian, she guessed. A little weird, too; he wandered around the hotel in bare feet, or sometimes just socks, even though he wore a complete suit with a tie. Maybe it was some Russian custom she didn't know about. She had no idea what he did, or how he came to be in this particular place at this particular time.

Of course, she had no idea how *she* came to be in this particular place at this particular time.

She listened intently for another sound of any kind from next door. Some scuffling, maybe, voices. Not much else. Was that good or bad? Should she go check?

No, no she shouldn't. She was here in her own world, in her Gray Zone, comfortably cocooned away from contact with others. She needed this.

But then: yes, yes she should. She should check because . . . well, because something just didn't seem right.

Yes, it was surely stupid to just walk next door, knock on the door, possibly walk into a situation she knew nothing about.

But she'd done stupid things before. Got married. Had a kid. Those were biggies, and would certainly be difficult to top. It wasn't that she hated the idea, or felt like being a wife or a mother was beneath her. Just the opposite: she wasn't up to being either. She herself was just a scared, weak little girl inside, and there was no way she could be the person a family needed. She couldn't be that person because—

(You got the dead blood, child)

Well, yes. She couldn't be that person because she had the dead blood. Good old Mom had instructed her in the ways of dead blood, in both word and deed.

Before she could think too much about it, she went into the hallway in her bare feet, walked to the adjacent apartment, knocked three times on the door. The door was locked, she knew; the doors were always locked in this building. But, being in an old building, the doors were also off center and mismatched. Whoever had closed the door last hadn't latched it all the way, and when she knocked, the door creaked open a few inches.

No answer from inside.

She pushed open the door, cleared her throat, ready to yell a "Hello?" and check on the Russian guy.

But when she pushed in, she instead saw the lower part of his body—those odd, bare feet—visible just beyond the small wall to the left of the entryway. No more than a dozen feet away. She knew the layout of the room very well; it was just like her own.

So Russian Guy was having a seizure, something like that, and had fallen in his apartment. That was the thump she'd heard. She rushed the ten feet or so past the wall on her left, coming into the main room, and saw, for the first time, another man. Russian Guy was half-on, half-off the dirty couch in the room, his body herking and jerking. Another man was on his knees, trying to put shoes on Russian Guy's twitching feet.

And next to that man lay a pistol.

No good could come of this. She'd just stumbled into something very bad. The man with his back turned hadn't seen her yet, he was too busy trying to squeeze a shoe onto Russian Guy's bare foot.

But then, here was Russian Guy, now lying eerily silent on the floor, a thin line of foam trickling from his mouth. She couldn't just abandon him right now, the way she'd abandoned Kenneth and Tiffany back in—

Stop. Just stop.

Okay, so she was a poor wife, a poor mother. And now she wanted to try being a poor hero. Fine. Just do it.

"Hello?" she said, feeling as if she needed to say something to let the guy with the shoe know she was there.

He stood quickly and turned to face her, shoe still awkwardly clutched in his hands. The room went silent for a few moments; even Russian Guy's thrashing and gurgling ceased.

She couldn't stand that, seeing the world around her frozen, a pregnant pause—

(don't think that word)

—and so she moved across the floor, dropped to her knees beside Russian Guy, and started CPR. Chest compressions. She'd decided to take classes after Tiffany was born. What if her baby started choking and she didn't know what to do? Everyone would know, instantly, she was a Bad Parent, because she had the dead blood, and because she'd never learned CPR. So she'd signed up. It was important, so important, to make sure other people didn't know she had the dead blood.

She concentrated on the compressions, not wanting to even look at the guy standing there. Let him think she hadn't seen the gun on the floor. If she guessed right, he'd get out of the apartment as soon as he could.

She was surprised when the guy didn't bolt. He simply stood there, saying nothing. As if waiting for something else to happen. Or maybe trying to decide what to do next.

After a few moments, he dropped the shoe and moved, as if to step over Russian Guy's body.

(The gun, he's going for the gun, he's going for the gun)

"Come on," she said. "He's gonna die if you don't help me."

Without thinking, she reached for the guy's hand and grabbed it. Immediately, her blood began to itch. It was the only way she knew to describe it. An itch deep inside that would, years from now, become a hunger for heroin. But on this day, before heroin, before her adventures chasing the dragon, it was just an unusual, mildly electrical sensation beneath her skin.

Maybe it was just adrenaline. After all, she'd only grabbed his hand to stop his progress. And now, if she could get him involved in what she was doing, maybe she could keep him from going for the gun. Maybe she could escape her own stupidity for putting her nose in this.

The blood itch was insatiable, so insatiable now that she couldn't continue. She looked at the inside of her forearms, certain she would see her veins crawling like snakes just beneath the skin of her arms. But nothing was there, and as she let go of the guy's hand, the itch subsided. A bit. She scratched absently at her forearms, looked at the guy again, who was barely containing his revulsion.

He *knew*. She could tell. He knew she had the bad blood in her, he knew she was an imposter, a person who pretended to be a Good Wife and a Good Mother, but was instead a pitiful joke. She could see this *knowing* in his eyes, and she could see he despised her for it. Who wouldn't?

She blew the hair out of her eyes, tried to control the trembling she felt in her body. Still, she did not want to die. Not here. Not now. Get him involved. Keep him occupied.

He dropped to his knees, pulled by her insistent grip on his hand.

"You know CPR?" she asked.

"Yeah," he said, then shook his head. "I mean no."

Good. He was muddled. At least his revulsion might help her get out of this mess.

"How about a cell phone? You got one?"

"No."

"Figures." She winced as she said it. No need to push the guy over the edge, even though she felt a bit of anger rising inside. She knew it made no sense for her to be angry in this situation, but she couldn't help it. Maybe she was mistaking her fear for anger.

She pulled out her own cell phone, turned it on for the first time since she'd fled Montana four days ago.

"Here," she said, feeling she could return to the chest compressions. The blood itch had retreated a bit more, and she was getting her composure back. "If you don't know how to do chest compressions, you gotta make the call."

Just keep him busy. Keep him off his guard.

The guy controlled his revulsion enough to start dialing. She listened to him talk with the 911 operator as she repeated the compressions on Russian Guy's chest. One-and-two-and-three-and-four-and-five.

He set her phone down on the floor, then spoke. "They're on the way."

So matter-of-fact, which was striking her as more and

more odd all the time. He should be more jittery, panicky about her presence here, revulsion or not. Obviously, he was here to kill Russian Guy, or Russian Guy had tried to kill him—the gun on the floor just a few feet away wasn't part of the hotel décor, after all—and yet, when she'd stumbled into the room, this guy was putting shoes on the Russian. Didn't make sense at all.

But then, she knew people often did things that didn't make sense. (You got the dead blood, child) For instance, some mothers, whacked in the head, cut their daughters' arms to drain the dead blood out of them. And in turn, some daughters terrified themselves when they casually started wondering if their own daughters had the dead blood in them.

She shook her head. *Stop*. Right now, she just needed to keep him occupied. Keep him away from that gun, because if he went for it, she was going to have to reach it first. And she wasn't sure she could.

"It's not hard to learn," she said. "I can teach you."

Psychology 101: get him to think of the man on the floor as a person, get him to think of *her* as a person. Offer him something to pique his curiosity.

She sensed his reluctance, even without watching his face.

"I—" he said, but she cut him off.

Take control of the situation.

"Three fingers up from here," she said, demonstrating

as she placed her hand at the junction of the man's rib cage. "Hands together, steady pressure, kinda like kneading bread when you think about it."

She wasn't sure about the kneading bread analogy; this guy didn't seem like much of a baker. But maybe it would trigger thoughts of family, his mother, something. Get him to see her as something other than the failure she was. Positive associations.

"You try it," she said.

She grabbed him again, this time on the arm, and the blood itch returned immediately. Why was that? What was it about this man that awakened the . . . well, that awakened the dead blood inside?

Still, as uncomfortable as it was, it kept him where she could see him. She swallowed the acidic taste bubbling at the back of her throat, ignored the burn radiating throughout her body, and urged him to his knees again.

Amazingly, he followed her instructions and began doing compressions. Sometime in the last few seconds he'd slipped on surgical gloves, which did nothing to settle her discomfort. Surgeons wore those gloves, yes. And she didn't even want to think about the other kinds of people who used them.

He was too tentative, barely applying any pressure.

"Harder," she said. "You're massaging the heart, keeping the blood flow going." There. Reinforce him, let him know he's doing something to help. Keep his hands occupied.

The man did as instructed, putting more effort into the

chest compressions, and she began to think it might be her way out of this. With his hands busy, she could go for the gun herself, hold him off, back out of the room. She could do that now, remove herself from the situation, because an ambulance was on the way. She'd done her superhero bit.

She glanced quickly at the gun on the floor, then back to the stranger doing chest compressions.

Then her opening came.

Russian Guy gasped and began to breathe.

The guy doing chest compressions stopped for a moment, seemingly stupefied, as he stared at Russian Guy's face.

She took advantage. She slid to her left, staying on her knees, and cradled the gun on the floor in her left hand before slipping it into the waist of her jeans.

And still the guy kept doing the compressions, pressing on Russian Guy's chest like an automaton. He was really getting into it, as if he were the one whose life was being saved.

"Stop," she said, sliding back over and putting her hand on Russian Guy's wrist. There was a pulse there, erratic but definite.

"He's back," she said, trying to study Gloved Guy's face for a reaction. For a moment she almost thought he was having a heart attack himself; his skin went the color of oatmeal, and his eyes seemed to have trouble focusing. A two-for-one deal when the EMTs showed up.

Okay, do something. Don't give him a chance to look around for the gun. Don't let him realize it's missing.

She leaned back, pulled a pack of cigarettes from the back pocket of her jeans. She'd never smoked before, but after leaving her perfect little home in the woods in Red Lodge, she'd pulled over for a pack of Camels. She'd smoked a pack a day since then, was almost at the point where she could get through a cigarette without coughing.

She offered him a cigarette, but he refused, so she lit one for herself, trying to calm the jitters.

Immediately, he spoke. "You shouldn't do that."

She narrowed her eyes. "Shouldn't do what?"

"Smoke. You're pregnant."

She felt like a balloon with a slow leak for a few moments. She looked at her stomach. Too early; she wasn't showing yet. That's why she'd run away, after all, why she'd come to Seattle. To fix this second . . . mistake.

Slowly, keeping her eyes on his face, she stubbed out the cigarette on the floor between them. Both of them remained on their knees at Russian Guy's side, as if they were here to pray for a sick friend.

Change the subject, just change the subject.

"What's with the gloves?" she asked, blurting out the first thing that came to her mind.

He looked at his hands a moment before holding them up, a look of disgust in his eyes. Germ freak? Maybe. But she guessed that wasn't his only reason for the gloves.

"Long story," he said.

She stood, her knee protesting with a crack, before her attention was again distracted by the Russian Guy on the floor. He was moaning, a low, soft keening sound. The sound her veins had made when Gloved Guy had touched her with his bare hand. Maybe . . . he had the dead blood, too?

"Probably a heart attack," she said. "Or a stroke. His body's going to be in shock for a while. Probably won't fully come back around until he's in the hospital."

She wasn't sure why she was saying all this suddenly. Maybe just to keep talking, keep Gloved Guy occupied. Keep him from looking for that missing gun. Of course, if Russian Guy was going to live, that might not be such a good thing. After all, Gloved Guy was here to kill Russian Guy, she was now sure of that. The gloves, the gun . . . well, if those didn't say "hit man," what did?

(But what was with the shoes?)

Okay, just keep control of the situation. She could do that. She held out her hand, an offer to help him stand. She wasn't surprised when he refused and stood on his own. He was a twitchy one, for sure.

"I can take it from here," she said after he stood.

"What do you mean?"

"You've been itching to bolt ever since I got here. Probably would have, if I hadn't come over."

He remained quiet, probably considering his options.

She let her left arm drop to her side, where it would be

closer to the gun if she needed it. "And I'm guessing that's an even longer story."

Just leave, she said quietly in her mind now. She had the gun, so she was safe; she'd fired one before. Back in Montana.

His face contorted, and she guessed this was a guy with a few secrets in his past. Secrets he'd rather not think about. She could identify with that.

"So go," she said. "Most of the time, you only get one chance to run." She tried not to think about that too much as she said it.

He nodded, stumbled a bit on his way to the door. She relaxed just a bit as she watched him, but tensed again when he turned before opening the door. Just a few feet away.

She wasn't sure what else to do, so she gave him a small, knowing nod.

He turned and left her standing there, gun hidden and clutched in her left hand.

After she heard the front door click shut (mostly shut, she noted), she returned her attention to Russian Guy on the floor. She should probably find a blanket, cover him, keep him warm. They taught her that in CPR class too. But she was tired now. And hot, in contrast to her earlier shivers. And . . . scared.

Well, she'd been scared the whole time. But she was more scared now, because she didn't know what lay ahead of her. She was alone and pregnant in Seattle, not very pregnant, true, but pregnant all the same, and she needed to be *not* pregnant because you passed the dead blood to your kids and she'd already made a mistake with Tiffany and—

Something else caught her eye on the floor now. A piece of paper. No, a napkin. She bent down and picked it up, turned it over. It had one long number scribbled on it in a shaky hand: 1595544534.

She took the gun and the napkin, rushed back to her room, put them both into her purse. She reached into her pocket for the cigarettes, pulled one out, paused, then threw it into the trash can along with the rest of the pack.

What was she thinking? She'd run out on her life a few days ago because . . . because she was scared she was becoming her own mother.

Which was a contradiction in terms, of course.

She remembered the first time Dear Old Mom—Flo to everyone else—sat her down and gave her the dead blood talk.

Mom had dead blood in her veins because she had received the dead blood from her own mother. And dead blood was a bad thing, because it made you think crazy things—things doctors had long words for if you talked about them, but still just crazy things. And now Mom could see she'd given the dead blood to her own child.

To her.

"You got the dead blood in you, child," Mom said, and suddenly Mom had her arm pinned to the table, a kitchen knife in her hand. "Gotta get the dead blood out," Mom said, and she cut.

Not a deep cut. But not the last cut, either. Years later, when she was much older than ten, when she was much wiser, she heard someone use the term "a death of a thousand cuts." She didn't know what it meant, not at the time, but she found tears welling in her eyes instantly.

Yes, for six years, she'd died a death of a thousand cuts as Mom tried to get the dead blood out. And so when she'd met Kenneth, she'd seen him as a way out, an escape. She'd run away, far away from Dear Old Mom, not realizing the dead blood would follow her.

Even here, to Seattle.

She sat, staring at the floor of her hotel room. She couldn't get rid of the baby. Not now. Maybe she never could have; she'd been here for four days, after all, the number for an abortion clinic scribbled on scratch paper, and never called it.

She wasn't her mother. Never would be. Never.

So . . . maybe she could go back, smooth things over, just tell them she'd simply needed a long weekend away. She could sell it, because she was a good actress.

She had, after all, played the part of the Good Wife and the Good Mother for a few years. And she'd fooled everyone except herself.

24.

Drawn from the memory, Grace went back to her Dark Room, put down the water bottle, searched in her purse until she found it. The napkin, which she'd encased in a plastic sandwich baggie shortly after returning to her former life, if only briefly.

She'd run once, come to Seattle for a few days, but got cold feet. And she had gone back, apologizing to her family and vowing she would do better. She'd given birth to a second child, a son she named Joey, and for a while, she'd played the part well.

But then.

Well, then she found herself wondering about Tiffany. Looking at her forearms, wondering if she had the dead blood coursing in her veins, because it passed from mother to daughter, after all.

After she thought that for the very first time, she felt her whole body shaking. Shivering. And she knew she'd been a poor actress, because the dead blood still flowed in her own veins, after all.

Despite her mother's best efforts.

And so, saying she was going to the store for a pack of cigarettes (a habit she'd returned to after the birth of Joey), she found herself inexplicably back in Seattle. And along the way she'd found the comforting, magical napkin with the numbers on it, safely encased in a plastic sandwich bag, still in her purse.

She had been wrong, then. Sometimes you do get a second chance to run.

Grace shook her head, pushed away the plastic bag, tried to push away all the memories it represented. Untouchable memories, now that she'd slid deeper into oblivion.

All of it, in some way, could be traced to this napkin, this mysterious number. And after all that time, she still couldn't let go of it. Was life really that random?

It was midafternoon, and she was still good. Still happy. Still golden-creamy, far from that gray zone that always hungered for another hit of heroin. That gray zone didn't descend until late afternoon or early evening. Usually. If she felt the gray zone descending, she would leave immediately, return to her apartment. She never did heroin here. Not in GraceSpace.

Before she left, though, she could get a few more things done. Order some supplies. She went to her laptop, keyed in her password, fired up the browser. She was running low on cap tops especially, but she could also use more tubes, and maybe she'd look at some inks.

At her supplier's Web site, she went to the order form, pulled up her order history. Under inks, she had ordered item #8174-2296-75, which was Jet Black from Bail Ink; as well as item #8724-1289-44, Midnight Black from Chisel Color; and #7721-8954-30, Squid Green, also from Chisel Color. She paused, wishing she could find the perfect black. She'd tried inks from at least half a dozen manufacturers in the past couple years, and while she liked them all for different applications, she'd never stumbled on the perfect black. Not yet. She entered order numbers for some dispenser bottles and rinse cups, caps, and hit the checkout button. The screen asked her to confirm all the order numbers and quantities, and as she scanned them, something struck her.

All of the order numbers, she noticed, were ten digits. She pulled the napkin in the plastic bag toward her again, looked at it even though she didn't need to. She knew the number.

Curious, she hit the Keep Shopping button and entered the number from the napkin into the search box: 1595-5445-34. She felt her heart leap a bit as she read the result. An ink called Black Tar from a manufacturer she'd never heard of named Catfish Industries.

She clicked through to the description and discovered it was a special-order ink, shipped from a new company in China. An introductory special listed a bottle for $25, which was pretty spendy. Still, *Black Tar*. The street name for pretty much the best heroin you could find. How could she go wrong? She added a bottle and hit the checkout button.

26.

The UPS guy showed up at the shop just after she opened.

"Hey, Joe," she said. "What can brown do for me today?" It was a joke she always threw at him, and he always took it good-naturedly.

"Brown can deliver some other colors," he said, motioning at the boxes he carried on the dolly. He left them in a pile by the front desk, then shoved the electronic signature display her way.

She signed her name and handed it back to him. "You should come in for some work," she said. "I can do a UPS logo on your arm for you, get you a promotion for your dedication."

He smiled, tipped his hat at her. "I'd put the UPS logo somewhere else, and I'm pretty sure it wouldn't get me a promotion."

She smiled and waved him off as he walked out the door.

Okay, still an hour or so before Vaughn and Zoey would be here, and about half an hour before her first appointment showed up. She could put away these supplies before then.

She carted the boxes back into her space one by one, kicking herself for not asking Joe to just trundle them in on his dolly. She removed the packaging, checked to make sure the order was complete, remembering only then that she had ordered ink from a new manufacturer.

Quickly, she put the other supplies away in her converted dresser, then opened the last box marked Catfish Industries. Inside, the tops of ten bottles glistened back at her. Most ink—okay, *all* ink—came in plastic dispenser bottles. These were more exotic.

She lifted one out of the box, held it up to examine it. Was it glass? Maybe. Crazy. She swirled the ink, noting its consistency, and was instantly excited. The light danced off the ink like stars, the substance inside thicker, heavier than normal. Like . . . well, like tar.

She popped off the top of the bottle, smelled. Like most ink, it smelled a bit like paint, but she detected a whiff of difference under the paint smell. Something mossy, organic. If she could just lay down some of this stuff, play with its consistency, she could get a better sense of its color.

Pigskin. She needed pigskin, which would let her lay a few practice lines, discover more about this ink and how it behaved. Ray wouldn't be at the butcher shop yet, so that was a no-go. Thick-skinned fruit—oranges or grapefruit—were options, but not horribly realistic. Besides, she didn't have any oranges or grapefruit in her refrigerator right now, only apples. Maybe when Vaughn or Zoey got in, she'd send one of them to Ray for some pigskin.

"Hey, Grace."

She jumped, startled by the voice. It was Candy, her ten o'clock appointment. She glanced at the clock on the wall. Ten before the hour. Somehow she'd been sitting here, absently holding this new ink, for fifteen minutes. And it felt like fifteen seconds.

"Sorry," Candy said, gum popping in her too-white teeth. "Didn't mean to scare you."

Grace put down the bottle, pushed the carton with the rest of the Black Tar back beside her dresser. "No problem," she said. "Just concentrating a little too hard, I guess. Didn't hear you come in."

"The bell clanked."

Candy was referring to the cowbell above the door, an inside joke among the three of them in the shop. Whenever anyone walked in, one of them would say "More cowbell."

"Guess I just didn't hear it. Come on in. Take about ten minutes to set up and get you started."

Candy walked to the chair in the middle of the Dark Room, a dentist chair Grace had carefully researched and purchased. Not many tattoo shops spent money on their chairs, just going with standard office seating. But Grace always thought the chair was part of the process; when potential clients saw it, they thought, unconsciously, of medical facilities. A very good thing.

"Just have a seat."

"What's that?" Candy asked as she watched Grace bend

and start to slide the black ink into the empty slot of the carton.

"Some new ink. Never used it before; just checking it out."

"What's it called?"

Grace smiled. "Black Tar."

Candy's gum stopped popping for a few seconds. "Wicked cool."

"Yeah."

"You gonna use it?" Candy said, settling into the chair.

"No. Haven't worked with it yet. Going with the Midnight Black—good stuff. Relax. Thousands of people walking around with it in their skin."

Candy settled into the chair, shifting around. "You think I want the stuff everyone else has? Gimme the Tar."

Grace was surprised to feel her throat constricting a bit with excitement. She had to admit, she *did* want to use the new Black Tar ink. But she couldn't, not without knowing more about it. She shook her head. "Can't. I'm not gonna stick you with anything I haven't tested."

Candy rolled her eyes, looking closer to fifteen than her true age of twenty-two. "Thousands of people walking around out on the streets with ink from the office store in them, and they're fine."

"Most of them."

"Yeah, well, is it specifically tat ink?"

Grace paused. "Yes."

"So it's sterile. That's half of it. You get it from a place you trust?"

Another pause. "Yeah." She got all of her items from a single supplier, and she'd never, ever had a problem with the safety of anything she'd ordered.

Candy raised her eyebrows. "So let's live a little. Gimme the Tar."

Grace felt anticipation coiling inside her, not quite believing she was even considering it. But after a few seconds of thought, she nodded. "Okay," she said. "We'll take a look. If I like the feel, we'll try it."

"Too cool."

For a moment, Grace thought Candy was going to kick her heels together and say "Goody goody gumballs."

Grace turned away, donned sterile gloves, went to her worktable. She pulled out some plastic wrap and circled it around the new bottle of Black Tar, creating a moisture barrier, then put it on the back of the table with the other wrapped bottles and instruments. From a metal tray next to the worktable, she carefully selected packages of single-use needles and tubes. Other shops still went with autoclaves, but Grace was extra careful; everything in her shop was single-use.

She stripped the packaging off the needles and the tube, then turned them over and slipped them onto the sterile surface of her worktable. Finally she pulled off the gloves, threw them on the metal tray's pad, wrapped it all together, and threw the whole package into the waste container to be incinerated later.

She rubbed her hands with alcohol cleanser, slipped on a fresh pair of gloves, and looked at Candy. Candy smiled, popping her gum again.

At her worktable, Grace chose a jar of petroleum jelly and used a tongue depressor to slather a bit on the front part of the paper. She pulled a cap out of the dispenser, put it in the jelly where it wouldn't slide or fall off the work area. Then she assembled her gun, slipping the needle into the armature and positioning the tube and reservoir over the needle.

Finally she was ready for the ink. The Black Tar. She selected the bottle, now encased in plastic, poured a few drops of it into the cap. It was the darkest black she'd ever seen, a slightly thicker consistency than anything she'd ever used. Interesting.

"Okay," she said, turning to Candy. "Let's see your hip."

Candy wanted a biohazard symbol, about two inches across, just above her right hip. Black was the only color she'd need to use.

Grace rubbed the whole area above Candy's hip with a sterile alcohol pad, then looked up at Candy. "You ready?" she asked.

"Do it to it," Candy said.

Grace turned back to her worktable, picked up her gun, drew up some ink, and brought the gun over Candy's hip.

There were lots of stencils and flash art for tattoos out there, and many artists used them whenever they could. Grace was the opposite. She was a freehander whenever possible, and only sketched out the most intricate designs ahead of time. Freehanding, she thought, helped her individualize each project. Kept it more interesting.

She put the needle on Candy's flesh and triggered the gun, outlining a circle. The gun moved easily, smoothly, and the ink put down a strong, solid line. Grace barely had to wipe away any excess. "Wow," she said under her breath.

Up above, Candy lifted her head for a look. "Good stuff?" she asked.

Grace looked at the tip of the gun, at the circle she'd just tattooed into Candy's skin, and simply nodded. Smiling, she triggered the gun again.

27.

"That rocks!"

It was Candy's voice, coming from somewhere distant. Grace shook her head a moment, noticing that she was cleaning the tattoo with antibacterial soap. She paused, looked at the clock. An hour had passed, and she barely even remembered doing the tattoo. That wasn't good.

She looked at Candy. "That went pretty quick."

Candy nodded eagerly. "Tell you the truth," she said, "I kinda dozed off. It felt . . . relaxing."

Clients had various reactions to tattoos, but no one ever called it relaxing. And no one ever dozed. Grace looked at the tattoo in earnest for the first time and had to agree with Candy's assessment. It rocked. The color was dark, almost shined with an oily brilliance, and the whole thing seemed to shimmer, as if she were looking at it through a kaleidoscope.

(Bulimia)

The letters formed inside the tattoo, as if part of some intricate pattern, but as obvious as neon to her eyes—

(Bulimia)

—followed by an image of Candy, crumpled and crying beside a toilet.

"What is it?" Candy said, sensing something.

Grace shook her head. "Nothing," she said. "Just need something to eat, I guess."

Or maybe she was jonesing for some smack extra early today. She didn't feel her blood boiling, but that strange image in her mind had to be the drugs talking.

"That's the last thing I need," Candy said, snapping her gum again.

Grace looked at the bony hip jutting from Candy's skin, then back to her face, but said nothing as she applied a bandage to the tattoo.

28.

After Candy left, Grace put away the Black Tar. She had two other appointments that day, and Vaughn had an appointment to work on a simple barbed wire design she supervised. He did nice work; he was more careful, more patient than Zoey. A couple years from now, she knew, they'd both be good artists, probably move on and start their own shops. Maybe even sooner.

But even as she worked on the butterfly tattoo on Rae's foot, even as she watched Vaughn outlining the barbed wire on his client's arm, she found her eyes, her mind, wandering back to the bottle of Black Tar sitting on her worktable. Something about it was . . . intoxicating.

And the more she thought about the bottle, the more she thought about Candy. About bulimia. That image of Candy, a collapsed heap, refused to leave her mind. Where had that come from? The tattoo world was full of New Age mumbo jumbo, to be sure, people who looked at the whole thing as some kind of spiritual journey. More power to them, but she'd never been one of them. It was art, yes. But nothing more.

Certainly not clairvoyance.

She left the shop at four o'clock, but not before retrieving Candy's phone number and address from her database.

And then, without really planning to go, she was standing at the door to Candy's apartment.

Why? This wasn't her issue at all, and she had more than enough issues to go around. How was she going to be any help to this girl when she couldn't even help herself? Junkie Woman, the Superhero.

She closed her eyes, paused, knocked. From somewhere behind the door she heard shuffling footsteps, a muffled "Who is it?"

"Candy, it's Grace. From the tattoo shop. Just dropping by to make sure everything is okay."

She heard more shuffling, a toilet flush. Finally, after several more seconds, Candy opened the door, wiping at her mouth with the back of her hand.

Grace offered a smile, tried not to read too much into that. "Did I catch you at a bad time?"

"Hmmm? No, no, not at all. Just—just about to brush my teeth. Come on in."

"I'm sorry I didn't call first," Grace said. "I figured, you know, first time with that ink and all, I wanted to check, make sure everything's looking good."

Candy led her into a small efficiency apartment, showed her to a threadbare couch.

"Yeah," Candy said, uncomfortably standing while Grace sat on the couch. "I was kinda surprised to see you."

"Better safe than sorry," Grace said.

"Sure, sure. Actually, to tell you the truth, the tat is great."

As if to illustrate, Candy lifted her shirt, showing the area. The bandage covered the fresh tattoo, but Grace could see the swelling was minimal, if any.

"I've . . . uh . . . peeled it off a few times just to look at it," Candy admitted.

"That's no problem, as long as you're keeping it clean, keeping it bandaged for the first week. Just soap—no alcohol."

Candy smiled. "Yeah, I've heard your lecture before."

Grace returned the smile, peeled back the girl's bandage, stared deep into the dark recesses of the round propeller-like biohazard symbol. It seemed to glow in the low light of Candy's apartment.

"I feel like I could just wear it now," Candy said. "Doesn't really hurt at all—nothing like my other tats, to tell you the truth."

"That's good," Grace said, feeling a bit of regret as she had to cover the tattoo with the bandage once more.

Candy dropped her shirt, finally seeming comfortable, and sat next to her on the couch. "You want a drink or something?" she asked, obviously warming to the idea of company.

"Sure. Whatever you have."

"Diet Mountain Dew and . . . um, Diet Mountain Dew. Sorry. Lots of caffeine; jump-starts the metabolism."

A high metabolism. Sounded like an eating disorder talking, Grace had to admit. But she didn't have any evidence, any *real* evidence, yet. Just a flushing toilet and Mountain Dew, innocuous things she'd find in the apartments of many young girls.

"Sounds good." She paused. "Can I, uh—" She pointed toward the bathroom door. "Can I use your bathroom?"

She saw a flash of panic in Candy's eyes—just a brief flash as she glanced toward the bathroom—and then Candy nodded her head a little too vigorously.

"Yeah. Sure."

Inside the bathroom, Grace pressed the button in the middle of the knob to lock the door, but she was pretty sure it didn't truly lock; the door scraped a bit against the frame and didn't seem to fully latch. Most doors in her life, it seemed, never fully closed. Or never fully opened.

She went to the toilet and sat on its lid for a few moments. This was why she was here, wasn't it? To see . . . whatever it was she had to see.

She glanced in the garbage can. Several wads of tissue, an empty tube of toothpaste. Nothing too interesting. She stood, lifted the lid of the toilet, peered into the bowl. As if that would tell her anything. At least Candy seemed to keep it well scrubbed.

Grace moved to her right, stood in front of the medicine cabinet mirror, stared at her reflection for a few seconds. Was she going to do this? Was she going to thrust herself into the midst of this situation that didn't involve her, try to change the world?

She thought briefly, again, of Russian Guy's heart attack so many years ago, and realized her one tenuous thread in all of this—the napkin with the number written on it—was also tied to this current predicament.

A thread, indeed, stitching together her poor decisions.

It would be easier, so much easier, to just walk out of this bathroom, walk out of Candy's apartment, walk out of Candy's life, and head home to the comfort of her pipe and her white smoke. Chase the dragon, and let it chase her. A perfect, symbiotic relationship. This thing here, inside Candy's bathroom, was an entirely different kind of dragon.

She stepped back to the toilet, pushed the handle to flush it, counted to five, and turned on the faucet. With a last look in the mirror, she drew in a breath, held it, and opened the medicine cabinet door, swinging it slowly.

Inside, she saw things you might see in the medicine cabinet of any house. A bottle of ibuprofen, cotton swabs, a bottle of perfume, some bandages. These items lined the top three shelves of the cabinet.

But the bottom shelf held four bright-blue bottles she recognized instantly. Milk of magnesia. A laxative. Next to the blue bottles were half a dozen small brown vials of some kind. Carefully, the sound of the water in the faucet masking any sounds she might be making, she retrieved one of the vials. *Ipecac Syrup USP*, the plain white label said. She stared for a few seconds before replacing the vial. She recognized the name instantly, because she'd kept a bottle of ipecac syrup in her own medicine cabinet when she was a mother.

Ipecac syrup was used for poisoning emergencies.

It induced vomiting.

Grace closed the medicine cabinet and turned off the faucet. Yes, she was chasing the wrong kind of dragon. She unlocked the door, opened it, went back into the living room, wearing a well-practiced smile. She sat on the worn couch beside Candy, took the glass of green liquid over ice, sipped at it.

"Everything okay?" Candy asked. "You look a little . . . I don't know . . . pale or something."

"Just need a little caffeine, I think. Long day. So this really hits the spot. Thanks."

She took another drink, a long draw, lingering on the sensation of carbonation burning her throat. The same sensation ipecac syrup might create, for example. She set the glass down on the makeshift coffee table, pulled around her purse.

"Listen," she said. "I know I'm being a bit over-the-top with all this, but I want you to see a doctor about that tattoo." She pulled out a pen and wrote a name and number on the back of one of her business cards.

Candy took the card and looked at it. "Dr. Foss?" she said. "But . . . the tattoo doesn't even hurt. It's fine."

"I know, I know. But Dr. Foss is a good guy; I know him

from . . . a few years back. He owes me. And, you know, like I said, I just want to be extra careful with this—using that Black Tar for the first time. I'll pick up the bill for it." She tried a smile. "That's what you get for being the guinea pig. I'll call him and schedule something for tomorrow."

Candy seemed unsure for a few seconds, but then shrugged. "Okay," she said.

Grace stood. "Thanks for the drink; I'd better get going. Just wanted to make sure you were okay."

Candy stood with her, uncomfortable, awkward, thin; and abruptly, without meaning to, Grace hugged her.

"Okay," Candy said, following her to the front door. "Thanks for dropping by. And thanks for the tat. I love it."

"I'm glad," Grace said, opening the front door and stepping through. She stopped, turned back to Candy. "Take care of yourself."

Candy smiled. "No prob," she said, and closed the door gently.

Grace turned and walked quickly away, getting totally out of the building before she felt the tears running down her cheeks. She *did* know Dr. Foss well; that much was true. He'd treated her at the clinic after she'd got hold of some poorly cut smack and kept in touch with her since, calling every couple of months and asking if she'd thought about his offer to get her into rehab. She'd call him, explain Candy's situation, and he'd know what to do. Bulimia was treatable.

Just like heroin addiction.

As she walked down the street in the dusk, thinking about Dr. Foss, an odd thought struck her. Here it was, early evening, and her blood wasn't itching. Usually, by this time, her veins were thirsty for more Harry Jones.

But tonight, the hunger stayed quiet.

29.

Late that night, in her bed, Grace awoke from a nightmare she couldn't remember. Something that floated just on the edge of her consciousness, teasing her with its proximity before jetting away each time she seemed about to grasp it.

The blood itch was there, inside, and it was bad.

Except.

Except, it wasn't in her arms.

It was in her whole upper chest.

Okay, so this was the start of the withdrawals she'd been expecting. She hadn't hit the pipe since this morning, just before heading to the shop. Since her session with Candy, nothing.

Soon—maybe in a few minutes, maybe in a few hours—she'd start tremoring, and then her stomach would kick into reverse, and then she would get the chills as the shakes increased. That's what happened when you tried to stop.

Best to just head it off now. Go light up, take off the edge. Help her get over the nightmare.

Still lying in bed, she scratched at the itch in her chest and felt a peculiar wetness there.

Whoa. She was bleeding.

She threw back the covers and made her way to the bathroom, flicking on the overhead light. She stared at herself in the mirror a few moments, took a breath, and pulled the collar of her sleeping shirt down so she could see her chest.

It was ink. Black ink. (Black tar)

Just to the left of her sternum, right above her heart.

She touched the ink, feeling the wetness before drawing away her finger again. No residue on the finger. The ink felt wet to the touch, but it was, like any other tattoo ink, beneath the skin.

Still, when she touched it she felt a mild electrical charge inside her bones, unlike anything she'd ever felt before.

No, that wasn't quite true. She'd felt something very much like it when she touched that man's hand in Russian Guy's hotel room years ago. She'd never forgotten the sensation, and now it had returned to her.

Was that bad? Was that good?

She didn't know.

It was just the start of a tattoo, this mark on her chest. She could tell that. An upside-down U, with a couple lines dropping from it like harp strings.

216

She touched the ink again, felt the charge, realized this wasn't withdrawal. Quite the opposite. At this moment the thought of heroin—smoked or smacked—made her feel sick to her stomach. All she wanted to do was touch the beginning of this tattoo, be comforted by the low electrical hum.

Was that bad? Was that good?

She didn't know.

She returned to her bed, lay flat on her back, feeling the beginning of the tattoo beneath her fingers. Had she done it to herself in the stupor of this morning? Finished Candy's tattoo, then started on her own chest? Impossible, really.

Frightening, as well. At least, her mind kept trying to convince her of this. There was something wrong, very wrong, with a tattoo suddenly beginning to appear, electric and liquid, on your chest. It meant . . . well, maybe it meant all those years of shooting smack had taken their toll, damaged her brain in ways that couldn't be repaired. She'd always known at some point that could happen. In fact, after everything, she had counted on it happening.

And yet, something about the electric liquid . . .

(Black Tar)

. . . on her chest felt comforting, warm. And so she drifted back to sleep, hands folded across her chest as if she were an Egyptian queen just placed into her sarcophagus, the skin of her arms and hands tingling with hypnotic energy wherever it touched the beginnings of the tattoo.

Was that bad? Was that good?

She didn't know.

30.

Grace went in late the next morning, knowing she had no appointments scheduled. Vaughn nodded at her as she walked through the door.

"More cowbell," he said, grinning.

"The only cure," she answered, letting the door shut behind her.

She'd made it through the entire evening without lighting up. Dangerous, she knew; she'd been through withdrawals before—vomiting that was much worse than anything ipecac syrup might induce—but so far nothing had happened. She was curious to see how long it lasted, how long she could go without the tremors. So far, so good. A bit more tired than usual, but nothing major. Yet.

"Hey," Vaughn said as she walked past him on the way to her Dark Room, "you know anything about this Black Tar?"

She spun, looked at him. "Black Tar?"

"Yeah, a new ink. Had a phone call this morning, and a walk-in, both asking about it."

"Where'd they hear about it?"

He narrowed his eyes for a few seconds. "Well, they said a friend got a tat from you, using it. They both saw it and loved it."

She swallowed, hard. "Candy. You know her."

He nodded. "Sure."

"She was just in yesterday morning," Grace said, trying to sound nonchalant. "Not sure why they think the tat would look great—probably still swollen and puffy. And she should have it bandaged." But inside, even as Grace said it, she knew it wasn't true. Candy's tattoo was somehow hypnotic—dangerous and attractive at the same time, like . . .

Well, like heroin.

Also see: the tattoo on her chest.

Vaughn shrugged again. "Well, guess you're going to have to start paying Candy for marketing. She already got two people to drop by. One made an appointment for this afternoon." He looked at the clock on the wall. "Just a couple hours from now."

32.

"I'm Ryder," the young man said, extending his hand to Grace.

Grace smiled, took his hand. "Grace," she said.

"Love the place here," he said, looking at the art, the snapshots of past tattoos hung on the walls.

"Yeah, thanks. We do pretty well."

"That's why I'm here," he said, rocking a bit on his feet. "I called this morning, talked to—"

"Vaughn, yeah. He said you're a friend of Candy's."

"Texted me a photo of her new art last night," he said. "Just a snap from her cell phone, but wow . . ." He paused. "So here I am."

She nodded. "Well, Ryder, I usually do a consult up front—"

"That's cool."

"—and then I just let people think about it, you know. Take a day or two to make sure they know what they want."

"Oh, I know what I want," he said, his eyes sparkling.

"Really?"

"Been thinking about it for quite a while now," he said. "Barbed wire, right around the bicep here." He held up his arm, traced a circle around the upper part of his right arm with the other hand. "With the Black Tar."

She paused, felt a familiar itch starting in her veins at the mention of the name. Except . . . this itch wasn't for the heroin variant she'd become so up close and personal with over the past couple years. It was for the ink. Just like this kid.

"Well, I just got that in yesterday," she said. "Candy was

kind of a test case, you might say. I'd like to make sure she's doing okay."

"Yeah, she said you were pushing her to some doctor," he said. "But she said she feels great, said it didn't even hurt. Works for me."

Grace tried another smile, but she wasn't sure it came across as much more than a grimace.

"I'll pay double for the Black Tar," he said.

"It's not about the money. It's about the safety."

He shook his head. "So I'll sign a waiver or something. I don't think you need to worry."

"I don't see any other art on you," she said.

"Nope. It's gonna be my first. Like I said, I've been thinking about it a long time."

She looked at the floor a few minutes, thinking. The thing was, she wanted to do it. Maybe more than she could admit. She wanted to tap into that Black Tar, see what would happen. That's what the itch in her veins was.

"Okay," she finally said. "Step into my parlor."

She went into her Dark Room, hearing him chuckle behind her.

"I'm sure it's the first time you've used *that* line," he said, following her.

"Of course." She flipped on the work light at her table. "Have a seat."

She heard him settling into the dentist chair as she started preparing her work area, laying out the sterile papers before going to the cabinets and picking out a thick outlining needle and tube.

He watched silently as she went through her preparation ritual, eventually speaking again. "Candy said you were extra careful," he commented.

She grunted, concentrating as she grabbed the bottle of Black Tar ink with her freshly gloved hands, dropping some of it into the cap held by a smear of petroleum jelly. She slipped the surgical mask over her mouth, turned to him.

"Right bicep?" she said, and he nodded.

She cleaned and disinfected the arm, found herself actually humming as she worked. Finally, she looked at him again over the top of her surgical mask.

"Ready?" she asked.

"You bet."

She turned back to her worktable, picked up her tattoo gun, and began.

33. THREE

An hour and a half later, one word brought her out of a stupor.

"Wow."

It was the kid (Riley? No, Ryder) looking at his tattoo and exclaiming in wonder as she wiped at it with her sterile cloth.

She put down the cloth and stared at the tattoo for a few moments, the fierce pattern of barbed wire undulating as it wound around the arm. Just as Candy's had been, this tattoo was a magnet for the eyes. Attractive, yes, but also . . . dangerous. Which maybe added to the allure.

The wire was detailed, much more detailed than any other tattoo she'd seen—so much so, she wondered how she had done it. A slithering, buried voice answered her: *she hadn't*. At least, she hadn't done it alone. She peered at the tattoo and it seemed to move like a snake, forming letters in front of her.

(Fall)

Then the letters faded, and it was just the glowing tattoo again. She glanced at Ryder, but he obviously hadn't seen the tattoo or its hidden letters; he just smiled.

As she looked at his face, a flickering image floated in her mind, a slice of time frozen: Ryder, hard hat cocked on his head, hunched on the ground over another young man with a pool of blood beneath his head. Behind them, a forklift and scattered boxes.

Just as abruptly, the image disappeared, dizzying Grace for a few moments. She closed her eyes.

"You okay?" Ryder's voice asked.

She opened her eyes, turned to start cleaning her work area. "Yeah," she said. "Just need something to eat, I think."

(Ha ha, a little bulimia humor there)

She picked up the used needles and ink tube, transferring them to the medical waste bin.

"I'll need your phone number and address before you leave, just so I can make sure everything's okay." She peeled off the gloves, put them on top of the paper on her work area, now smudged with ink stains.

Ryder spoke from behind her. "Sure, no problem."

She crumpled the paper into a tight ball. "And I'll give you some instructions for taking care of the tattoo. You don't want it to get infected."

35.

After Ryder left, Grace retreated to the bathroom, locked the door behind her. Nervous, manic energy coursed through her body, and she was surprised to find she still didn't have any symptoms of withdrawal.

She stood in front of the mirror, peeled away her shirt. There on her chest, just to the left of her sternum, more of the tattoo had been filled in, a full outline now, and she recognized what it was.

An old arched door, the kind you might see in an ancient castle, with large iron bands. The door itself had rough-grained vertical planks and a metal plate with a large, gaping keyhole for a skeleton key.

An ancient door was tattooed just over her heart.

Locked.

37.

Two hours and eight jittery cigarettes later, she was in her apartment, searching the *Seattle Times* online archives, skipping over the front-page stories about the firebug that had everyone buzzing.

She'd instantly recognized the background in the freeze-frame photo that came to her mind when she looked at Ryder's tattoo. Anyone who lived in Seattle would know the piers.

She keyed in the words *pier accident* and hit Search, surprised at the number of results returned: stories about drug chases, a truck driver crushed, a faulty crane, a kid killed by a freight train. Then, on the fifth page of results, a story from last year.

"Dock worker injured in forklift accident," the headline said. She clicked on the story and scanned it, gleaning the basic details: forklift operator Joseph Copacino, a falling stack of palettes, serious brain injury to coworker Brandon Youngquist.

Accompanying the story were two headshots. One was captioned with the victim's name, Brandon Youngquist. The other photo was captioned with the name Joseph Copacino, but Grace knew him by another name.

Ryder.

The story finished with standard boilerplate about an

accident investigation, and then a line that caught her eye: *The victim's family has retained the services of attorney Antonio Genobli.*

She looked at the screen numbly for a few moments, then did a Google search on the attorney's name; seconds later, she had a phone number.

She called the number, asked the receptionist if she could speak to Antonio Genobli. When the receptionist asked who was calling, she hesitated only briefly before saying, "I'm calling about the Brandon Youngquist case."

She thought she detected a bit of hesitation, then a quick recovery by the receptionist. "Hold one moment, please."

And a moment was all it took; almost immediately a clipped man's voice answered. "Tony Genobli."

Grace realized she was itching at the door tattoo on her chest, forced herself to stop. "Mister, ah, Genobli. I wanted to talk to you about the Brandon Youngquist case."

"Who is this?"

What should she say? "Um, I'm a friend of . . . Joe Copacino."

She heard a long pause on the line. Then: "You're in contact with Mr. Copacino."

She looked at the slip of paper with Ryder's phone number on it. "Yeah."

"I'd like to meet you in person."

It was her turn to pause. "When?"

"Now."

38.

Under the cloudy skies of late afternoon, Grace sat facing Antonio Genobli in his office. She was surprised to discover his whole operation was decidedly low-key: basic office super-store furniture filling a suite of three putty-colored offices occupying the corner of a decaying building in Rainier Valley, southeast of Seattle proper. Rainier Valley had long been Seattle's own miniature melting pot, home to immigrants from all over the world.

Tony Genobli smiled at her from his rickety task chair. "I know," he said. "Not really what you were expecting for an ambulance chaser's offices."

She shrugged, uncomfortable that he seemed to be reading her thoughts.

"I grew up around here," he said. "Used to be a lot more Italians around here, you know. Still home to me. Plus, with my . . . clientele, I don't want to stuff a lot of money in their faces when they walk in here, you understand. I'm one of them. Always have been."

She liked him immediately. "I see what you mean."

"Now," he said, leaning in. "I'd be most interested in finding Mr. Copacino."

"You mind telling me why?"

Genobli leaned back in his chair. "I think I can help him."

"How?"

"I'm an accident attorney," he said. "He had an accident."

"I thought you were representing the other guy—the guy who got hurt."

"Brandon Youngquist. Yes, I am."

Grace could still see the image dancing in her mind. "I thought you'd be going after Ry—Joe."

"Mr. Copacino? No, no, not at all. What are we gonna get out of a young dock worker? We started by going after the Port Authority, auditing their safety records on the fork-lift in question, that kind of thing. But then we had a bit of a breakthrough."

"What kind of breakthrough?"

"I'm not at liberty to discuss that."

She sensed Genobli was eager to find Ryder, so she pressed her advantage. "Then I guess I should just leave," she said.

"No, no, wait," he said, stopping her before she had a chance to make a show of leaving. He gave a big sigh. "Okay," he said. "I'm gonna give you some of this for some—uh, some information in return. Share and share alike, *capisch*?"

She nodded her head.

"As I said, we were going after the Port Authority first. Get 'em for poor maintenance on the forklift or improper training on the driver—uh, Mr. Copacino—that kind of thing. But those were kind of dead ends. So then we started looking at the company who owned the shipping containers, poring over everything. The shipping containers, their place of origin, you know. Found they had improperly bound the palettes. Actually, more than that, they didn't have them bound at all. Big no no.

"So when Mr. Copacino was pulling out those palettes, they were just loose. A wonder they didn't kill Mr. Youngquist. This Catfish Industries, it's kind of a shell corporation for a large Chinese company, and they're involved in all kinds of bad stuff. Both coasts—shipping a lot into Newark as well."

"What kind of stuff?"

"You name it—lots worse than the lead toys or the tainted pet food you've heard about." He smiled. "But I'm tracking them down."

"So the other guy—Mr. Youngquist—he's okay?"

Genobli looked at her. "No, not okay. In a long-term care facility, but doing better. Pretty heavy damage, to tell you the truth. Hard time speaking and all that, but they started him on this new miracle drug a couple months ago, and they've seen some great progress already. Had an old lady at the same facility on the drug—dementia, something like that, for years—and she snapped out of it suddenly. Like a miracle. Hoping for the same kind of thing with Mr. Youngquist."

"So Joseph—the accident wasn't his fault," she said.

"No. That stack was doomed to fall, sooner or later. Not his fault at all."

"Does he know this?"

"I was hoping you could tell me. Haven't been able to track him down. Hasn't been in touch with his family, just dropped off the face of the earth after the accident. Tell you the truth, I kind of wondered if he'd skipped town. But if he's part of this lawsuit, I think we can negotiate a nice settlement."

The pieces started falling into place, and Grace felt gooseflesh rippling her skin. Ryder had gone underground, thinking he had nearly killed a coworker. A friend. And now, here she was, the person who could provide redemption. Just as she'd done for Candy.

"You okay?" Genobli's voice asked.

"Huh?"

"You keep scratching," he said, nodding at her. "You having an allergic reaction or something?"

She took her hand away from the tattoo on her chest. "Yeah," she said. "I'm golden. Mr. Copacino goes by the name Ryder now. If you have a pen, I'll give you a phone number."

41b.

When Grace showed up at her shop the next morning, a young woman was waiting outside the door. The woman helped her roll away the security gate, then simply said, "I want a tattoo."

Grace turned to look at her. Might be a BRB—someone who came to ask about a tattoo, then said she was going to the cash machine and would Be Right Back. BRBs rarely came right back.

Inside the shop, the BRB offered her hand. "I'm Corrine," she said.

Grace shook the young woman's hand. "Grace," she said.

She looked at the woman's hair, a rather obvious wig. It was dark. Elvira, Mistress of the Night dark. Black Tar dark.

They stood staring at each other while her answering machine beeped. She glanced at the machine's digital read-out, hoping Corrine wouldn't notice. Six messages. After business hours. Unusual, to be sure, but she couldn't check them right now.

Another beep from the machine.

Corrine smiled, looked at the phone. "Better check your messages," she said as she sat in one of the wooden chairs in the waiting area.

"You sure you don't mind?"

"Not at all."

"Okay, sure," Grace said, crossing the floor to pick up the headset and then punching the Play button. The first message was someone asking about a Black Tar tattoo. So was the second message. And the third. All of them.

She hung up the phone, feeling excitement—not pain—boiling in her veins. A hunger for a new kind of Black Tar.

"What's Black Tar?" Corrine's voice asked behind her.

Grace spun around to face the pasty-faced woman with impossibly dark hair.

"Sorry," Corrine said. "Your headset—I couldn't help but hear it."

Grace nodded, pasted on her own smile. "Black Tar is a new ink I'm using," she said. "Good coverage, darkest black you'll ever see."

Corrine chuckled. "I've seen some pretty black stuff."

Grace paused, knowing already she was going to use the Black Tar ink on this woman. It was . . . fate, after all. She was supposed to use the Black Tar on the people who came seeking it. To offer them salvation, hope. A paradoxical shining light created by the darkest black.

She was becoming addicted to this new Black Tar, yes. But this wasn't a Black Tar that killed. It was a Black Tar that gave life.

"Let's do it," Corrine said. "Let's use some Black Tar."

"Okay, well, I usually do a consult on a design—give me an idea what kind of tattoo you're looking for, where it's going, that kind of thing. Then we schedule a time."

Grace said all this, knowing none of it was going to make a difference. This woman, Corrine, wanted a tattoo. And she wanted to give it to her.

Corrine nodded before she spoke. "Here's the thing," she said. "I made an oath to myself a couple months ago to be more impulsive. Only I haven't been. Until now. Until last night, actually. I decided I wanted a tattoo, so today I'm getting a tattoo."

"Well, that's part of why I do the consult. Make sure you're not doing it on just an impulse, make sure you're comfortable with something that could last the rest of your life."

An odd look came across Corrine's face, and she took a deep breath. Grace absently wondered what sort of story was spooling inside this woman's mind.

"I, uh . . . I was diagnosed with incurable cancer a couple months ago. That's when I decided to be more impulsive, like I said. And . . . I guess I'm running out of time to be impulsive."

Great. She'd given the "decision you'll regret for the rest of your life" lecture to a woman with terminal cancer. If nothing else, that sealed the deal. That also explained the wig. Chemo. She mentally stepped back, took a breath. "What were you thinking of doing?" she asked.

"I don't know. Impulsive, like I said. Call me a blank canvas."

A blank canvas. No rules. And Black Tar. Grace felt a fire dancing in her belly, the kind of fire only smack could usually bring. "Okay, then," she said. "Let's do it."

She led Corrine into her Dark Room and began preparing the work space. Grace kept her back to Corrine, giving her time to adjust, see the facilities, trust that she was in good hands. She often did that with first-timers: introduced them to the room, then just sat quietly and worked until they had time to get comfortable with the idea.

Ready to go, Grace fastened a surgical mask over her face and turned back to Corrine, who still hadn't moved from the doorway. She just needed a little coaxing. "Time to be impulsive."

That seemed to thaw Corrine; she walked across the Dark Room floor, slid into the seat. She was still tense, nervous, but they were progressing. Baby steps.

Grace turned back to her workspace to lay out the single-use needles and tubes, and to give Corrine more time to get comfortable in the chair.

She waited patiently a few minutes, then grasped the tattoo gun and turned back to Corrine. She smiled. She knew Corrine couldn't see the smile beneath her mask, of course, but it was an old trick she'd learned. You could always hear a smile in someone's voice.

"This is the tattoo gun. I attach the needle here, draw ink into the tube up here. Just relax."

She watched Corrine take a deep breath, offer a tentative smile, nod her head.

"Okay," she said. "Any more thoughts on what you want? Where you want it?"

"My arm," Corrine said immediately.

Good; the timidity was melting away quickly.

"Something big. Something strong."

Grace nodded, adjusted the task light so it was focused on Corrine's arm. "Maybe slip this arm out of your shirt," she said. "So we don't stain it."

She didn't tell Corrine that getting a full-arm tattoo as your first one was typically a Very Bad Idea. One of the most sensitive parts of the body was the back of your arm. She didn't say any of this, because she knew this wasn't going to be a typical tattoo.

"Now," she said, looking at Corrine and trying to keep the smile in her voice, "like I said before: just try to relax."

She triggered the gun, began tracing a swirling line on the upper arm with the Black Tar, and thought to herself: *What am I doing?*

It was a question she'd asked herself so many times before. Every time she chased the dragon.

42a.

Chasing the dragon. That's what she'd been doing on Corrine's arm, she decided, as she came out of the increasingly familiar stupor. She looked at Corrine, who seemed to be dozing, as she washed the skin of Corrine's arm with soap. The whole thing had taken four hours, and in that time, she had created a dragon.

The head of the dragon stretched from the shoulder

almost to the crook of the elbow. Glints of blues and greens and golds filled in the scales; Grace looked at her work area, noticing that, sometime during the tattoo session, she'd added other colors to the mix in her work area.

Chillingly, it looked like the dragon was eating Corrine's arm.

"A catfish," Corrine's voice said.

She looked at Corrine, whose eyes were open and wide now. "What's that?"

"I said, a catfish. A beautiful catfish," Corrine repeated.

Grace stared at the tattoo. "I was thinking more like a dragon," she said. Somehow, the idea of this work of art being mistaken for a catfish insulted her. It was a dragon.

"Same thing, really, in Chinese culture," Corrine said. "To the Chinese, the catfish is a dragon, a fighter, a symbol of strength. It's perfect."

Grace continued to scrub the tattoo, choosing to say nothing. Instead, she looked at it, and as she did, patterns inside the scales moved, swam as if the catfish itself were swimming beneath a rippled surface.

Slowly, inked numbers began to shimmer and glow inside the scales at the tip of the dragon's snout. She read the numbers in order and recognized them instantly: 1595544534. The numbers written on the napkin she'd kept for eight years. The numbers that had led her to the Black Tar ink only a few days before.

Once again, an image flashed in her mind: Corrine sitting in a dark room, an IV in her arm, a single tear trickling from her eye. But the IV in her arm wasn't hooked to a bag of fluid. It was hooked to a computer screen, with blood flowing down the front of the screen. On the screen itself, a single word, followed by two exclamation points, steadily flashed: *DISASTER!!*

Grace didn't fully understand the image, just as she hadn't fully understood the images of Candy or Ryder. But she understood the message clearly. The numbers weren't hers any longer; they were Corrine's. Because if she didn't give the numbers to Corrine . . . well, *DISASTER!!*

She spoke softly. "I . . . uh, need to give you something," she said as she turned and threw the used needles and tube into the sharps container.

"Yeah? What is it?" Corrine asked from behind her.

"You're gonna think it's weird, but it's . . . I guess it's a memento of something I've been holding on to for a long time. Call it a good luck charm."

Now Grace crumpled everything into the paper that lined the top of the table, threw it into the garbage behind Corrine.

She returned her attention to the other woman's face; she seemed to be . . . disappointed, somehow, for a few seconds. Then her face brightened again and she nodded.

"Hang on just a second," Grace said. She went into the

front office and pulled the napkin in clear plastic from her purse, then returned to the Dark Room and held it in the light of the task lamp.

"What is it?" Corrine asked, taking the bag from her and examining it.

Well, that was a question, wasn't it?

"It's a . . . I don't know. I've held on to it for years now, and . . . anyway, I want you to have it. Sometime, after you've beaten this cancer, you'll hand it to someone else who needs a good luck charm."

Corrine smiled, and Grace knew everything was going to be okay. Evidently, she'd said something right.

Corrine clutched the plastic bag in her hands, saying, "It's *Fu*."

"*Fu?*"

"Chinese symbol for good luck. So this is your symbol for good luck—your *Fu*."

Grace smiled. "No, it's your *Fu* now."

Even so, as Corrine thanked her profusely and left, Grace wished she had the napkin. Just to hold one more time.

45.

That night, Grace dreamed of Tiffany and Joey, her children back in Montana. And Kenneth, her husband. In the dream she chased the dragon, lighting up some Black Tar, taking the smoke deep into her lungs, exhaling and letting the white tails of smoke caress her body.

But in the haze, through the dragon tails, she saw the faces of her children. Her husband. They called her name— her real name, not the fake one she'd used since moving to Seattle to become a junkie.

"Janet! Janet!" she heard Kenneth say, louder and deeper than the voices of her children calling out for their mother.

"I'm here!" she tried to scream, but she couldn't talk. Every time she opened her mouth, her vocal cords froze.

And still her family called out to her, trying to see her through the haze of the white dragon tails.

Eventually the smoke coalesced, massed, took shape, and Grace (Janet) knew she was now surrounded by real dragons with real teeth. Real dragons that could bite.

Still, her family called to her, and the noise they made drew the attention of the dragons. She opened her mouth again, trying to tell her family to stop, trying to scream something at the dragons to draw away their attention, but the only thing that came from her mouth was more thick, steaming smoke.

She grasped at the tails of the dragons, trying to hold them back, feeling the grit of the scales sliding off under her fingernails. But there were too many dragons, dozens of them.

They were hungry. They knew where her family was.

And they rushed toward her family with mouths open, saliva stringing heavily from white teeth.

47.

Grace awoke, tears in her eyes. She'd been crying as she slept. Was such a thing even possible?

The dreams of her family had fueled the tears, she knew. How long since she'd dreamed of them? How long since she'd even thought of them? A couple years, at least. Like so much of her life, her family had become nothing more than trash, kicked to the curb by the ever-hungry dragon.

When all was said and done, that's exactly why she used the heroin. To inoculate herself against everything she'd left behind.

And now she'd gone a couple days with no smack at all. Nothing to smoke, nothing to shoot. Her body felt strong, and no withdrawals were ravaging her body.

She scratched absently at the spot above her heart. There was the mystery tattoo, yes, appearing magically like some kind of oily rash. The door. But even that image was somehow correct, somehow fitting. It was a thick, heavy door, solidly locked.

But now memories were returning, along with a yearning for the family she'd left. How else to explain the dreams?

Going back was out of the question; they'd never take her. Abandoning family was like stepping off a cliff; once you stepped off the edge, you left the world at the top of the cliff behind forever. You were destined only to fall.

Also, there was the little matter of dead blood, and what she might do to her daughter in the name of said dead blood.

She looked at the clock, remembered she had an early appointment at nine. Dane. She'd finish his tat then make some calls. No, she hadn't experienced any true hunger for smack, any withdrawal symptoms. But her mind still needed the escape hatch the junk provided. She could score something, and by late afternoon she'd be blissfully floating high above any ghosts of her past, caramel-smooth and creamy.

She needed the smack to kill the memories. To kill the guilt. To kill who she once was.

49. NINE

Dane showed up about ten minutes after she rolled up the shop's front gate, an ear-to-ear grin on his face.

She'd inked four previous tattoos on him and scheduled a fifth one for his upper back. He wanted a phoenix, a bird rising from the flames, on his upper right shoulder.

Dane was a good kid, but maybe a bit overeager. Whenever he came into the shop, she almost felt like he was going to start hopping everywhere, a human pogo stick. He had that manic energy in his eyes, as if getting a tattoo were the most wonderful experience anyone could ever have.

Personally, she thought he should just switch to decaf.

"Great day, isn't it?" Dane said as he closed the front door behind him, turned, flashed that toothy grin her direction.

His smile made her whole face hurt. "Morning, Dane," she said. "We're doing a phoenix, right?"

He nodded vigorously, stripped off his jacket, and threw it onto one of the wooden chairs in the lobby area. He was well built—not beefy, but solid—and the tattoo of a flaming sword on his upper arm was impressive. Not Black Tar impressive, but still one of her better pieces of early work.

He followed her into the Dark Room and settled in the chair almost before she was seated at her work area. She smiled. At least it would be nice to work with an old pro.

"You're gonna have to turn over for this one," she said, and he did as instructed, peeling away his shirt and putting it on the floor.

She prepared her inks and needles, listening to him chat about the Mariners, the commute on I-5, the miserable working conditions at the seafood restaurant where he cooked.

She nodded and said yes at all the appropriate pauses as she prepared, her mind retreating from Dane and embracing the Black Tar. Dane hadn't said anything about it; evidently, he was one of the few without connections in the sizable Seattle area body-art grapevine. So really, there was no reason to use it in his case, was there? He just wanted a black phoenix on his upper shoulder.

And yet, did he deserve any less than the others? The Black Tar, she now knew, was meant to be part of a sacred ritual for her, a sacred ritual to be shared with others. Look what had happened with Corrine. She'd been able to channel something secret inside the woman's life, deliver the numbers, save her from *DISASTER!!*

Dane was a good kid. He should have her best.

She looked at the bottle. She was already at the end of the eighth bottle—partly because the Black Tar bottles were unusually small, partly because Corrine's dragon tattoo was unusually large—but no matter. Grace had the stock number, and she could order more. She could create wondrous tattoos for clients every day, offering them salvation from the past sins that haunted them.

She understood she must do this because she could not be saved from her own mistakes. Images of Tiffany, Joey, and Kenneth, fresh from her dreams, danced in her head for a moment.

She noticed Dane had gone quiet behind her. Evidently pausing to take a breath.

Corrine smiled, picked up the bottle of Black Tar, squeezed the last of the ink into a cap, and stuck it in the smear of petroleum jelly.

"Are you ready to see a phoenix rise from the ashes?" she asked.

Dane fairly giggled behind her. "I was born ready," he said.

FIF 50.

Just over an hour later, she snapped out of her daze. The phoenix, turned in profile inside a large circle with flames licking at the bottom of it, glowed in the beam of her task light. She turned to get the antibacterial soap and began washing the area; as she did so, Dane stirred.

"How's it look?" he asked.

Grace wasn't the kind of person who took easily to bragging, but she said, "I think you're gonna love it." And she knew he would.

She continued to wash, waiting for a word to form inside the tattoo, waiting for an image to flash in her mind. She was ready, willing, to help Dane. It was her burden to carry.

After a few more seconds of scrubbing, she saw letters begin to resolve inside the inky blackness of the tattoo: F. I. R. E.

Fire.

Immediately an image came to her mind: Dane standing in the foreground, a Zippo lighter in his hand, opened and burning, familiar manic energy dancing in his eyes. Behind him, in the photo, a building burned.

The image dissolved abruptly, and Grace had to take a few seconds to catch her breath.

Dane, intuiting that something was wrong, lifted himself from the chair a little, turned on his side so he could see her sitting behind him. "You okay?" he asked.

She smiled. "Didn't eat breakfast," she said. "I'll be fine." Wow, how many times was she going to use that line?

Dane stood, grabbed his shirt.

"There's a mirror out in the front lobby," she said.

He turned and smiled at her, and she could see his eyes, his teeth, glistening in the darkness of her room.

"I know," he said. "This isn't my first time here, you know."

Shirt in hand, he walked out her door and disappeared from view.

She felt her lungs wanting to panic, wanting to hyperventilate, but she controlled her breathing.

She'd just given a tattoo to the arsonist who had been burning down buildings all over Seattle. The man who had lit at least a dozen fires, killing five people, and propelling himself to the top of the local news cycles. The person all of Seattle knew simply as "the firebug."

Numbly she walked out into the front lobby, saw Dane with his back to the mirror, head turned to the side to admire the burning bird on his shoulder.

"It's not even sore at all," he said, rotating his arm. "I don't think I need a bandage." He pulled his shirt on, turned his too-wide smile her way once more.

She nodded, brushed a hand through her hair, feeling hot and uncomfortable in his gaze.

He handed her cash, including a rather large tip, and she accepted the money without looking at his eyes. She couldn't. Not now.

He paused. "You better get something to eat soon," he said. "You look rough."

"Yeah," she said, turning away, crossing her arms in front of her as if trying to cover herself from sight. "I hope I'm not coming down with something."

Behind her, she heard the squeak of the front glass door opening.

"Take it easy, Grace," he said.

She pulled her arms closer, hugging herself, then turned to face him one last time. "You too," she said. "Thanks."

She kept the fake smile on her face until he disappeared from view. A copy of today's *Seattle Times* was still sitting on the floor by the front door, where she'd kicked it to the side when opening shop. She grabbed the *Seattle Times*, sat on one of the wooden chairs just inside the door, and opened up the paper. A small bar on the front page proclaimed that there were "no new clues in firebug case." The *Seattle Times* had obviously fallen into the typical pattern of tracking a big story: big headlines when there was some breaking event (photos of blazing infernos were a plus with an arson case); small sidebars with filler on days when they had no real news to report. But always keep a mention on the front page.

She scanned the small article, skipping to the end to find the information she knew was there. Every story about the firebug ended with a mention of the tip line set up by local law enforcement, working with FBI assistance.

She noted the number before she ran to her bag and found her cell phone.

A pleasant female voice answered after the second ring, simply saying, "Task Force."

Grace paused, suddenly realizing she had nothing real to tell the tip line. She panicked and hung up. What was she going to say? "Hey, I know who the firebug is, because I gave him a tattoo this morning with some of my magic ink, and it told me he was the one setting the fires." Then the Task Force would check out her background, discover a heroin bust on her record, treatment at the clinic for an overdose, and quickly write her off as Just a Junkie.

No, she needed something on Dane, something con- crete she could take to the police.

This dragon, she knew, just might swallow her whole.

54.

Late that afternoon she was outside Dane's duplex apartment, an unassuming cedar structure tucked among trees and overgrowth on the edge of Tukwila, not far from SeaTac. As she sat and watched the duplex, the rumble of jets ascended and descended overhead, artificial thunder.

She'd started by calling the seafood restaurant where Dane complained about working, a local joint called Northern Bay.

The girl on the line gave a huff when she asked about Dane. "It's his day off," she said with irritation, as if this was a bit of information that should be painfully obvious to anyone.

She thanked the girl and hung up. Made sense to come in for his ink on a day off. She'd looked through the contact database on her computer, coming up with his file and jotting down the address.

Then she'd driven to the street, parked down the block. And this was where she had been since. Dane's car sat in the driveway in front of the garage door, a beat-up heap that had once been silver, with rust eating holes in the fenders.

She'd seen Dane pop outside once to pick up the mail from his box, but he'd been inside, out of view, since. That meant six hours with nothing to show for it. It would be dark soon, and she was starting to worry someone had noticed her, sitting alone in a car all day. Maybe she'd be reported as a stalker.

A thought occurred to her as she sat there, smelling the heat of the day dissipate around her: concoct some kind of story to lead police to Dane's apartment. Say she'd been inside his duplex, seen a stack of gasoline cans in the garage. He parked his car in the driveway, after all, which likely meant his garage was filled with deep, dark secrets.

But then, how many anonymous tips must the Seattle Police Department receive in a day? She'd have to report anonymously, after all, because—well, because she lived her whole life anonymously. True, they had the tip line, and they were likely to follow each and every lead that poured in, but how quickly? Not tonight, for certain, and something told her Dane was getting ready to do something tonight. He would do that, because he had a fresh tattoo of a phoenix on his shoulder, further fueled by the odd energy of the Black Tar ink. He would want to celebrate the occasion, mark it with something special. And what could be more special to a pyromaniac than a grand display of fire?

As Dear Old Mom might say, Dane had some dead blood in him.

She would wait. It was all she could do.

55a.

Light in her eyes awakened her, and she shook her head, fighting off the sleep and the dreams of dragons. She was in a spotlight, she realized suddenly; someone had reported her finally.

Then the lights were gone, past her, and she realized the light didn't come from a spotlight. It had come from headlights brushing by her parked car.

It took a few moments to clear her head. Muddy, she was muddy. Maybe from the dead blood, maybe from withdrawal. She turned her head to the side, straining to get a good view of the car that had passed, leaving a stench of dirty oil in its wake.

Dane's car.

She didn't see him at the wheel, too dark for that, but she recognized the rusty car, bathed in the sick orange glow of the streetlights. It moved to the next street intersection and turned.

Panicky, Grace turned the key in her own car, started the engine, wheeled around to follow. A glance at the clock on the dash told her it was almost midnight. The last time she remembered checking the time, it had been about ten thirty. She must have dozed off at some point. And by dozing, she'd nearly let Dane get away.

She turned at the intersection, came to the main artery, and his car came into view again. Oily smoke belched from its exhaust, looking so much like the dragon tails she knew and loved so well.

She turned to follow, unsure how much distance to keep between them. At this time of night, traffic would be light, and it would be easy to spot someone tailing you.

She was relieved when she saw him making his way to the I-5. At least that would make him easier to follow; the I-5 had traffic on it any time of day. Or night.

Her hands felt jittery. She wasn't a cop. She was making this up as she went along. Really, she didn't know if she should actually follow him or if she should just try to break into his house, call, and report a fire. She smiled. That would have been good. Ironic.

She couldn't do that, though. He was the phoenix now, rising from the ashes, in search of more flames. At midnight, he wasn't heading to work at a restaurant; he was heading out to do his true work.

She had to follow him. She had to stop him. Junkie Girl the Superhero, out to keep the streets safe once again. Maybe this, above all things, was what the numbers, the Black Tar ink, had been pointing toward all along.

Her true work.

She turned and glanced at the purse on the seat next to her as she passed another bank of streetlights on one of the interstate's exits. It reflected a powdery pink in the artificial light.

Once she'd been Janet the Pretend Wife and Mother, long before she'd become Grace the Tattoo Artist and Heroin Junkie. That path had come to its first fork eight years ago, and she'd ended up in Seattle for reasons she still didn't fully understand. That fork in the path had led her to the hotel room next door, a .38-caliber revolver, and a strange note of jotted numbers.

Terrified by what had happened to her in that room, she'd returned to Red Lodge. She'd scrambled her way back up the face of the cliff, returned to her family.

But seeds had been planted inside her then, hadn't they? Those seeds—the numbers and the revolver—had grown some bitter fruit, and it was time for her to harvest it.

Darkness folded over them as they drove north for several minutes, and by the time Dane turned onto the exit at Northwest Eighty-fifth Street in Ballard, half an hour had passed. Almost twelve thirty in the morning.

Dane pulled into the parking lot next to an old iron sign that said *Villa Apartments*. Next to the old sign a new one hung on a chain-link fence: *Coming soon: Lake Villa Condos.*

If Dane didn't know she was following him, she'd be pushing her luck by pulling into the lot right behind him. She continued down the street and parked in front of a section of older homes, then got out of the car and hurried back under the cover of night.

Now inside the fence, she looked for Dane's car but

couldn't see it; she saw a few lights on poles by the covered parking lot, but they weren't working. Bulbs burned out long ago, she guessed.

Ahead, weak lights illuminated the front doors of the building, which was little more than a glorified four-story motel; black iron railings hid front doors and windows on each of the four levels, and the main entry into the building— two dirty glass doors—opened onto stairs that connected all four floors. It was the kind of place where more meals were cooked on hot plates than in ovens, and Grace thought she could almost smell the aroma of some fatty meat wafting toward her even now, at this time of night.

As Grace stared, Dane appeared at the door, paused a second, then opened the door with a key. Within moments, he'd disappeared inside the building. Her last view was the back of his head, descending stairs that obviously led to the basement.

None of this was going as planned, she thought, as she ran across the unmowed grass to the front door. Maybe because none of it was planned in the first place, at least not from her end. She was quite sure Dane's end had been well planned, dreamed about for days. Likely even as he sat in her chair this morning, dozing while she tattooed a dark phoenix on his shoulder.

She tried the door and found it locked. Well, duh. That's why Dane had used a key. Somehow, he'd stolen a key from one of the apartment residents or maybe even made his own copy. For all she knew, he'd once lived in these doomed apartments.

Her heart hammered in her chest as she looked around. On the pebbled concrete wall next to the door, a call box with apartment numbers on each of the buttons hung crookedly in its metal frame. She punched a button at random but neither heard nor felt the buzz she should. She punched a few other numbers, but none of them worked. Evidently the call box had gone the way of the parking lot lights; what else would she expect at a complex that was going to be torn down and turned into condos?

Okay, now what? She could try to break in, she supposed. The door was glass, and the frame seemed flimsy; if nothing else, she could maybe put a rock or something through the glass. Such an action would attract the attention of Dane, of course, but she couldn't do anything about that.

Wait. Her cell phone. She pulled it out of her purse, dialed 911, told the operator a fire had started at the Villa Apartments. At least she could give rescue workers a head start.

She turned off her phone and slipped it back into her purse. If she could figure out a way to avoid the fire altogether, stop Dane before he started . . .

Maybe she could try getting the attention of someone in a ground-floor apartment, see if they'd give her access to the inner courtyard and the stairs. She glanced down the row of windows; a few apartments down, she saw lights behind pulled drapes in one of the windows.

Grace turned and ran for the apartment; seconds later, she heard the front door open behind her. She turned, ready to sprint back to the door before it closed.

Instead, she was looking at the face of Dane. Even worse, he was looking at her.

He furrowed his brow for a few seconds, then tried a smile. "Grace? Is that you?"

She took an involuntary step back as he moved toward her. "Yeah," she said, trying to look nonchalant, trying to put on that funny-to-randomly-see-you-here look. "Just, uh . . . dropping by to see a friend here." She pointed at the poured concrete building behind him.

"Oh, I don't think that's a good idea," he said, and his eyes seemed to twinkle in the low light. Behind him, a dull *whump* rattled the front doors.

He made a comical face, rolled his eyes to look at the door behind him. "Ooh, that didn't sound good," he said.

She could barely see his face, but that grin—that manic, unbearable grin—shined at her in the low light.

"I know who you are," she said. "What you are."

Behind him, smoke had begun working its way up the stairs from the basement and was filling the area behind the glass doors. Grace stared at the smoke uneasily. The parking lot lights and the call box had been broken; would the alarm system inside the building make it three for three? She guessed it would, if the building had any kind of alarms at all.

"Oh, you don't know me at all," he said. "Dane's not even my real name."

"I've called the police," she said. "They're on the way." Not quite true. She'd called the fire department, but the police would surely accompany them.

He shrugged. "Time to move on," he said, moving away from the door and trying to disappear into the night. A phoenix in search of its ashes. He stopped, turned her way again. "I've been in Seattle too long anyway."

She scrambled, finding the gun in her purse. "Stop!" she screamed, pointing the gun at him and dropping her purse without meaning to. She thought about picking up the purse but opted instead to put both hands on the gun grip.

Dane smiled at her. "Please," he said. "You expect me to believe that's loaded? To believe you've ever even fired it?"

Smoke was billowing out of the apartment complex now, and she needed to make a choice: keep Dane at bay or try to help people inside the apartment.

Or . . . maybe both.

She dropped the aim of her gun, pulled the trigger, fired a round into his upper thigh. He dropped instantly, howling in pain.

Keeping the gun trained on him, she walked over to where he lay on the grass, blood seeping from a black hole in his leg. She leaned close to his ear and spoke through gritted teeth. "You don't know me at all," she said. "Grace isn't even my real name."

She pulled the front key to the apartment from his hand, ran to the apartment complex, and retrieved her purse from the dewy, sparse grass. Then she unlocked the twin glass doors on the front of the building and did her best to prop them open.

Inside, she heard smoke detectors beeping in a couple of apartments, but no fire alarm.

He disabled the alarm and the sprinklers, a voice inside said. And suddenly, she knew that was correct.

Okay, she should start with the top floor, because it would be most difficult for them to get out. She ran up the four flights of stairs and began going down the row, ringing doorbells and pounding on the doors as she did. Her breath was coming in ragged gasps as she went, and she felt tears squeezing from her eyes. Not just from the smoke.

People began coming to their doors, but by the time they did, she was already at the next door. Her lungs felt like they were torn, and she wasn't sure what she'd say, anyway. The gathering smoke did all the talking necessary.

Two other people joined her, pounding on doors and ringing the doorbells of apartments where no one had answered yet.

She went to the third floor and repeated the process, recruiting more help, then on to the second and first.

She paused briefly to see if Dane was still on the grass

outside. He was sitting there, his belt now wrapped around his leg, but his face had a look of utter and complete wonder as he stared at the smoke boiling from the building.

Maybe he was a phoenix, but she'd chased worse. She'd chased dragons.

Flames began to eat their way out of the basement, working their way into apartments on the first floor. Most of the doors to those apartments were hanging open now, the occupants moving safely away from the building. But two doors remained shut.

She couldn't see what was happening on the other floors, but she had to trust that the people who had joined her were making sure everybody got out.

She went to the nearest closed door on the ground floor once again, rang the doorbell several times, pounded on the flimsy door.

She heard something inside that made her whole body go cold, even though the heat of flames continued to spread around her.

A child crying.

"Hey!" she screamed at a man running away from the building in a T-shirt and boxers.

He stopped and looked back at her.

"Give me a hand!" she said. "I hear a kid inside."

He looked like he was debating for a moment, then he ran over to where she stood. Up close, she could see the sweat on his face.

"Help me get this door open," she said. She rang the bell and pounded on the door several more times, rattling it in its frame.

The man looked around. "How about a garbage can?" he asked. "We could use it to bang down the door."

She nodded, tried to put her shoulder into the door. Inside, the child continued to sob, and Grace felt her own tears beginning to stream down her cheeks.

The man in boxers returned, dragging a large steel barrel behind him. She ran to him, helped him lift it.

"Okay," she said, "let's bust the door down. One, two, three, go!"

Together they rushed the door, using the can as a crude battering ram. The door gave a huge shudder, and a crack appeared near the bottom hinge, but still the door held.

The smoke thickened, and the man in boxers coughed a few times. "Again!" he said between coughs, and Grace lifted and counted again.

"One, two, three, go!"

They hit the door a second time, and it jumped away from its hinges, hanging lazily open a few feet.

Grace pushed at the door and rushed in first. Now every drop of blood in her system felt like dead blood, because the child's crying had stopped. She wished she had a flashlight.

Should she crawl? Isn't that what they said to do in fires? Yeah, but the fire was in the basement, so what good would it do?

Shaking her head, she decided to drop to her hands and knees, realizing instantly that it was the right choice. Smoke, little more than heated air, would rise, collect in the top part of any floor.

After a few seconds of crawling, she made her way to the child, crouched and unconscious in a corner. She grasped for the small body, scooped it into her arms, stood and turned to head back out the door. No way she could crawl now.

She kept her eyes on the door, which looked like a gaping wound into the darkness outside. On the way, she tripped on something and almost went down. Another person, she realized. Also unconscious.

"Hey!" she screamed, hoping the guy in boxers was still outside. "There's a woman in here!"

"Got her," came the short reply. He was obviously inside the apartment too. That was good; it meant he had run into the fire with her. And then Grace was back out the front door again, cradling the child against her, sobbing as she looked for signs of life.

(It was a girl, she could see now, a beautiful five-year-old girl like her Tiffany had once been, like—)

She squeezed her eyes shut once more, squeezed thoughts of Tiffany from her mind, opened her eyes slowly again.

She whispered to the child, incomplete, incoherent words, willing the young girl to open her eyes, *just open her eyes*.

"I'm sorry, Tiffany," she said, seeing that the child was Tiffany—the same ruddy cheeks, the same wild hair that wouldn't stay out of her face (that was impossible, of course, that was impossible)—and then: "I know you don't have the dead blood."

Suddenly, miraculously, Tiffany opened her eyes. And smiled at her.

(Not Tiffany)

A tap on her shoulder. It was the guy in boxers. At his feet lay an unconscious woman.

"I think she's stoned out of her mind," he said.

Grace glanced down at the woman and saw the needle marks on the woman's arms.

She closed her eyes, turned, gently rocked the child to soothe her. And as the tears continued to stream from her eyes, the cleansing tears that were helping her see clearly for the first time in years, she sank to her knees because she knew she could no longer stand.

And as police cars and fire trucks poured into the parking lot in front of her, the dragon did some chasing in the apartment behind her.

56. SIX

Later, after getting control of her sobs, after telling a police officer she'd seen the wild-eyed man on the lawn come crashing out of the apartment just before the fire erupted (though she said nothing about the gunshot wound, her mind was still clear enough to steer away from that entanglement), she returned to the tattoo shop. It was late. Or early, depending on your definition—that hazy dead zone between the quiet, still darkness of late night and the awakening of first light in the eastern sky.

Her clothes still smelled like smoke. Her tears still traced clean tracks down her ash-covered face. Her stomach still felt sick and empty.

The police wanted her to come to the station and make a statement at eight o'clock that morning, just a few hours away, knowing she knew more than she'd let on, but evidently trusting her enough to let her leave. She would do that. She would tell them all she had seen. Even the part about the gun.

Well, maybe not all of it. She'd already concocted a story about how she became suspicious of Dane because of his tattoos—all of them fire related. How he talked about fires and burning throughout his last tattoo session. (This was an outright lie; neither she nor Dane had any memory of their last tattoo session, she knew.) How she had followed him and had her suspicions confirmed when he lit the fire in the basement of the apartment complex.

They might slap her wrists, give her the old lecture about not taking the law into her own hands, that kind of thing. But they would let her walk out of there after a few hours.

And she would keep walking. *She* would be the phoenix.

She unlocked the gate at the front of GraceSpace, rolled it away, unlocked the front door, turned on the lights inside. First she wrote a note to Vaughn and Zoey, letting them know their apprenticeships were over and telling them the shop was all theirs. She was making other plans, moving other directions.

She took all the cash from her Dark Room's safe and transferred it to her purse. Then, she took the .38-caliber revolver from her purse, put it in the safe, and locked it again. Finally, she retrieved the last bottle of Black Tar, slipped it into her purse. Yes, it was the last bottle. But she had the stock number; she could order more.

She could order so much more.

Out in the front lobby area, she passed the mirror Dane had used to admire his new phoenix tattoo fifteen long hours ago. Her reflection stared back with red, unmoving eyes.

After a few seconds of staring, she unbuttoned her shirt and looked at her chest. The tattoo of the door was there still, but now it was different. The door was open.

Unlocked.

And in the thin sliver of space behind the open door on her chest, she saw hidden letters, now glowing. *F-A-M-I-L-Y.* She touched the letters, saw an image of her children, Tiffany and Joey, laughing as she chased them across a manicured lawn, dappled sun shining through the thick canopy of leaves above. This tattoo moved, hypnotically cinematic, a movie in front of her eyes. The children were older now, yes. But still children. Still *her* children.

After her statement to the police, she would return to Montana. To Red Lodge. Once, dead blood had flowed through her arteries, but now every drop was alive.

She smiled at her reflection.

In that moment, she stopped chasing the dragon.

And it stopped chasing her.

Final Stanza

Minus Midas

4.

They wanted him to kill a woman here in the District.

Not that he had to, of course. Killing was completely voluntary; he could quit at any time.

All he had to do was die himself.

And that would mean one other person close to him would die as well.

And so, because he had to keep living, he had to keep killing.

He smiled as he cradled the mug of coffee in his hands, and blew on it a bit before sipping. It was a habit he'd developed, this blowing on coffee before every sip, imprinted into his brain because he'd worn gloves so long. Sometimes leather, sometimes latex, sometimes leather over latex. Hold a mug of coffee in your hands while you're wearing gloves, you don't know how hot the drink is. If you're not paying attention, you burn your lips, maybe blister your tongue. So it became a habit to blow on any drink before he sipped it, and the regularity of the act comforted him.

There really was no alternative. He couldn't take off the gloves while he was out in public. Ever.

He glanced at the clock on the wall, one of those old

analog jobs you don't see around much these days: bright white face, black hash mark for each minute, wedgelike ebony hands pounding out each and every second, 24/7. Part of why he liked this diner.

The guy was fifteen minutes late. He'd have to make a note of it afterward, let people know. Maybe get the guy's knuckles cracked, a small victory for him. After all, these Handlers (and that's what the Organization called them—Handlers, as if he were some kind of celebrity being escorted on a press junket) were paid to keep him on a leash. A tight leash. Noting their missteps was one of the few small ways he could show a little control over his situation. Keeping with the leash analogy, it was the only way he could snap his jaws, bite the hands of the guys taking him out for a walk.

He smiled. *Analogy.* Mrs. Brown back at P.S. 238 would have loved to hear him use the word. Every once in a while he found himself thinking about her, thinking about the guys like Kurt Marlowe and Neil Kramden, even thinking about Mr. Sherman himself, who had changed his life forever in what he'd come to think of as the Great Sherman Tank—so named because his life had tanked hard after that incident.

Man, had it tanked.

He blew on the coffee, sipped it again. It was lukewarm at best, but he could no more stop himself from the habit than he could stop himself from breathing. It was part of who he was.

A sizzle escaped from the back at the grill, followed soon

by the scent of onions frying. Probably an order of steak and onions, maybe a Philly sammy. It was still pretty early for lunch, midmorning, but that's another reason why he liked the Blue Bell Café. You want lunch at 10:00 a.m., no one bats an eye; they just throw your order on the grill. You come in with a broken arm or a face that looks like hamburger, no problem; they just throw your order on the grill. You wander through the front door with your clothes caked in blood, no questions asked; they just throw your order on the grill.

Not that he'd ever come into the grill with blood on his clothes, of course. But he *could*, and that's what counted. Blood wasn't really his style, which was what made him so valuable to the Organization.

He lived everywhere and nowhere, on the road every month of the year. But because the Organization had put down its roots in the DC area, this was as close to home as he got. Three, four times a year he did jobs here, giving him some degree of familiarity. All of the other job sites he usually visited only once.

The door hinge squeaked open, and he knew without looking that it was his guy, his Handler, finally showing up. Close to twenty minutes late. Oh yes, he'd note that for later.

He closed his eyes, cradling his chipped porcelain mug of coffee in both gloved hands, inhaling the earthy scent of the dark liquid inside. A few moments later, he sensed the man standing next to him.

"Mr. Bleach?"

A thin, reedy voice. It shocked him a bit, not the voice he'd expected, not the kind of voice he always heard from these guys, but he showed no reaction. Keeping his eyes closed, he smiled. "Not Mr. Bleach. Just Bleach."

"Just Bleach?"

He opened his eyes, seeing for the first time the kid who matched the voice. Young, maybe twenty, tall and thin, big patch of red hair up top, couldn't even grow a full mustache yet. Not that it had stopped him from trying; the kid had one of those peach-fuzz excuses on his top lip, which probably included the first hairs that had sprouted on his face a few short years ago. In a hurry to grow up. Too much of a hurry.

Still, he felt sorry for the kid. Maybe because of the voice. He nodded at the empty seat across the booth. "Yeah," he said, "just Bleach."

Of course, his real name wasn't Bleach; nobody had a last name like Bleach. Inside, he was still Stan Hawkins. Still thought of himself that way. To everyone else, he was Bleach.

But he would always, to himself, be Stan.

The kid sat down quickly, all elbows and awkward sharp angles. "I'm sorry I'm late Mr.—ah, I'm sorry I'm late, Bleach. I just—this is—"

"Your first time," he finished for the kid. He blew at his coffee, took another sip. It was starting to go cold now, but the waitress would be back to warm it up any minute.

The kid nodded his head, overeager. "Yeah, yeah. I just—

man, you wanna do good your first time out, and you go and do something like this, end up being late, you know?"

The kid should be aggravating him, probably would be under normal circumstances. Another smile creased his face. *Normal circumstances.* As if he'd ever been in any such thing.

Okay, he had to admit it. He found himself liking the kid, in spite of it all. He decided he wouldn't say anything about being late.

It was the kid's voice that did it.

When the kid spoke, his voice cracked like brittle sugar candy. Just as his own had done, once upon a time.

Stan put down the cup of coffee. "What should I call you, kid?" he said, looking over at the counter and nodding to the waitress.

"Well, my name's Brian," he said, a bit uncomfortably.

The waitress was coming over with a fresh pot now, so he turned his attention back to the kid. "They didn't give you a name yet?" he asked.

"Well, yeah." The kid waited while the waitress poured more of the coffee in Stan's cup, shook his head when she asked if he wanted anything.

After she left, Stan spoke again. "But you don't like your name," he said.

"It's . . . Carrot."

Stan smiled, blew on his fresh cup. Much hotter now, much better. "Yeah, well, kid, that's the whole idea of the name: you're not supposed to like it." He paused a minute while the kid stared at the table. "Let 'em see that the nickname bothers you, it'll only be worse."

The kid smiled and looked at him, getting a bit more comfortable now. "Sticks and stones, all that jazz?"

Stan returned the smile, knowing it came off more ominous than genuine—especially if the kid knew anything about him—but unable to help himself. "In the Organization, it ain't sticks and stones that will break your bones."

The kid's smile faded. Carrot. A little obvious, maybe, but the Organization always knew your weak points. Each and every one.

"What about your, um, name?" the kid asked.

"I told you: just Bleach."

"I know. I mean, how'd you get it? I guess I maybe expected you to be an albino or something."

Stan huffed a bit. More like a leper than an albino. "Ever use bleach, Brian?" he asked.

The kid shrugged. "Yeah, I guess. Get stains out of clothes, that kind of thing."

Stan blew on the coffee again, sipped. "That's what I do. I clean up stains." He paused. "That kind of thing."

The kid swallowed hard. So the Organization *had* given him a bit of background on the man they called Bleach. Just as well, really. The kid's fear should keep him out of the way.

"So where to, Brian?" he asked as they left the diner and walked to the car. He already knew where they were going, of course, but he wanted to help the kid relax, get his feet under him a bit.

"Apartment down in Anacostia."

"Okay."

"Bad news. Don't really want to wander over there unless you have to."

"Really."

"First time in DC?"

He smiled. Where'd they get this kid? "Yeah," he said. "First time."

The kid, amazingly enough, was pretty quiet during the first part of the ride. Stan had been sure he would be one of those jittery kinds, twitchy and itchy, constantly talking to keep the nerves in his stomach calm. Even so, he knew a few questions would have to come. They always did.

As the kid wheeled the car off the Beltway and into the concrete jungle, he spoke. "What'd she do?"

Stan smiled, looking out the window at some rusting hulks in the old navy shipyard. He thought it might be what concentration camps looked like. "Don't know, kid."

"You don't know? You're here to . . . do this, and you don't know what she did?"

"I never know. Makes it easier. Sometimes."

"But not all the time?"

"Not all the time."

The kid waited in silence for a few more seconds. "And it doesn't bother you? Not knowing, I mean?"

Stan looked at the kid, who kept glancing back and forth between him and the potholed street ahead. "'Course it bothers me. Nothing about this doesn't. But no one ever asks. 'Cept kids like you."

The kid sniffed. "I'm not a kid."

Stan smiled, turned to look out the window again.

The kid's voice came again. Softer. Quieter. "Can I watch?"

Stan pulled in a deep sigh. Everybody wanted to see someone else die. Until they did. Then they never wanted to see it again. Having seen it a few dozen times now, Stan certainly wished he never had. But that ship had sailed a long time ago.

"You don't really want to watch," he answered.

"Yes, I do."

"You just drive. That's why you're here. Meet me, pick me up, drop me off so I can catch my flight."

"I won't get in the way or anything. You won't even know I'm there."

Stan offered a grim smile as he watched the reflected cement spin by on the inside of the windshield in front of him. "I'll know you're there, Brian. I always know."

He thought it was a nice touch, using the kid's first name again. Just the right amount of sincerity.

The kid pulled the car to the side of a secondary street, hitting another pothole just as he put the white Chevy into Park.

Stan sat a few moments, studying the decaying building next to them. "This the place?" he asked, already knowing the answer.

"Yeah. She's in apartment . . . uh . . ."

"Number 955."

"Right."

Stan opened the car door, shut it behind him, and began walking toward the building. He didn't pause, didn't look at the kid, didn't do anything to encourage him. Still, he wasn't surprised to hear the kid's car door slam behind him as he walked away. He closed his eyes for a moment, then pushed toward the front door of the crumbling tenement.

No call box, but there was a hole where one used to be. A decade ago, maybe. He paused, considering, then went to the doors and tried them. They opened with barely a give. Not surprising. From the looks of it, security was the bottom of the priority list for this particular building. Right below plumbing and electrical repairs. Maybe even below razing the place and starting from scratch.

He felt the kid behind him now, coming through the door as he walked into the lobby area. He ignored him and walked past the long row of mailboxes, more than half of their tarnished brass doors broken open, abandoned long ago. Some people probably still got mail—maybe even the woman in 955—but he guessed this wasn't a plum route for mail carriers.

Stepping over some trash on the floor, he moved

toward the concrete stairs, hearing a loose-limbed shuffle behind him.

The kid's voice echoed in the hollow shell of the building's core. "Don'tcha wanna take the elevator?"

Stan continued as if he hadn't heard the kid, stepping on the first stair and continuing, one foot after the other. A few moments later, halfway up the second flight, he heard the kid's footsteps behind him again.

He scaled the stairs to the ninth floor, feeling himself breathing heavier—becoming heavier—with each step. But he didn't allow himself to stop. That was the key on these assignments; you kept putting one foot in front of the other, going until it was all done, not letting your mind get a hold of what was happening.

If you did that, you might let that unwelcome thing called a conscience trip you up. And that, in turn, might get you killed.

He was walking down the hallway now, making his way past a few open doors. The first two opened into abandoned rooms, populated only by the ghosts of their former occupants and a few leftover pieces of furniture. The third room offered the muffled sounds of a television, but no one seemed to be watching. A few closed doors after that, and then he was at 955.

The kid was about halfway down the hall behind him, and Stan heard him clear his throat.

"You gonna—" the kid started to say, but this was no

time to stop and talk. No time to stop and plan. No time
to stop.

He grabbed for the handle of the door, twisted, feeling
the latex of his glove move against the faux-brass doorknob.
It was unlocked, which initially came as a bit of a surprise
to him, but then struck him as fitting. This woman—this
Leslie Thomson—had to know the Reaper would someday
be at her door, had to know that locking it wouldn't stop
or slow anything.

Maybe, in an odd way, she even welcomed it. Often, it
seemed they did.

He walked through the door, not bothering to shut it
behind him, moved through the living area littered by beer
cans and fast-food wrappers, past the unused kitchen with
empty spaces where the oven and refrigerator used to be,
and into the small hallway at the back. Three doors. One
would be a bathroom; the other two, bedrooms.

He put his hand on the first doorknob and twisted, and
knew he had the right room as he opened the door. It was
warmer in here, moister. A bare window, painted shut from
the looks of it, hung above what passed for a bed: two ratty
mattresses stacked on top of each other. On the mattresses
was a woman in a T-shirt, a soiled blanket around her legs
and a lit cigarette clutched in her fingers as she sat propped
against the wall.

She looked at him, unsurprised perhaps, but nonetheless
fearful. Yeah, he decided, she was probably one of those

people. One who almost looked forward to the end, an escape from the endless maze they'd built around themselves.

"You the one?" she asked as he entered the room, and that almost stopped him. No one had ever asked him anything like that. He knew what she meant, what was inside that question, but he also knew he could not, would not, stop to answer it and give her comfort. Keep moving, keep swimming forward. Like a shark.

He began peeling off his right glove, rolling it back over his hand, as he walked into the room and approached her. She stared, her pupils dilating into large buttons, but she made no move to stop him.

He was over her now, and he reached for her with his hand—his bare right hand—lightly touching the skin of her forehead with a gentle stroke, as if giving her a loving benediction.

But that's not what it was. He felt the brief iciness of the skin-on-skin contact, and even before he drew his hand away, her eyes rolled back into her head as her body went into violent convulsions.

A massive heart attack. A stroke. Sometimes both; he'd seen autopsies of past victims, the doctors' notes wondering how people with otherwise healthy vascular systems could have such sudden and violent ends as veins in their body literally exploded under pressure.

He didn't have to wonder why. He knew too well.

He turned away from the woman, thankful her convulsions were at least quiet. It wasn't always that way. Sometimes people uttered small moans or guttural grunts. Sometimes the joints of their bodies cracked and snapped under the tension. One man had even managed to grab his arm before he could pull away, digging yellow fingernails into the flesh of his forearm. He'd carried bruises and scratches for weeks.

The kid was standing in the doorway of the bedroom, his jaw slack as he stared at the convulsing woman on the bed. Stan pulled on his surgical glove once more, slowly and carefully, before pushing the kid out of the way and walking out the door.

He took the stairs again, not hurrying as he descended to the ground floor. Now was the time when the images always flooded his mind. Not this woman; this one was better than most, because he had turned his back before most of the convulsions took her. And he hadn't spoken to her. He'd made that mistake before.

Some of those people still haunted his mind. The ones who tried to talk themselves out of the situation. The ones who cried when they saw him. The ones who begged him to take pity.

But most of all, his grandfather and Sherman. Them, every time. Them, every day.

He pushed the ghosts from his mind as they fought to be seen and heard, focusing instead on the one image that could always drown them out. The catfish.

The catfish ruled them all, its brown tail sweeping away

the murky images of past memories as it swam across the surface of his mind.

He was at street level now, and he pushed his way back onto the street outside, eager to get out of the building. Outside, the air felt even more stale, but the catfish could help that too. He concentrated on the image of the fish swimming, staring into its black eyes.

At the car, he slid into the passenger seat, closing his eyes and modulating his breathing. Blocking all outside stimuli. It was over now, and he wouldn't be doing it again for . . . well, who knew how long? But certainly not in the next week. The Organization didn't want such things to be spaced too closely together, didn't want seemingly unrelated deaths to be connected by association.

Slowly the catfish began to swim away from his consciousness. When he was desperate, when he was drowning and reaching for the image, the catfish was giant, filling his entire mind with its dark eyes and round mouth. But as he calmed, the catfish always swam away from his vision, getting smaller and smaller, moving away through the brown water until it was lost in the murkiness.

He heard a car door open, then close, beside him. That would be the kid, returning. Still he kept his eyes closed, waiting for the catfish to disappear completely before he would open them again.

The kid spoke. "She was . . ." He let the sentence trail off, unsure how to finish it.

The catfish receded into nothingness. Stan opened his eyes, turned his head, stared at the kid, who was looking down at his hands on the steering wheel. Same as it always was; the kid, like so many others before him, was looking deep inside himself, wondering why he'd ever wanted to see such a thing.

Stan, himself, never wanted to see such things. But he didn't have a choice, did he?

He wanted to pat the kid on the shoulder, tell him everything was fine. But he didn't want to experience that inevitable flinch, watch the kid pull away like he was some kind of monster.

Of course, he *was* a monster. The kid wouldn't have found that out if he'd only stayed in the car.

"Yeah, kid," he finally said. "She was."

5.

That night, after catching a flight, he checked into an airport hotel in Cincinnati. The Organization had a rather sophisticated travel system built for him. Flights were always booked on planes flying at less than 50 percent capacity; the Organization kept track of flight loads and seating assignments, somehow forging tickets that always got him onto the flights. He was literally untraceable, because he never officially showed up on the manifest list for any flight. Amazing, really, that airports and the airlines didn't have more stringent security.

Wherever he stayed between assignments, he always received packages by overnight courier, consisting of flight tickets, identification, and forged credit cards for his new identity. His hotels, meals, and other travel expenses went on the never-ending array of cards. He guessed some accounting wonk in the Organization kept track of his spending, but no one ever asked questions. The Organization also included $1,000 in each package. Another mystery for him; with most of his costs covered by the credit cards, he rarely went through more than a hundred bucks between jobs. Viktor never demanded it back, never asked how he spent it, so: let sleeping dogs lie.

After an assignment, his next ticket always took him to a major hub; most of his time on assignment was spent at Days Inns in Detroit, Hampton Inns in Atlanta, Radissons in Salt Lake City. The Organization knew how to plan these things a month or more in advance, keeping him on flights with major airlines, always under new aliases. After each assignment, he destroyed the documents he'd been given, replacing them with new ones.

He'd never traveled under the same name twice in the two years he'd been doing this. The Organization lived up to its name in that regard: it was organized, always keeping him shuttling from one location to the next. Once a month or so it was a new city and new assignment, followed by a few weeks in transfer cities, then on to the next assignment.

After checking in to the hotel, he put his small case on the fake wood-grained desk that seemed to be in every mid-range hotel room, then swept the bedspread and blanket off the mattress and shoved them into the corner.

He never trusted the bedding; you never knew how often the blankets and bedspreads were washed, if ever. Sheets, yes. Those had to be laundered. So he slept only in sheets, even when he was in cities like Denver in the dead of winter. It helped that he never got cold, because his body seemed to run hotter than normal. Had been that way ever since puberty. Ever since Sherman. Ever since his grandfather.

He knew, deep down inside, he would never be cold in this life or the next one, as if his metabolism were preparing him for the eternity he would surely spend in hell.

Stan lay down on the sheets of the bed, spreading out. He considered turning on the television but decided against it. What would he see on the TV but car accidents and robberies on the local news, criminals tracked on crime programs billed as entertainment, lives of misery caught forever by the lenses of ever-present cameras? Just a year into the new millennium—the twenty-first century so many had feared would be the end of the world—and things were still spinning down.

No, the world hadn't ended with Y2K, as so many people had feared. But he'd known all along that wouldn't happen. What he knew about this life, this existence, told him the end wouldn't come in a sudden blast. It would come in slow, shuddering gasps, extracting the most pain possible.

And every time he watched the television, his theories were confirmed. Y2K wasn't the end. But it certainly was the beginning of the end.

He hoped.

He closed his eyes, thinking of sleep but knowing it wouldn't come. Not yet. After a few moments he stood again, went to his travel bag on the desk, pulled out a plastic bag containing a large white prescription bottle. This was the one thing the Organization had given him that had been salvation. He twisted off the top, shook two of the giant lozenges into his hand, paused a moment before shaking out a third and popping them all into his mouth. He fought the urge to keep going, to keep popping every pill in the bottle until it was empty and he was full. He would welcome the oblivion.

But then, the Organization knew where his mother was. They kept a close eye on her in a long-term care facility. They always reminded him they were paying for her care as part of his employment, as if this were a benefit like a retirement plan or paid medical. But Stan knew why they were so careful to give him frequent updates on his mother and her progress. If he were to stop his assignments, if he were to disappear unexpectedly, if he were to overdose on these miraculous "sleeping" pills, his mother's health would take a sudden downturn.

Stan went to the bathroom, looked at the ghost staring

back at him in the mirror, drank a glass of water. After that, he returned to the bed and lay on top of the sheets. He closed his eyes once more, feeling the pleasant heaviness overtaking his body, and breathed deeply.

In moments, he was asleep.

1.

Stan killed his first victim when he was only twelve years old, and he did it by barely lifting a finger.

Ha-ha. A little black humor in that. Lifting a finger.

Because that's what the Killing Curse was all about.

Mr. Sherman only had himself to blame, really. His first and only year as a PE teacher at P.S. 238, and yet it was clear to every boy in his gym class that Mr. Sherman had never really grown past sixth grade himself. Balding, slumping, glowering—nothing that spoke of the joy of physical activity —Mr. Sherman carried the weight of his past around on his shoulders. Stan would later find out Mr. Sherman had been a star basketball player in high school, even had a shot at a small college upstate. But Mr. Sherman had flunked out in a year, moved back to the city, and quietly earned a teaching degree at a city college.

Stan found all this out, of course, long after he'd killed Mr. Sherman. He'd found out many things about Mr. Sherman after killing him. More than he'd ever found out about the man while he was alive.

"Hawkins!" Mr. Sherman barked out in his husky voice on that morning, picking him from the lineup of eighteen boys in gym class. Mr. Sherman was a big believer in last names only. You were never Craig or Mark or Stan; you were only Krasinski or Franklin or Hawkins.

Stan stepped forward from the line, and Mr. Sherman shouted another name.

"Kramden!"

Mr. Sherman's voice was deep, guttural, as if finished with deep-grit sandpaper. Stan had been feeling that kind of grit in his own throat lately; when he spoke, he didn't recognize his own voice.

Kramden stepped forward, and Mr. Sherman tilted his head back, staring down the line at the two boys as if trying to study them from a better angle. This was one of those odd things Mr. Sherman always did, something the boys imitated in the locker room after class.

"Pick your teams," Mr. Sherman finally said. "You got first, Kramden." He tilted his head forward again, lifted his clipboard to look at it.

"Um, Mr. Sherman?"

It was Kramden, speaking up to ask a question. Odd enough. Talking wasn't something encouraged in Mr. Sherman's gym class. Especially talking *to* Mr. Sherman.

Mr. Sherman let his gaze slide from the clipboard back to Kramden.

"Um," Kramden stammered, as if now deciding he really shouldn't ask.

"Just spit it out, Kramden."

"I was just, um, wondering . . . what we're playing."

Mr. Sherman squinted, walked across the gym floor toward Kramden, his sneakers squeaking on the successive coats of lacquer.

The cavernous gym was quiet for a few moments as Mr. Sherman eyed the squirming form of Kramden.

"That what this is, Kramden? Playing? A game?"

Kramden tried not to look at Mr. Sherman. "I . . . I . . ."

"Hawkins," Mr. Sherman said, still holding Kramden in his gaze the way an eagle might hold a rabbit in its talons. "This class a game?"

"No, sir," he said. He wasn't sure what Mr. Sherman considered the class, but Stan wasn't stupid. He knew how to answer.

"See, Kramden? It's not a game to Hawkins. To Hawkins, it's a competition, a way to learn about life in the real world."

Kramden looked like he wanted to answer, but he was quaking too much.

"You go ahead and pick first then, Hawkins," Mr. Sherman said. "We're *competing* in basketball today, although I guess Kramden here is *playing* basketball."

"Yes, sir," Stan answered. During all this, Stan had been looking straight ahead, scanning the rest of the boys in the class as they stood in a line. Most of them, wisely, had their gazes dropped to the floor. No sense attracting the attention of Mr. Sherman when he already had the scent of blood in his nostrils.

Everyone, that is, except Kurt Marlowe. Kurt Marlowe, who was looking at Stan expectantly. Kurt Marlowe, who wet his pants in Mrs. Carter's third-grade class and never outlived it. Kurt Marlowe, who had some kind of nasal problem that made him sniff constantly. Kurt Marlowe, who was invisible most of the time, and probably wished he was invisible when he wasn't. Kurt Marlowe, who was always picked last in gym class.

Kurt Marlowe looked at him expectantly, eyes moist and bright, and Stan felt . . . what was it he felt? Pity? Maybe. But as he thought about the event that would follow, he knew it wasn't pity that fueled his decision. It was something else. Staking out new territory, maybe. Doing the exact opposite of what Mr. Sherman expected because . . . precisely because that's what it was.

And all of it was fueled by that pathetic look from Kurt Marlowe. All of it.

"I'll take Kurt," he said.

Silence for a few moments. Not even the squeak of shoes on the floor, as every boy, and Mr. Sherman himself, froze in place. Even Kurt Marlowe seemed stunned. But after a few agonizing seconds, Kurt jogged over to stand behind Stan, offering a nod.

Stan refused to look at Mr. Sherman. "Your pick, Neil," he said, referring to Kramden, the other team captain, by his first name. Mostly because Mr. Sherman never did. Enjoying his new role as class contrarian.

Kramden seemed to shake himself out of shock and made his pick. "Robbie," he said.

An obvious choice. Robbie Lane was always one of the first two boys picked.

Stan didn't hesitate; he'd picked this path, and now he was determined to walk it. "Sam," he said. Always one of the last picked, Sam was a freckled kid with a patch of dark-red hair and awkward, lanky limbs.

Kramden—Neil, he should call him Neil—picked Max. Now he had the two boys who never played on the same team, because they were always the first two picked.

Smiling, Stan picked Joe, Eddie, Ron, Harold, and Tim with his remaining choices. His last two, Harold and Tim, were actually pretty good athletes; he'd already filled his team with the gym class rejects.

Through it all, Mr. Sherman stayed quiet. Stan was careful never to look in his direction, fearing he would lose his nerve, be reminded of his own stupidity.

No one was left, even though Kramden still had a pick.

"We're one short," Kramden said to no one in particular.

Stan heard Floyd snort from Kramden's team, then mutter under his breath, "Yeah, right. We're one short."

Scattered bits of laughter.

"I'll jump in for this one," Mr. Sherman said.

The room went quiet again; Mr. Sherman had never participated in any of their gym class activities.

Stan felt his gambit starting to reach a dangerous new level. He finally turned and let himself look at Mr. Sherman, who was moving toward Kramden's group.

Mr. Sherman spoke, his back to Stan. "Evidently, Hawkins doesn't think this is a *game*. He thinks it's a joke." He turned and stared at Stan. "You're skins."

Expected. Every gym class involved a team sport of some kind—never individual sports and never anything non-competitive, because it wasn't the Sherman Way—and every team sport always split into Shirts vs. Skins, because this definitely *was* the Sherman Way. One team kept their shirts on, while the other team took off their shirts and became the Skins. It was an added level of anxiety for boys starting to go through so many physical changes, and Stan was sure, deep inside, that Mr. Sherman knew this and enjoyed it.

Quietly, the boys standing behind him, most of them the gym-class castoffs no one wanted to pick in lineups, began peeling off their shirts. Usually at this time a bit of posturing would begin. Some of the boys would be clapping, trading high fives with other team members, getting into the spirit of the competition, as Mr. Sherman might like to say.

But today was different. Today silence ruled, save for the occasional squeak of shoes on the polished gym floor. Four boys took the floor from Kramden's team, with Mr. Sherman himself at midcourt.

"Pick your starters, Hawkins," he said, and smiled. "Then you and me can tip off."

Stan turned to his team, led them off to the opposite side of the floor. Harold grabbed his arm as they went to the wood benches.

"What are you doing?" he asked in a whisper. "We're gonna get slaughtered."

What was he doing? He wasn't sure.

"I—" he started, but his voice squeaked as he said it.

His voice was changing, getting that deeper timbre, and yet the irony of it all was that a fair number of his words became high-pitched squeals. Usually such a squeak would raise a few snickers, but none of the boys on the team seemed to notice. Or care.

Stan cleared his throat, shifted gears, decided he wouldn't try explaining what he couldn't. "Yeah," he finally said. "We're gonna get slaughtered."

He peeled off his shirt and stood looking at his charges. "Now, who wants to get slaughtered with me?" he asked.

Kurt Marlowe's hand went up immediately, followed by Eddie, Ron, Tim, Joe, and finally, Harold.

Stan smiled. "Okay," he said. "Let's do this." He walked toward Mr. Sherman and certain doom waiting at center court, feeling as if his whole life were downshifting into slow motion.

Mr. Sherman's smile was as wide as ever, but it wasn't a smile of pleasure or reassurance. It was a smile of hunger, of pain. That was why he always felt uncomfortable whenever Mr. Sherman smiled, Stan suddenly realized.

Stan took his place opposite Mr. Sherman, forced himself to return the gaze.

"Who's gonna ref?" someone asked, but Stan didn't look to see who it was. Harold, maybe. It would be something Harold would do: worry about the rules being broken while the world crumbled around him.

"We don't need a ref, do we?" Mr. Sherman said, staring at Stan. "Just a friendly game of basketball."

Now Stan smiled. "That's what this is to you, Sherman?" he said, using his gym teacher's last name only for the first and only time. "A game?"

Mr. Sherman's smile faltered, but only for a moment. "Lane," he said, "throw this jump ball so we can get started." He held out the basketball, and Robbie approached to take it gingerly.

Robbie held the ball in both hands, looked at Stan as if trying to solve some deep problem, glanced at Mr. Sherman, then balanced the ball on one hand. He threw the ball into the air, straight and true.

Mr. Sherman jumped, went after the ball, but Stan stood still. Mr. Sherman tipped the ball behind him, toward Max, but Stan didn't follow the path of the ball.

He simply stood at center court, waiting.

Sherman had come back to the ground and turned to follow the game, but now he finally seemed to realize things weren't progressing according to plan.

And oddly enough, the other four starters on Stan's team had remained still as well. No one moved, even as Max took Mr. Sherman's tip-off and made an easy layup. The ball slid through the net with a *thwik* and then bounced on the floor, slowly rolling away and coming to a stop. No one from Stan's team made a move to retrieve the ball and inbound it.

Maybe they were all too stunned by the events leading up to the game. This was unexplored territory, and they were probably wishing it had remained that way.

Too late for that.

Mr. Sherman's eyebrows furrowed, and he moved back toward Stan at center court. "What are you doing?" he asked, anger now starting to flash in his eyes.

Stan made no answer, but he held Mr. Sherman's gaze.

Mr. Sherman reached out to grab Stan's arm, but Stan backed away before he could.

"Don't touch me," he said through clenched teeth.

Mr. Sherman stopped his advance for a few moments,

then began it again with renewed force. His hand shot out, not to grab Stan, but to hit him.

Stan sidestepped, unconsciously, and put out his hand to stop the progress of Mr. Sherman's blow. His hand clasped at Mr. Sherman's sinewy forearm, and as he made contact, Stan felt an icy shock. Like the static electricity that builds up on a carpet then releases when you touch a friend's hand, perhaps, but stronger. More . . . internal. The shock originated not at his hand, the point of contact with Mr. Sherman, but from somewhere deep and dark inside his own gut. He felt his insides roll in reaction to the sudden sensation.

Immediately, Mr. Sherman fell to the hardwood floor, spasming. His arm, now limp, slipped from Stan's grasp, and his face—his *face*—literally bounced on the floor like the basketball had only moments before.

Blood began to stream from Mr. Sherman's nose, and another hushed quiet fell over the room as Mr. Sherman continued to convulse in front of them.

"Someone go get help," Stan yelled, and a few seconds later, Harold ran through the double doors at the end of the gym and disappeared.

A phone started ringing somewhere, its insistent tone breaking the stillness. Stan looked around him, at all the boys still motionless, his gaze finally stopping on Kurt Marlowe, who simply nodded.

Ring. Not one of those old-fashioned rings, but the ring of a cell phone, out of place in this setting.

"You told him not to touch you," Kurt Marlowe said to him.

Ring.

6.

Ring.

Stan opened his eyes, Kurt Marlowe's words still in his ears. He reached for the cell phone that had pulled him from his never-ending dream.

"Hello?" His eyes were open, but his mind was still flooded with dream images.

"Good morning, Bleach." The voice on the line spoke with a slight Eastern European accent, and he recognized it instantly.

"Good morning, Viktor. Surprised to get a call from you."

"I would expect you'd be used to our calls by now."

Stan squinted his eyes against the daylight streaming in through the pulled drapes. He stifled a sigh, not wanting Viktor to hear.

"Just not used to calls from you specifically."

"I know, and I apologize. I really should try to communicate more often. You are well?"

"No worries, Viktor."

"You are sleeping well?"

"Great."

"And your mother. She is doing well." Viktor said it as a statement, but there was a question hidden in the last word.

Eyes still closed, Stan rubbed at his temple, considering his words. "Yeah, Viktor," he said. "My mother's doing fine."

"Good, good. As I say, I do not take the opportunities to talk with you as I should. To make sure you are happy in our employ."

Stan shook his head. Viktor always spoke with a slight air of formality, remnants, he was sure, of having learned English as a second language in Russia. Or wherever it was he came from. Stan always assumed it was Russia; it only made sense Viktor would have connections with the Russian Mafia.

He stifled another sigh. "What can I do for you, Viktor?"

"Ah, always so accommodating, Bleach. How considerate. I have a project for you in . . . ah . . . Seattle."

"Washington?" He winced. As if there were a hundred Seattles spread across the country.

"Yes."

Usually Viktor had him working in large cities across the East and Midwest. Chicago, St. Louis, the Twin Cities, New York, Boston. Evidently, Viktor was stretching his reach into the West. Still, Stan made no comment. You don't say anything more to a guy like Viktor than you have to.

"Okay, Viktor. You got it."

"You will leave tomorrow. Commercial flight, the usual routine. Your new documents should be at the front desk right now."

"Okay." Stan waited, feeling as if he was supposed to be saying something else. What, he wasn't sure. "Anything else I can do for you, Viktor?"

A pause on the other end of the line. "Only this, Bleach. Only this."

"You got it." He hung up without waiting for a reply.

He lay in bed, and the words of Kurt Marlowe in the dream returned to him: *You told him not to touch you.*

Good advice.

Stan pulled himself out of bed and into the shower, then dressed in the new clothing. He never had to pack or buy anything; fresh clothes, food, and other essentials always waited for him at his next suite, apartment, or hotel room. The Organization shuttled him from location to location following each job, always taking care of the logistics. One day a month, Stan carried out an assignment. The next three or four weeks, he stayed boarded up inside a room somewhere—always someplace different—until it was time to rise once more, like a deadly phoenix, and kill again.

But before this next assignment there was one other person he needed to see back on the East Coast.

7.

It had been a few months since his last visit to Aspen Meadows, and little had changed aside from the season. Last time the tree limbs hung heavy with spring blooms, and the gentle breeze carried the aroma of honeysuckle, earth, wood. Birds chattered in the air. Now the mixture of smells had been replaced with the heavy aroma of freshly cut summer grass, the bird calls were more infrequent, the trees and plants wilting in the late summer heat.

He shut the door on the rental car, walked across the asphalt to the front of the facility. The automatic doors whisked open, pushing a chill of conditioned air against his face as he entered.

A parrot in a cage squawked as he walked to the front desk, perhaps bothered by the tabby cat playing with a ball on the floor. He still had a hard time adjusting to the animals and pets in the common areas of the place; yes, he'd listened to the counselors tell him how therapeutic pets were for patients, but he couldn't quite bring himself to that way of thinking.

The presence of the animals made it seem as if the whole facility—cats, dogs, birds, fish, humans—was just a giant unwanted pet center, filled with animals waiting for families to come by and pet them, give them some attention.

He pushed the thought from his mind, uncomfortable with how well it fit. He visited his mother here every few months, and he was one of the more frequent visitors. Some of the people here, wards of the state, never had any company.

Luckily for them, this center for homeless pets didn't euthanize.

The young woman behind the glass at the desk was new, and pleasant enough—almost too pleasant—as she asked him to sign in and gave him a visitor pass, hesitating only briefly when she saw his hands encased in the latex gloves.

He smiled. "I'm a bit of a germ freak," he said, holding up both hands, as if this somehow illustrated an obsession with cleanliness.

She just nodded, asked if he needed directions, and he politely told her no. He had been here before, often, including many times before this young woman worked here. She was the new person here, not he.

Stan walked down the hall, purposely avoiding eye contact with the various souls sitting idly in the rec area, pushing themselves aimlessly down the hallway in wheelchairs, staring out the doors of their cavelike rooms as he passed.

He tried to ignore these obvious things, instead focusing on the many wonderful aspects of Aspen Meadows: a dining area with dinners shared among residents; games and activities in common areas; the cute pets, of course; an activities calendar outside the main recreation room filled with things to do. This was a center for both relaxation and stimulation, the marketing people and administrators at Aspen Meadows would be quick to tell you.

The people who lived there would tell you something else. Those who could talk.

He came to his mother's room, paused, went inside. The door was open, as always. The curtains inside were pulled away from the window, the fresh flowers he sent every week in a vase on the window shelf.

His mother, in a large brown recliner, sat staring into space.

He crossed the room, put his gloved hand on her shoulder, leaned in and kissed her. "Hi, Mom," he said, pulling one of the chairs from the small table out so he could sit on it and face her.

Her eyes, Bassett hound eyes in an impossibly sunken, bony face, turned and focused on his for a moment. It looked as if she was about to say something of great interest, but then her eyes refocused on nothingness again and she fell back into her usual thousand-yard stare.

She hadn't spoken in five years. The last two she'd been here, the bill footed by the Organization. Provided he was a good boy, and did as he was told.

He looked out the window, watched one of the grounds-keepers work a weed trimmer along the base of the giant brick fence encircling the fortress.

"Just wanted to drop by, see how you're doing," he

said, still staring at the man outside. "You're looking good. Obviously, someone's feeding you."

A voice spoke from behind him. "Yeah, my only problem is, I'm a little too good at feeding myself." He turned, knowing he would see the smiling voice of Janna.

"Hi, Janna," he said, standing and putting his hands in his pockets. It was a tic, another habit he'd picked up over the years. Like blowing on any drink.

Just one of the hazards of being a contract killer who murdered people with his bare hands.

She ignored his discomfort, came into the room, enveloped him in a warm hug. "You coulda called and let me know you were coming."

"Yeah, sorry. I didn't know it was going to be today until . . . um . . . today."

"Still flying all over the country, then?"

"Yeah, just took a small detour." He smiled.

Every so often he took a quick flight to visit his mother, courtesy of the Organization's seemingly endless supply of counterfeit credit cards.

Just one of the benefits of being a contract killer who murdered people with his bare hands.

She patted his back, pulled away, turned to his mother. "You keep your voice down now, Cleona. Don't want to disturb the neighbors."

Stan smiled. Part of why he liked Janna. She wasn't afraid to acknowledge the obvious or even poke fun at it. Some people would be offended by it, he supposed, but he found it refreshing in a world that tried to ignore so much.

"You gonna stay for lunch?" Janna asked. "I think it's meat mush today, instead of vegetable mush."

"No, I don't think so. Gotta head out soon."

"One more thing," she said. "You think about that clinical trial I told you about?"

"Um . . . haven't had much of a chance."

"It's a pretty exciting treatment—they've had good success, bringing people back with it." She paused and dropped her voice a bit. "We'd be able to move Cleona. Get her out of here—Midwest, maybe even the West Coast. No one else would have to know." Janna looked at him, intent.

Did she know his situation? If so, how? Could he trust her? He felt himself start to ask a question, but then it hit him: she was fishing. Viktor had pushed a few bucks her way, told her to try to pick him for some information, try to trip him. Classic Viktor strategy. That had to be it.

She continued to stare, her gaze asking questions he wouldn't answer.

"I'll . . . I'll think about it."

"Okay, then. You just let me know when you're done thinking so much," she said. "I'll leave you two."

She backed out of the room, closing the door behind her, seeming disappointed. Probably because she didn't have any dirt she could take back to Viktor. Stan stared at the closed door a few moments, then went over and opened it again. Keeping it open felt more comfortable.

"Keeping busy with the day job, Mom," he said, sinking into the chair again. "Places to go, things to see, people to do."

He smiled at his joke, but his mother's stare remained steady. She hadn't moved since he entered the room.

"Heading out to the West Coast in a few days, do some more business out there. Then I'm off for another month or so. Rinse and repeat."

A small table sat next to her chair. A pen. Some napkins. An empty glass.

A cat wandered into the room from the outside hall, came to where Stan was sitting, brushed against his pants. He bent and stroked its fur as he looked at his mother.

She was still in there somewhere, the woman who had raised him. The woman who had held him and read Dr. Seuss, the woman who had herded him to piano classes, the woman who had later herded him to weekly counseling sessions to talk about what therapists alternately described as OCD, social disorder, paranoia, or a heady mix of all of the above.

Good old Mom.

"I'm sorry about Grandpa," he said suddenly, not sure why. He hadn't spoken to her about his grandfather since she could actually hold up her end of the conversation, hadn't spoken to any of the therapists or counselors or social workers about it ever. "I figured it out after him, you know. Why it happened. How it happened. Too late, I know."

The cat abruptly gave his leg one last brush and ran out into the hallway again. His head still down, Stan heard a scribbling sound. He lifted his head, saw his mother writing something on a napkin with the pen. It was a number: 1595544534.

He took the napkin, looked at her. This was the first human movement he'd seen from her in . . . months. Had Janna started her on the new drugs, secretly?

Within moments, she had returned to her usual statue state. Her dry eyes stared straight ahead, as if taking in something she found slightly disappointing.

Stan ran a hand through his hair before he stuffed the napkin into his pants pocket. So she'd scribbled on a napkin. Like that meant anything. Probably just the misfiring of a brain warped by disease, numbers left over from some scrambled past.

Still, she had moved. On her own. He pulled his chair toward her, leaned in close, close enough to smell the scent of her breakfast. Oatmeal, he guessed. Grain mush, as Janna might call it.

She stared, a bit of drool pooling at the corner of her mouth. He wiped at the drool, the wetness of it feeling odd through the latex gloves, like gelatin.

"You even alive?" he asked, whispering. He licked his lips, then: "Am I?"

She didn't answer.

Yeah, he was doing all this to keep his mother in the thin, hovering zone between life and death. And really, how much of a line was it?

For that matter, how much of a line was it for him? He'd been a zombie for a couple years now, allowing himself to be controlled by his own pity and a Russian mobster starting to build a network on the North American continent.

He could kill himself, avoid killing other innocent lives. If he wanted his own mother to die. Or at least finish dying.

But he couldn't do that. Even now, so many years after his grandfather, so many sleeping pills and painkillers later, he couldn't dull that gnawing hole deep inside. Not now. Not ever.

He'd killed one person he loved. And God knew he couldn't repeat it.

This was his circle of hell, and he was confined to it until the bitter end. No magic tricks to make him disappear, no easy way to slide off this mortal coil.

His thoughts returned to Janna. Maybe she was telling clever lies. Or maybe, just maybe, Janna *did* know something of his situation, and was offering a way out.

In either case—devious turncoat or a naive dreamer— Janna was dangerous. He liked her, but he'd have to make some calls, see if he could get her removed from the staff. He could do that, through the Organization. Make things like that happen. Maybe it would even be a smart move. If she were working for Viktor, he would immediately see that Stan wasn't going to fall for any poisoned bait.

He stood, turned to the door, and left without looking back at his mother.

Yes, he was a zombie. And zombies fed on the living. Always.

8.

The flight to Seattle was uneventful enough, and this time his Handler met him at the airport. Always much better that way. It wasn't the end of the world when he met Handlers at restaurants or bars or other locations after checking in at the hotel, but it was always much . . . cleaner . . . to just start the whole job from the airport. The dynamic didn't shift that way; the Handler felt comfortable being a driver, and Stan felt comfortable being a rider. Meetings in other places led to small talk and conversations, which led to the Handlers asking questions, which led to people seeing things no human should.

They called him Bleach, after all. He liked things clean.

Clean or not, though, he was also tragic. Who was that mythical Greek guy? Well, yes, Midas; he was obvious, and Stan had read many accounts and translations of Midas's exploits over the past couple years. (Reading was one of the things you could reliably do while hiding in hotel rooms. When you weren't otherwise occupied chugging sleeping pills, that is.) But he was now thinking of the guy who constantly rolled a rock uphill. Sisyphus, maybe? Always he moved uphill.

His Handler was quiet, simply nodding when he recognized Stan coming out of the Jetway. The Handler didn't offer his hand for a shake. Good. Even with his gloves on, it made him uncomfortable, itchy, to touch the skin of others.

He rarely had to search for his Handlers, he knew, because the Organization gave them photos of him ahead of time, along with explicit instructions on where to take him and when. Ignore those instructions, and the Handlers would receive a visit from less savory members of the Organization. Maybe even a return visit from Stan himself.

He followed the Handler to a white sedan double-parked outside. They opened the doors and slid inside without a word. As the Handler wheeled onto the street, Stan saw a newspaper folded on the dash. He picked it up, looked at the Handler.

"Thought you might like something to read on the way," the Handler said without taking his eyes off the road. "Your first time in Seattle, I'm guessing."

"Yeah, thanks." He unfolded the paper to look at the

front page. *August of 2001 Hottest on Record*, the headline said. He glanced at the article, scanning the various atrocities August had inflicted upon the fine Seattle landscape.

"Even the weather's going down the drain," he said, not fully realizing he'd spoken out loud until the Handler answered.

"Just twenty months late. Or eight months late, depending on your point of view."

He looked at the Handler. "I don't follow."

"Y2K. Everybody thinking the world was going to end when we rolled to a new century. 'Cept it wasn't really the new century—2000 was the *last* year of the *twentieth* century. New century didn't start until this year."

Stan smiled. "Well, we still have four months left in 2001. World might end yet."

The Handler turned and looked at him for the first time. "I'm starting to think that would be the best news we could get," he said.

Stan sighed, folded the newspaper again, and threw it on the dash. "Amen, brother. Amen to that."

9a.

His target was holed up at a ratty old hotel in an area the Handler told him was called Fremont. They passed through a bit of a historic district on the way. Stan noticed faded paint on the sides of brick buildings: ads for nonexistent drinks, signage for meat packing plants that were now homes for shops and restaurants.

The Handler wisely parked in an alley around the corner from the hotel, and Stan got out to walk. This Handler, whatever his name was, didn't follow. Good. No replay of the incident with the kid.

Humidity and heat combined to make the air feel heavy, and after the quick walk to the front door, he felt his long-sleeved shirt clinging. He liked to wear long sleeves, because they drew less attention to the gloves—thin driving gloves, unless it was an assignment day like today. Then he switched to latex. They were disposable, and that was important for these projects; the thought of reusing gloves after an assignment seemed wrong. Backward. Sickening, in a way.

At the front door of the hotel, he retrieved the small envelope he'd folded and tucked away in a back pocket. The envelope, which held two keys, had been part of his most recent delivery packet.

He picked one key at random and tried it in the protruding lock of the oak door. No go. He fished out the other key and tried it, feeling it slide home and turn as a bird twittered from one of the floors above. Birds in the city—not pigeons, but real songbirds of some kind. Maybe seeking shelter from the oppressive heat in the shade of the eaves. He liked that.

Inside, he moved confidently, striding across a lobby that smelled oddly of limes and urine. The decay inside said it wasn't just on the wrong side of the tracks, but nowhere in sight of them.

He passed the elevator doors and took the stairs. Always, he preferred the stairs.

On the fifth floor he surveyed the area for a moment before walking down the hallway. Ten yards down, he came to the door marked 534.

Odd to get keys. Usually, he didn't have such quick access to his targets. More often, he was simply given an address and trusted to find a way inside. Maybe an unlatched window or an inadvertently unlocked door, maybe a scheme as a deliveryman, maybe a tail that let him follow the target to an office or location away from home. But he almost never had keys or other means of easily getting into homes. Or hotels, as was the case here.

He placed his head against the door of the room and listened to a conversation on the other side, recognizing it immediately as a daytime television program. He sighed, considering. Take off the gloves now, or wait until he was inside? Tough choice, but he decided not to think too much about it and peeled the gloves off his hands, taking care to make sure the latex didn't snap, and stuffed them into his pocket with the other key.

Fingerprints weren't a worry. They were never a worry,

because he'd never had his prints taken. For that matter, the scenes of his hits were never treated as homicides, because his victims seemingly died of natural causes. If you wanted to call it that.

Stan put his right hand on the doorknob as he slid the key into the deadbolt. In most movies and books, people breaking into homes always moved slowly, creeping into the place without being noticed. Stan knew better. This wasn't a game of stealth, but of power. You made less noise, created more surprise, by moving decisively.

He closed his eyes for a few seconds, took a deep breath, turned the key in the lock, and swung open the door. Without pausing, he closed the door behind him and walked in, past a short wall that opened into the main room on the left. A couch sat on the far wall as he walked into the room.

And on the couch sat a dark-haired man, nervously pointing a gun at him.

Stan continued walking toward the man, as if this were the most natural thing in the world for him. And maybe it was.

"Stop!" the dark-haired man said, his voice rising a bit.

Stan was skilled at picking out changes in voice inflection, what those inflections meant. He'd had a couple years of practice at reading people in extreme situations.

The man narrowed his eyes, turned off the television with the remote he held in his left hand, put both his hands on the stock of the revolver.

Stan stopped, waited. The man's hands threatened to start shaking, but remained steady for the moment. Stan noticed his bare feet, his black, thick-soled shoes neatly sitting beside the bed even though the man was fully dressed in a suit and tie. Maybe a bit of a neatnik, didn't like people wearing shoes inside his apartment. Stan could identify with neatniks.

"Viktor sent you?" the man asked.

Now Stan was able to pick out an accent in the man's voice, an accent that sounded eerily similar to Viktor's.

"He did," Stan said, holding his hands up in the air to show he was unarmed.

"Who are you?"

"Nobody important."

The man grunted. "I know this feeling well."

They stared, regarding each other, for a few seconds.

"So what now?" the man on the couch said. His voice wavered a bit as he said it, almost as much as the tip of the gun he pointed at Stan.

Stan shrugged, partly because he himself didn't know what was going to happen. Not that it mattered. The end result would be the same. He'd been through this kind of thing too many times to worry much about the details.

The man pointed his gun toward a single wooden chair across from the couch. "Take off your shoes," he said.

Stan cocked his head to the side, unsure he'd heard the man correctly. "What?"

The man motioned to the chair again. "You will sit down and take off your shoes."

Stan stared for a few moments, then went to the chair and sat. He bent and began unlacing his shoes. Okay, this guy really was way too worried about dirty shoes in his apartment.

"Aren't you going to ask why?" the man said. His voice was cracking a bit, but Stan pretended not to notice.

"Why?" Stan said, humoring him.

"You're American. You know the phrase 'die with your boots on.'"

Stan removed his first shoe, set it to the side. He looked at the man, shrugged. "Yeah."

"This—this is one thing we have of America, Viktor and I, when we are young. Our mother wants us to learn English, yes? So she smuggles illegal things to teach us. Mostly books. We love torn books about cowboys and Indians."

"Dime novels?"

The man seemed excited by this. "Yes! Yes! In these books, the cowboys say to die with your boots on, and that becomes—what would you say?—something special between two people."

"A pact?"

"A pact, yes. We promise we die with our boots on."

Stan glanced at the man once more. "Viktor's your

brother," he said, although he'd meant it as a question. Viktor had obviously practiced his English a bit more.

"Viktor does not tell you this?"

Stan shrugged, shook his head. Killing his own brother. Hell probably had its own circle reserved exclusively for Viktor Abkin. Right below his own circle. Or maybe they'd be roomies, which would be oddly fitting.

"Those aren't boots," he said, jutting his chin at the man's black-soled shoes on the floor.

"And you are no cowboy. But Viktor understands. I take off my shoes, because I do not die without my boots on, you see?"

"Kind of a superstition, then."

The man's eyes narrowed for a moment, and Stan saw a bit of anger flare. "No superstition. It just is," he said simply. He gestured with the gun again. "Other shoe, please."

Stan bent and began untying his other shoe. "So you're making me take off my shoes as a message to Viktor."

"Yes. He finds you dead, with no shoes, he knows I send a message. He knows he cannot decide to remove me simply because I make problems for him."

Stan nodded, continuing to stare at his now-untied shoe. He knew what his next move was, had known it ever since he'd been told to take off his shoes.

He slowly slipped off his second shoe, stood and hurled it at the man's face, then dropped to the floor and rolled, coming up in a crouch even as Viktor's brother ducked and slouched on the couch. He saw fear in the dark eyes as the man tried to swing the gun back around toward him, but Stan was already grabbing the wrist with his hand.

His bare hand.

A very good thing he had decided to remove the gloves before entering the hotel room.

Instantly the man's eyes rolled back into his head and he went into convulsions. The gun dropped, allowing Stan to step back and release his grip. Viktor's brother, his body still heaving with tremors, slid to the floor in front of the couch, a bit of foam escaping his mouth.

Stan stared for a few seconds, watching the man's hand spasm as it tried to grasp one of the black-soled shoes he'd neatly placed in front of his couch. Only minutes before, probably.

Like most of his victims, the man wasn't dying quickly; usually, it took a minute or two of thrashing and convulsing, and Stan had to stand there and watch. It was part of the curse.

Stan gave a deep sigh. Well, what of it? Was there any real harm, letting the man die with his shoes on? He could do that, couldn't he? A small act of rebellion against Viktor.

He dropped to his knees, picked up one of the shoes, noted the tag on the inside of the shoe's tongue: an oddly-formed letter that looked like a reversed numeral 3. Beneath the three he saw other characters he guessed must be Russian. Made sense. This guy, Viktor's brother, was wearing shoes from Russia, or Eastern Europe, or wherever they were from.

Kneeling beside the quivering form, he began to put on the left shoe. No skin-on-skin contact. Not that it mattered; he'd already touched this man, already killed him.

The man's limbs were stiff, the muscles of his legs quivering as he convulsed, so Stan had to concentrate to get the shoe on the inflexible foot as he—

"Hello?" a woman's voice blurted from the short hallway behind him.

Stan stood and half turned, looking at the woman who had spoken.

Her eyes flickered, looking first at Stan's face, then at the shoe he still clutched in his hand, then at the form of Viktor's brother, half on the couch, half on the floor, body quieting from heaving convulsions to mere twitches.

He tried to think of something to say, but really, what could he say that would make sense of this scene? And in the end, what did it matter? He'd done what he came here to do. His target was dead (okay, *dying*), and he could simply move on to the next hotel or apartment, sequester himself for a few weeks with a few bottles of painkillers, kill the dreams that tried to seep into his conscious world.

He let the shoe fall to the floor, put his hand in his pocket, feeling the latex of the gloves brush against his fingers. All he had to do was get these gloves on, get to the door, and get away. No need to explain anything to this woman.

She moved quickly, coming across the floor and dropping to her knees next to the man on the floor. Viktor's brother. Didn't even know his name.

Stan paused for a moment, pulled the latex gloves from his pocket, pulled one of them on, lifted his foot and stepped over the man's legs.

But as he did so, the woman did something unexpected. Without looking up, she grabbed his hand—his bare hand—and began pulling. "Come on," she said, her voice sounding eerily calm. "He's gonna die if you don't help me."

That statement might have made him smile in other circumstances, the irony of it all (he's gonna die if you don't help me), but all he could concentrate on was his hand. Her hand.

Touching.

(You got the dead blood, child)

And nothing happening.

The mild electrical itch was there, but the words were new, something he'd never experienced before.

(You got the dead blood, child)

He tried to get a glimpse of her face, but her head was down, concentrating on Viktor's brother. Those words weren't spoken, he knew, but he heard them, loudly and clearly, in his mind. And he knew, as her insistent grip pulled him to his knees, that those words were somehow being pushed to him by their touch.

"You know CPR?" she asked.

(No, it wasn't her voice; the voice in his mind was older, scratchier.)

"Yeah," he said, his brain feeling muddled. "I mean no."

She resumed the compressions on the man's chest. "How about a cell phone? You got one?"

"No." Wait; he did have one, but . . . but his mind wasn't working. The voice in his mind, the woman's touch, had rattled him.

"Figures." She stopped a moment, pulled a cell phone from the back pocket of the jeans she was wearing, shoved it toward him. "Here."

He looked at the phone as if it were poisonous. He still didn't have both gloves on, and he couldn't risk another touch; something had obviously gone wrong the first time, but—

"If you don't know how to do chest compressions, you gotta make the call," she said, waving the phone a bit.

He took the phone, being careful to avoid contact with her hand, and dialed 911. Then he cradled the phone against his shoulder, pulling on the other surgical glove.

The operator answered, asking the nature of the emergency. "Heart attack," he said. And what was the address? He gave it to her, recalling it instantly from his memory. And what was his name?

He hit the end button on the cell phone and set it down on the floor, returning his attention to the woman repeating chest compressions, counting silently to herself.

"They're on the way," he said.

She continued the compressions as he watched a drop of sweat form on her forehead. He needed to get out of here. He'd done his job, killed this man. He'd never see this woman again in his life, and all he had to do was get up and walk out the door. She'd stay and do the CPR; even though Stan knew it was hopeless, she didn't. And so she would try.

That thought was abruptly pushed to the side by another: she had touched his bare hand and lived. Why?

"It's not hard to learn," she said. "I can teach you."

"I—" he began to protest, but she cut him off.

"Three fingers up from here," she said, demonstrating as she placed her hand at the junction of the man's rib cage. "Hands together, steady pressure, kinda like kneading bread, when you think about it."

Not that he'd ever kneaded bread.

"You try it," she said.

He tried to think of the catfish, the comfortable image that swam in his mind and calmed him after his assignments. But the fish refused to come.

Barring that, he wished for sleeping pills or pain pills. Or both.

He started to protest, but she grabbed him again, this

time on the arm. His long sleeves prevented any skin-on-skin contact, and at least she couldn't touch his hands now. That was when he noticed, for the first time, that she also wore long sleeves. A fellow traveler.

Uncomfortable, he clasped his hands the way she'd shown him, trying a few tentative pushes on the man's chest.

"Harder," she instructed. "You're massaging the heart, keeping the blood flow going."

Blood flow. *You got the dead blood, child.*

He pushed harder, and after a few more compressions, the man's eyes actually fluttered open. He looked lazily at Stan, then at the woman, then closed his eyes again. His mouth opened, and his lungs sucked in a deep breath.

"Stop," she said, putting her fingers on the inside of the man's wrist.

Now, now, now, his mind screamed at him. Now was the time to leave. Except . . .

Except he'd just killed a man, touched a woman without killing her, and brought a dead man back to life in the span of two minutes. He was adrift on an ocean of confusion.

"He's back," the woman said, looking at him again and blowing the unruly strand of hair away from her face. She leaned back, and a pack of cigarettes appeared from somewhere. One of her sleeve cuffs shifted with the movement, revealing scars that looked like old cuts.

She shook out a cigarette, offered him one. He refused,

and she lit her own, then blew it out the side of her mouth as she squinted through the blue smoke at him.

"You shouldn't do that," he said.

She stared. "Shouldn't do what?"

"Smoke. You're pregnant." The statement shocked him as much as it obviously shocked her. He hadn't known she was pregnant, hadn't planned to say anything; his mouth opened, and the words just came tumbling out before he knew what he was saying.

He watched as she slowly, methodically stubbed the cigarette on the floor next to her.

"What's with the gloves?" she asked.

He looked at his hands, held them up, as if noticing for the first time that he was wearing gloves. Obviously, without really thinking about it, he'd somehow slipped them on again. How could he answer that question, especially to a woman who should be dead right now? She'd touched the bare skin of his hands, after all.

"Long story," he said.

She started coughing, seemingly uncomfortable with the cigarettes. Or maybe she was just uncomfortable with him. She stood, her knee cracking as she did so.

Stan half wondered if he'd be able to stand himself; his whole body felt drained.

"Probably a heart attack," the woman said from above him. "Or a stroke. His body's going to be in shock for a while. Probably won't fully come back around until he's in the hospital."

He looked up at her, and she offered her hand. He stood without taking it.

"I can take it from here," she said.

"What do you mean?" He brought his hand to his face, scratched at his cheek, even though it did nothing through the thin latex of the gloves.

"You've been itching to bolt ever since I got here," she said. "Probably would have if I hadn't come over." She glanced over at the chair where he'd been sitting, now on its side. "And I'm guessing that's an even longer story."

It felt like he was the one who'd had the stroke; his mind, his body, refused to move.

Catfishcatfishcatfish, he said to himself, trying to call the comforting image to his mind: the dark-gray image of the fish surrounded by burning orange. But the catfish refused to enter his thoughts, refused to calm him.

"So go," she said. "Most of the time, you only get one chance to run."

He nodded, stepped backward, stumbled as his knee gave a slight hitch. He turned, concentrating on the front door, which hung open just a few yards away from the open center of the living room.

He went to the end of the short wall leading to the front door before he stopped to look at the woman again. As if one last look would make everything perfectly clear. She gave him a quick nod, her arms folded across her chest as if she were hugging herself against a chill.

In the distance, Stan heard the thin whine of a siren rising as he closed the door behind him.

2.

A few weeks after Stan killed the gym teacher, the Sherman Tank began in earnest with the death of his grandfather.

Heart failure.

That's what everyone said. Doctors, family, friends. Even Stan himself said it when asked. But deep inside, Stan knew it wasn't a heart that killed his grandfather. It was a hand.

His own hand.

He hadn't meant to, just as he hadn't mean to kill Mr. Sherman. It just happened—happened, in fact, before the storm created by Sherman's death had even passed. He was still getting stares in the halls, whispers behind his back. And of course, he was still hearing that odd statement from Kurt Marlowe, rattling in his mind again and again: *You told him not to touch you.* That phrase had been a constant companion in the few weeks since Sherman's death.

It especially came to him when he touched other people with his hands. He had done that, of course. Members of his family, the few friends who would still come over after school, the grief counselor who made a habit out of taking Stan's hands in her own and talking about how SORRY she was this HORRIBLE THING had happened to SUCH A FINE YOUNG MAN.

They all lived, of course. But that was only because Stan didn't understand the curse clearly yet. He wouldn't understand that until Grampa Mick died.

Grampa Mick introduced him to catfishing. All kinds of fishing, really—wet and dry flies, spinners, bait—but it was the catfishing that stuck with Stan. Mainly because it was magical, a certain kind of alchemy with mud and water.

To pull catfish from the murky depths of the mighty Missouri River, you didn't even need a fishing rod or specialized line. All you needed were several large hooks, a length of twine, lead weights, and bait. Sometimes blood bait, sometimes garlic, sometimes plain earthworms.

Stan clearly remembered the last catfish setline he checked with Grampa Mick. Near Fred Robinson Bridge in the Missouri Breaks, just a few hours from his grandfather's small farm on the undulating waves of eastern Montana's plains.

Stan was a city boy, but each summer he got shipped out to the rural reaches of Montana to spend a few weeks on his grandparents' farm.

For Stan, those were weeks filled with magic. And after the incident with Mr. Sherman, he was especially ready. Following a couple weeks of harassment and silence and counseling at school, his mother had decided maybe he could just skip the last week of school to go visit Grampa Mick and Grandma Velda.

Stan enthusiastically agreed; he was ready to leave his life in the city behind, pretend nothing in the world existed except his grandfather, grandmother, and the whispering wind that sighed through their creaking farmhouse.

So when Grampa Mick told him they were going to spend a weekend at Fred Robinson Bridge, Stan knew what it meant. It meant fishing for sauger, sure, but it also meant putting out setlines for catfish.

Anticipation filled him on the ride to the bridge. It was early June, right before the big paddlefish snagging season, which meant few people would be on the river. Just a few locals, like Grampa Mick. They talked about the city, about disappointments and hopes, about books they'd recently read and movies they'd recently seen.

But not once did Grampa Mick bring up the incident with the gym teacher. No "Tell me how you're feeling" or "Anything you want to talk about?" or "It's okay to be angry." Grampa Mick just treated him like he was . . . normal. Grampa Mick, perhaps alone among all people on earth, had an innate understanding of what happened inside Stan's own mind.

Which was to say he always remembered there were things you'd rather forget.

When they finally reached the bridge, they pulled into the campground and picked a spot to park Grampa's rusty old Dodge pickup. The campground stretched away from the river, a few swaths of trees lining the riverbanks of the muddy Missouri. Grampa Mick set up their camp in silence, and Stan was glad to just listen to the current of the river, smell the caked muck on the breeze, stare into the dusty blue sky in that silence.

Eventually Grampa Mick spoke. "Maybe try for some sauger later this evening. Could put out a few catfish lines now."

Stan nodded eagerly. He loved the simplicity of catfishing, the elemental feel of it. They walked through grass that was still green (but would be brown in a matter of weeks), making their way to the bank, Grampa Mick clutching the twine, hooks, and blood bait.

When the river came into view, it was high—higher than Stan remembered it being the year before.

"Late runoff this year," Grampa Mick said, as if reading his mind. "Snow stayed in the mountains to the end of May."

Stan nodded, staring at the muddy brown water of the Missouri as they walked along the riverbank. In the distance, downriver, they saw a few boats creasing the water's surface.

"Too early," his grandfather said.

"For what?" Stan asked.

Grampa Mick nodded at the boats drifting on the current. "For paddlefish. River has to drop some first."

Stan stared at the boats in the distance. One was adrift

on the current, spinning slowly; the other was anchored, a man on the deck casting line from a huge pole and reeling it in, again and again.

Abruptly, Grampa Mick dropped to his knees on the overhanging bank, pulling out his twine and hooks along with the blood meal pellets that would be bait. He began measuring lengths of the muddy white twine by stretching his arms. "Paddlefish probably won't start hitting heavy until next week—later than usual. Ah, but the catfish . . ." He snipped the twine and looped a mass of hooks and leaders on the end. "The catfish will always be here, won't they, Stan? Couldn't get rid of 'em if you wanted to."

Stan nodded, still staring at the boats on the river. He turned his attention back to his grandfather as he began to let the setline drift out into the current. They repeated the process four times, both upstream and downstream from their camping spot, before Grampa Mick asked if he wanted to have a little lunch.

Stan nodded, and they returned to camp for ham sandwiches and crackers. They ate in comforting silence, and Stan thought about the boats in the current, the fishermen on the decks, casting and reeling, trying to snag a paddlefish. So much different from catfish and setlines. Paddlefishing was pure chance: you had to hook a paddlefish, lying on the bottom of the river, pull it to the surface with one of the large snag hooks.

Catfish, on the other hand, emerged from the bottoms

on their own. They came to the blood meal, to the bait, following their instincts and their hunger.

After he and Grampa Mick had finished lunch and read in the camper for a while, Stan asked if they could go check the setlines. Something inside him was eager to see the setlines, to pull them from the muddy river and discover what might be waiting.

Grampa Mick looked at his watch. "Barely been two hours," he said, as if protesting.

But he wasn't. Not really. Grampa Mick wanted to go too; Stan could tell.

"No harm in checking 'em, though," Grampa Mick said through a broad smile.

They returned to the bank and their setlines, dull excitement brewing in Stan's stomach. The first three lines were all empty; some muck and vegetation attached to the hooks, but the blood meal, now soggy and mud-colored itself, remained undisturbed.

But as his grandfather pulled on the fourth setline, it began to pull back and move on its own.

His grandfather smiled, working the line. "Looks like we got one."

Stan watched, fascinated, as his grandfather fought the catfish on the line, man versus nature. After about five minutes the catfish came to the surface, revealing its whiskered face and silver backside.

"Good size," his grandfather remarked. "Get that gaffe."

Stan gripped the hook in his hand, waiting. His grandfather motioned him to the edge of the overhanging bank, handed him the twine.

"Hold this tight," Grampa Mick said, taking the gaffe from him. "He won't make this easy."

The words stuck with Stan for years afterward.

Stan did as instructed, holding the twine, feeling his tenuous connection with the creature from the deep, its every motion and movement telegraphed to him. He watched as his grandfather went to his knees and raised the gaffe. For a moment, he wanted to cry out "Stop!" when he saw his grandfather raise the gaffe, but the moment passed and the gaffe swung down, catching the fish behind one of its awkward front fins.

Grampa Mick pulled the fish from the water, swinging it behind him and onto the bank in one fluid, practiced motion. He pinned the catfish's head to the ground, working at the hook deep inside the mouth.

Stan stood, transfixed, sure the catfish was gazing at him, as if expecting him to stop the inevitable.

Within moments, it was over. Grampa Mick went back to re-baiting the setline, and Stan tried to ignore the catfish flailing in the tall green grass of the bank, its every movement taking it farther down the incline. Farther away from the water.

Later, back at camp, Grampa Mick showed him how to clean the catfish, remarking how this particular one—"about seven pounds"—was the perfect size for eating.

First, Grampa Mick made a long cut down the stomach. Then he turned the fish over and nailed it, stomach down, to a dead tree stump and made two more cuts along the back, around the dorsal fin.

Through it all, the catfish writhed, its round mouth taking in gulps of air as it fought to stay alive.

Stan closed his eyes, unable to watch as his grandfather filleted the fish. He answered politely whenever Grampa Mick explained what he was doing—filleting the sides, cutting away the cheeks—but his eyes remained closed.

Even so, he still felt the fish struggling.

That evening, his grandfather cooked the fillets and cheeks of the catfish, and they sat beside the campfire with plates balanced on their knees.

Stan pushed around the meat on his plate, but he didn't eat. Instead he looked into the campfire, staring at the remains and the carcass of the fish burning in the flames.

He won't come easy. His grandfather's words, echoing in his head.

As he watched the fish's carcass burning in the spitting flames of the fire, he could swear he still saw it struggling. Moving. Trying to escape.

Trying to swim through the fire that consumed it.

"How's it?" his grandfather asked through a mouthful of meat. Stan looked across the campfire at Grampa Mick, staring at the face etched in hard relief against the light of the flames. He thought he could see white pieces of the catfish's flesh stuck in his grandfather's teeth.

Stan smiled, opened his mouth to speak. "It's—" Instead of his normal voice, a choked squeak escaped. He cleared his throat and tried again. "It's good," he finished.

His grandfather smiled, set his own plate down, stood with some effort, came around the fire. Stan tried to ignore the skeleton of the catfish still burning.

Grampa Mick patted his shoulder, ruffled his hair. "That's my favorite boy," he said. "That's my favorite boy."

Stan smiled, tilted his head as he watched the fire, brought his hand to Grampa Mick's arm and touched the leathery skin.

A simple touch. A loving touch.

A last touch.

10.

Another city. Another extended-stay suite. Another binge of pills that would let him sleep the dreamless sleep.

Except none of that was happening, because his cell

phone was ringing. He'd ignored its first two outbursts, but now the third one was starting, and there was no way he could ignore it forever.

Viktor, on the other hand, would keep calling forever. He knew that.

Stan took a deep sigh, picked up the phone.

"What happened, Bleach?" Viktor's voice asked.

"Hello to you, too, Viktor."

"You will tell me what happened in Seattle," Viktor repeated.

"Sounds like you already know."

"I will hear it from you."

Stan sniffed, scratched at his arm, remembering the puckered pink scars on the woman's arms. "You could have told me he was your brother."

For a few moments, only the sound of Viktor's steady, measured breathing. Then: "He is no longer my brother. Only a liability."

Stan smiled grimly. In Viktor's world there were only assets and liabilities. Mostly liabilities. He sighed, made himself stop itching his arm. "I don't know what happened, Viktor. Some woman."

"Some woman?"

"She . . . she wasn't there at first, but maybe she was a friend or something, dropping by to check on him."

"What about her?"

"After . . ." Stan swallowed, finding it difficult to continue for a reason he couldn't put his finger on, ha-ha. "After I did the job, this woman showed up. And she did CPR, brought him back."

"CPR?"

"Cardiopulmonary—"

"Yes, yes, I know the term. I was just confirming. Her name?"

"I . . . didn't ask."

"What did she look like?"

"Well, uh, pale. Stringy hair, blonde, more like uncombed than stringy. Dark, hollow eyes, cut marks on her arms."

"Cut marks on her arms."

Viktor sometimes had the odd habit of repeating things you said, as if he were practicing to become a parrot. Now probably wasn't the time to let his irritation show, though. Stan stared at the closed drapes covering the window, fluttering in the air from the air conditioner. He wanted this call to be over.

"You owe me another project," Viktor said.

Stan shook his head. "Because of your brother," he said.

"I told you, he is no longer my brother."

Stan itched his arm again, shrugged to himself. Like another project mattered at this point. "Whatever."

Viktor was quiet on the other end of the line for a few moments. "And how is your dear mother?" he asked.

Stan could hear forced sweetness, coming across as pure menace, in Viktor's voice.

Stan found the bottle of sleeping pills on the nightstand, shook a few more out, popped them into his mouth. "I'm not going anywhere," he said into the phone. "Everything's okay. One fluke doesn't mean I'll be bailing."

"I hope so. And your mother, I'm sure, hopes so too. They take such good care of her at that facility. It would be a shame if she took a sudden turn for the worse."

"Yeah, Viktor, I can tell you're all broken up about it."

"You will leave next week."

"Next week? It's only been—I dunno—a couple days."

"When you fail to do your projects as scheduled, it throws off my own schedule. We must get back on schedule."

"Fine."

"Your documentation is at the front desk. You will fly to San Francisco next Tuesday, the eleventh."

"Tuesday the eleventh. Got it. Just one question."

"Yes?"

"What city am I in right now?"

"Newark."

Newark.

11.

After he ended the call with Viktor, he immediately dialed another number.

A clipped voice answered after three rings. "Aspen Meadows."

"Is Janna working today?"

"I'll connect you; one moment, please."

Evidently that was a yes.

A couple short clicks, and another voice came on the line. "Janna Schillinger," the voice said, and Stan felt inexplicable relief at hearing her voice.

"Hi, Janna," he said, hoping his voice sounded brighter than he felt.

"Stan," she said. "I'm guessing you've been thinking about that clinical trial."

"Huh?" he said, then remembered. "Oh, that. Well, no, I'm actually just calling to see . . . I mean, is she all right?"

"Just saw her at lunch. Same as it ever was. Can't get her to eat much of anything unless I sit there. Not that I'd want to eat much of this stuff myself."

He swallowed. "Okay, I just . . . wanted to check."

He heard a chair scrape, as if Janna had shifted in her seat a bit. "You got a pen?" she asked.

"Why?"

"I'm gonna give you a number."

"A number for what?"

Janna sighed. "I really think you need to look at this clinical trial. You're on the road, you can probably find a computer with a modem somewhere."

"Yeah, I suppose."

"I'm gonna give you the protocol number for this trial, and you can read about it. I just need an okay and . . . I can make everything happen."

Did he detect a bit of subtext in what she was saying? Once again, so hard to know. He sighed, unsure how to feel about Janna. He liked her, but she scared him.

"Okay," he said, pulling a pad of paper and a pen from the nightstand beside his hotel bed. "Give me the number."

He heard paper shuffling. "Okay, it's 159554—"

He felt his blood turning to ice. "534," he finished.

A slight pause on the line. "So you *have* been reading that information I sent you."

Stan ran a jittery hand through his hair, wishing for a couple more sleeping pills. Not just yet. The protocol number for the clinical trial was the number his mother had shakily written on a napkin. He stood, searched his pockets, came up empty: no napkin. But that was the number. He remembered it well. His whole body was numb, and he felt like a piece of fragile paper inside a Category 5 hurricane, powerless to stop the world whirling around him.

Still, wasn't this some kind of sign? Why else would his mother scribble that exact number on a napkin? It had to mean something, because there was no way it could mean nothing. Not in these circumstances.

"Okay, I'll do it," he said.

Janna seemed surprised, taken aback. Maybe for the first time in her life, he guessed.

"What?" she asked.

"The clinical trial. I'll sign her up for it."

She took a deep breath. "Okay, Stan. You'll need to send me the signed consent form."

"I think I have the papers you sent me," he said. And he did; they were in the single briefcase he carried from project to project.

"I can do . . . fax machine or something. From the hotel here."

"Okay, that will be good." She gave him a fax number, and he wrote it on the notepad.

After another pause, Janna spoke once more. "She'll be moved, Stan. To another facility. You understand that?"

"You said it before."

"Yes, I did. But I want to be sure you think about that, what it means."

He waited. "So what does it mean?"

"It means, I think, you'll be able to move too."

He smiled, hoping she wasn't a traitor. He had to put his trust in her now.

"Give me a couple days and call back," Janna said. "I'll have some more information for you." She hung up the phone without waiting for a response.

Stan listened to the dead air of the disconnected line before closing his cell phone again.

12.

After he picked up the package for his next assignment at the desk, he asked the clerk if she could fax a page for him.

"Certainly, sir," she said, taking the page from him. "I'll be back in a moment with a confirmation."

He waited, wondering why he felt nervous, until she returned with a printout confirming his signed acceptance form had been sent to Janna.

Stan thanked her and returned to his room to examine the contents of his new package.

The unsmiling visage of his own face stared blankly from his new passport. *KURT MARLOWE*, it said, and he immediately recognized the name from somewhere. He had known a Kurt Marlowe at some point. Not one of his assignments. Even though he received names and background information on each assignment, he never let himself commit any of it to long-term memory. Their faces already haunted him; it would be unbearable to be haunted by their names as well.

Wait. *Kurt Marlowe*. Yes. From P.S. 238. From his old school days. Hadn't he even had a dream about that kid recently? The sleeping pills formed a dull curtain of haze around most of his days, but he thought that yes, he did remember just such a dream.

Kurt, or Marlowe, if you were a Mr. Sherman kind of guy, was the kid who was always picked last in gym. The kid who was there when he killed Sherman. The kid who had said *You told him not to touch you.*

What a fitting summary of his life since. No one could touch him. Not since puberty, since his voice changed, specifically. Stan had figured out that much. His voice had squeaked, then shifted timbre to his lower, adult tone for a brief moment just before he touched Sherman and his Grandpa. His changing voice, his passage into adulthood, had somehow awakened this deadly power inside. When his voice changed, when he became a man, he became a monster who could kill people just by touching them.

(You got the dead blood in you, child)

Yes. Well. The voice from the woman at the hotel nailed that.

And now he had come full circle by becoming the weird kid who had unknowingly summed up Stan's entire adult life in just seven small words: *You told him not to touch you.*

The identities he received were always entirely fictional, he knew. But when you became a dozen different men in a year's time, there were bound to be some confluences with reality. But with the numbers from his mother, the touch and voice from the woman at the hotel, and now this reopened wound into his ancient past, he was experiencing a sudden torrent of unreality.

Occasionally, he faintly recognized names. Once or

twice, he had to smile at the black humor behind his identities. He'd been Jonathan Hinckley once, the same name as the man who shot John Lennon—but common enough not to raise too many eyebrows. He'd been William Clinton during the last presidential election; someone was evidently a fan of the outgoing president.

The identities were usually unimportant. They were rarely checked anywhere, since he always traveled in the United States. His boarding passes always carried his fake names, of course, but rare was the gate agent who actually looked at the name on any printed boarding pass.

It was easy—too easy, really—to be a ghost of the skies, a man with an ever-changing past and future.

Kurt Marlowe. Surely the man making his identities didn't have access to his past. He assumed it was a man; most people in the Organization were. No. Even if the guy knew his past, Kurt Marlowe would be a minor character. He wouldn't pick up on that.

Stan put the passport in his pocket, then glanced inside the accompanying folder. His cover this time: he was traveling to a truck driving school in Oakland, California. He smiled. Truck driver. Right. He folded the letter of acceptance from the HIGH ROAD TRUCK DRIVING SCHOOL and put it in his pocket with his passport.

Next item in the folder, some background information on the real reason he was traveling to Oakland: a man named Franklin, who looked like some kind of drug scum.

Finally, he looked at his forged boarding pass. He always wondered why the Organization booked him on commercial flights; it would be so much more efficient, it seemed, to charter them. Or maybe not. Maybe charters could be traced, whereas his ghost identities on more than a dozen flights each year were more invisible. Probably so. Which was why he was about to fly—he checked the ticket—United Airlines, leaving Newark, bound for San Francisco on September 11. Flight 93.

Kurt Marlowe was ready for the friendly skies.

13.

His driver's license and admission papers for the truck driving school tucked into the front of his jacket, Stan—or the newly minted Kurt Marlowe—handed his boarding pass to the gate agent. She tore off the top and handed back the stub without looking at him. Or the pass, for that matter. Same as it ever was.

He was a bit sorry to be leaving the Northeast in September, in the midst of the fall blooming all around him. Not that color meant that much to him, but it penetrated his senses occasionally. One of the few things. Hadn't even remembered where he was, and had to ask Viktor when he called.

He walked down the Jetway to board the plane, another giant 757 set to take him to the West Coast. He entered the jet, looking at his ticket. Row 5, which put him in first class. Odd; he'd never flown first class. His Mystery Travel Agent had given him an upgrade, which seemed a little . . . too visible.

He settled into the seat, tugging at the new money belt he'd bought to carry his extra cash. If he was going to stash the money from the Organization, he might as well be more, well, organized.

He closed his eyes as he waited for the other passengers to board. The upgrade didn't matter, of course. Nothing mattered.

Maybe it would matter even less in a few days, when his mother would be at another facility, taking part in a clinical trial, hidden away from the prying eyes of Viktor and the Organization. Could such a thing even be possible? His gut told him so, because his gut also told him Janna knew exactly what she was doing.

That would mean he'd be able to walk away, disappear like a true ghost. True, he'd have to plan carefully. And he probably wouldn't be able to contact his mother for a long time. Maybe a few years. He'd have to wait for his trail to go cold.

Yes, after this he would disappear. Somehow, he would think of a way to do it. Somehow he knew Fate, or God, or whatever, was going to show him a way.

He fished in his pocket, took out his prescription bottle,

shook a few tablets into his mouth. Wasn't sure whether it was the painkillers or the sleeping pills. Like it mattered. Either one, he hoped, would keep away the dreams that continued to haunt him. The old dreams of Sherman, of Grampa Mick. Of Kurt Marlowe. And the newest sensation on the dream scene: that woman in the hotel room. The one who had lived after his touch. The first and only person to do so since he'd become an adult. What did that mean?

Maybe most of all, the dreams of her needed to be quieted.

Some time later—couldn't have been more than a few minutes—he was jolted from a stupor by the sound of the flight attendants running through the obligatory safety check. He must have been dozing.

He sat up in his seat, noting that the plane was about half-full. The first-class seat next to him was empty, but both seats across the aisle had passengers.

Stan turned and looked at other passengers behind him, taking note of whom he saw. It wouldn't be unlike Viktor to send along someone to keep watch, especially after the . . . unfinished project.

He didn't spy anyone taking an unhealthy interest in him, although the guy behind him, in row 6 of first class, seemed nervous. Sweaty. Maybe afraid of flying.

He turned, thinking he could maybe take another sleeping pill. Or pain pill. Or whatever. No way he was afraid of flying.

A few minutes after everyone had boarded the plane, the pilot informed them their departure had been delayed.

No worries. No worries at all. Stan was already flying, thanks to the pills.

But the pills couldn't control his thoughts, occupied now by the woman in the hotel. Her hand tugging on his arm, pulling him to his knees. Her arms wrapped tight around her, her eyes staring at him in wonder.

She'd felt the touch, too, hadn't she? Something inside it had scared her as much as it had him. (You got the dead blood in you, child)

His eyes opened once more as his foggy brain made a connection it should have seen before. They had connected, he realized, because she carried a curse like him.

The Dead Blood, as her inner voice had told him. He most certainly was haunted by it, but she, in some fundamental way, was haunted by it as well. And so his touch had no effect on her.

Finally the plane began to roll. Stan checked his watch and was surprised to discover they'd been delayed more than forty minutes; maybe the drugs had made the time pass quickly for him. In a few minutes they were airborne, banking and turning west.

He let his lids flutter shut once more, concentrating on nothing, embracing the emptiness of the drugs in his system.

A scream woke him.

Stan's eyes sprang open. His vision swam in lazy circles a few moments. No worries; he was in a hotel room, surrounded by cool air and emptiness, stretched out on the cool sheets of the bed and—

Sobbing filtered through his consciousness. No, he wasn't in his hotel room. His vision came into focus, and he remembered: he was on a plane, bound for the West Coast. In the aisle, the flight attendant appeared; behind her, a man held a knife at her throat.

"Move to the back of the plane," the man hissed, staring at Stan.

Stan stood from his seat slowly. Eye contact seemed to make the man nervous, so Stan looked down as he moved into the aisle and toward the back of the plane. A few other people, five or six at the most, stumbled down the aisle ahead of him. At row 23, Stan turned and sat slowly, awkwardly, in a new seat. The rest of the passengers—a couple dozen at most—had all been pushed to this area at the back of the jet.

He looked up the aisle at a hijacker. That's what he was, wasn't he? Had to be.

As if to confirm, a voice came over the intercom. "Ladies and gentlemen: here the captain, please sit down keep remaining seating. We have bomb on board. So sit."

The voice spoke in a heavy accent, broken English. Like Viktor's brother, only more broken.

Stan tried to access his memory banks. From what he remembered, the captain hadn't spoken in broken English when they were sitting on the tarmac in Newark.

"That's not the captain," he heard someone hiss from behind him, as if to confirm his own thoughts.

He leaned into the aisle. Three men, all of them wearing red bandanas, had moved the rest of the passengers behind row 20. But now only one of the hijackers, wearing a red belt with wires sprouting from it, was visible.

Around him, other passengers chattered nervously. The drugs made it difficult for him to concentrate on individual voices, and they all coalesced into a constant din. As if they were voices of ghosts, speaking to him. Some of them cried, which was a sound he'd heard more than a few times on assignment. A few were on cell phones, or the air phones built into the plane's seats.

Above the babbles and sobs, another announcement blared over the intercom.

"Ah. Here the captain. I would like to tell you all remain seated. We have bomb aboard, and we are going back to airport. We have our demands. So, please remain quiet."

The English seemed marginally better this time; was it a different person speaking? Still not the captain, though.

His plane had been hijacked. Would Viktor orchestrate such a thing, to get back at him for the botched hit on his brother?

No. It made no sense. No sense at all. Even Viktor wouldn't go this far; the other passengers, the plane itself, were too much collateral damage. Too visible.

He turned and caught the eye of a man who had just hung up his cell phone.

The man said something, but Stan couldn't make out what it was.

"What?" he asked.

"I said, two planes just crashed into the World Trade Center." The man's face looked tired, gray.

For a few moments, the area around them went quiet and still. No more screaming. No more sobbing.

Outside, the thin atmosphere rumbled past their windows as the jet set its new course.

Another man crept up the aisle on his knees, leaning down to speak to them. Stan chanced another glance toward the front of the cabin, where the lone hijacker continued to clutch the neck of the flight attendant. That red belt couldn't really be a bomb. Stan was no explosives expert, but the belt wasn't very convincing.

"That's not a real bomb," the man in the aisle said. "We gotta do something." Crouching in the aisle, the man looked at each of them in turn. "We know what's happening here."

Stan nodded, swallowed hard, still trying to process it all. He looked at all the other scared faces of passengers around him, recognized the people across the aisle from row 5 in first class.

But Stan wasn't scared; he was a disinterested participant, a mile high on the plane and a mile high on the pills he'd popped before boarding the flight. Let the plane crash; he would welcome his personal slide into oblivion.

Wait. People from row 5 in first class. He sat up straight as the first numbers clicked into place. Three fives: him, and the two others in row 5.

"What row were you seated in?" he asked the man in the aisle.

The man looked at him, a puzzled look on his face. "Fifteen," he said.

Stan turned the numbers over in his mind. A fifteen and three fives. "Anyone from row 9?" he asked. A woman raised her hand.

"What about 44?" he asked.

A man behind him spoke. "Only thirty-four rows—I was in that one."

Stan closed his eyes. "Row 4?" he asked, then opened his eyes again. Two people raised their hands. He didn't recognize them, though they'd been in the row directly in front of him. Probably part of the haze created by the pain pills— a haze that had now burned away as all the numbers glowed in his mind: Fifteen. Nine. Five. Five. Four. Four. Five. Thirty-four.

1595544534.

The number on the napkin, once again. He hadn't seen the napkin since . . . since the woman in Seattle. But still, he knew the number. From somewhere else. He looked at the other passengers, and a strange sense of calm descended on him. Now it made sense. He was meant to do this; his mother had seen something, scribbled the mysterious numbers on the napkin as a warning. As a command to do something.

"I'm in," he said to the man in the aisle.

In answer, the man in the aisle held out his hand. Stan raised his own hand, his gloved, latexed hand, and shook.

"I'll lead the way," he said, beginning to peel the latex off his fingers. Like shedding an old skin.

"You sure?" the man asked.

"I'm sure."

"How we gonna get in the cockpit?" he asked.

Stan stopped, looked at the man. "No idea," he said.

From somewhere behind him he heard a man utter the words "You guys ready? Let's roll."

Stan rose, feeling the air rush around his face, feeling the wheels of the universe click into place, feeling whole for the first time in his life. The drugs had somehow sharpened his senses now, making him more alert, more aware.

He pushed down the aisle, feeling the plane shift. The man with the red belt screamed something unintelligible at him, but Stan merely smiled as he reached out with hands, hands now bare and exposed. The bomber swung his metal knife—

(not a knife, not a knife, a box cutter)

—at him, and Stan let the cutter bite into his bare skin, because with his other hand he grasped the man's bare arm, stopping the movement.

For a moment, the bomber looked into his eyes. Stan felt the current building inside, and then . . . nothing.

For the first time, Stan wanted the curse. And for the second time, it had failed.

The bomber struggled to break his grip, but Stan's body coursed with strength he'd never felt before. His fingers found the windpipe and blocked the man's air, his hands tight, unmoving.

Finally, the bomber collapsed.

Stan stared at his hands. Somehow, the curse had left him. At this, of all times. And yet, he felt . . . perfect. As if his whole life had been preparing him for this moment.

And in a way, it had.

Blood pouring from his cut hand, Stan stepped over the bomber's unmoving body, catching a glimpse of the wires on the man's belt. No way those wires would complete a circuit and detonate a bomb of any kind, even if—

Stan stopped, and the man behind him, the man in the aisle whose hand he had shaken, bumped into him.

A circuit. That was the explanation. When he had

touched the woman in the hotel room, he had felt the electrical connection. She had felt the electrical connection. But it wasn't the normal connection he usually felt; it was a short circuit. Both of them had the dead blood, the curse, which meant both of them were like positively charged batteries. Somehow, touching her, connecting with her dead blood, had killed his curse inside.

He smiled. And somehow he knew, the woman now had the napkin with the numbers on it. Someday, perhaps it would lift the curse from her.

Ahead of him he saw the door to the cockpit. Everything was falling into place so perfectly. He had escaped his curse. He could escape this existence. And his mother could escape her prison.

The numbers had led him here, and all he had to do was bust through the final doorway blocking his path.

The plane tilted hard to the left, then to the right. Behind him, Stan heard a few more screams from people being thrown around.

Chaos surrounded him. Two of the men who had followed him down the aisle had worked their way around him while he choked the fake bomber, and now they were pounding on the cockpit door. Finally the door cracked, coming off its hinges and gaping as the plane continued a hard roll. The air around smelled like blood and smoke, felt like hammers and knife blades, sounded like terror and destruction.

The door was fully open now, and Stan pushed his way toward it. As he came through, the man at the plane's controls turned, locking gazes. It was the one who had been sitting behind him in row 6, the one who seemed afraid of flying.

Now he seemed more afraid than ever. Anger flashed in the man's eyes, followed by terror as Stan grasped his shirt in his bare hands.

Stan understood his entire life for the first time. When his voice had changed, he hadn't become a man. He'd become a victim, because he'd let the curse take over everything about his life. He let it define him. He let it swallow him. He let it *become* him.

But ironically, that curse, with all of its pain and anguish, had brought him to this very moment in this very airplane on this very day.

He had seen the bait through the murkiness, and now he would rise for it. Perhaps he would die in the effort, burn in the flames like Grampa Mick's catfish etched forever in his mind, but for a few brief moments, he would never be more alive.

The fake pilot struggled to pull free, but Stan's hand became a vise; with his other hand, his right hand, he reached for the man's face, grabbing it by the jaw, feeling the bristling whiskers of the unshaved skin as he twisted the man's face toward him again.

He tightened his hands into a chokehold, smiling as the

man's eyes rolled back into his head, leaning down to whisper one word into the fake pilot's ear.

"Catfish."

14.

He awoke, the stench of fire and fuel in his nostrils. He opened his eyes to see a blue sky overhead, punctuated by thick, roiling smoke. Somewhere behind him, a monster roared.

Dazed, he sat up and looked at his surroundings. The roaring monster was a fire, a giant curtain of flame several yards away. Chunks of metal hung on smoking trees. Searing wind pushed the flames toward him. The panorama spun wildly for a few seconds, then steadied again. He lifted a bloody hand to his head, pushed himself to his knees, and stood. Immediately he fell again; neither of his legs wanted to work.

Hell burned around him.

He pushed himself to standing again, and his legs worked this time. He had no memory of what had happened—something horrible, certainly—but he had to get away. He began to walk, trying to ignore the wreckage around him.

Then he ran. Because he had to.

At last, lungs feeling as if they'd been dipped in rubbing

alcohol, he stopped to catch his breath and thoughts. He stood on a gravel road leading away from a barren field—the field where the fire had burned—to a dark thicket of trees.

He didn't want to, but he turned to look at the destruction behind him before he disappeared into the trees and concentrated a few moments on the pillar of black smoke rising to the heavens above. In the distance, the sound of alarms pierced the air around him.

He had no idea what had happened—had no idea, in fact, who he was or why he was here—but he knew, as he took in the scene of carnage, that it was important to keep moving forward. Like a shark. (Or a catfish?)

He felt a lump in his pocket and retrieved the items held there. A driver's license with his photo, from the state of New Jersey. Kurt Marlowe. The familiarity of the name struck him immediately. Yes, that had to be him. The license was wrapped in a sheet of paper indicating acceptance to a truck driving school in California.

He folded the paper back around the driver's license, slipped both into his pocket again, took one last look at the burning inferno, and turned to walk down the gravel path.

Behind him lay death and destruction, yes, but ahead of him, down this lonely gravel road, lay everything else.

And he would not look back again.

Acknowledgments

Special thanks to God, for helping me see the opportunities in every challenge; to my Lovely Wife and Lovely Daughter, for continuing to be lovely when I'm lost in schemes to torture characters in new and interesting ways; to Allen Arnold, Amanda Bostic, and the team at Thomas Nelson for planting the seeds that became the stories in this book; to editors Ed Stackler and LB Norton for helping those seeds take root and grow; to Lee Hough for his constant guidance (yeah, I had to give up that seed metaphor before it went too far); to Todd Michael Greene, for lending his name to Kurt's therapist; and to you, dear reader, for lending me a few hours of your time.

Words fueled by the music of Adele; Broken Social Scene; Fountains of Wayne; David Crowder Band; Peter Bjorn & John; Robbie Seay Band; Better Than Ezra; Clodhopper; Starfield; Sweet; Pixies; Future of Forestry; and Wilco; among many others.

Reading Group Guide

1. Why do you think the book is called *Faces in the Fire*? What are the "faces" the title references? What are the "fires"?

2. *Faces in the Fire* is told through a series of seemingly disjointed scenes that take place out of order. Why do you think the author chose this narrative technique? Did it add anything to the stories for you? Did it detract from the stories?

3. Scientists have described the human brain's tendency to identify patterns in seemingly unrelated data as "patternicity." In other words, we see faces in clouds, identify coded messages in long texts, and detect conspiracies tying together coincidences. Each of the main characters in *Faces in the Fire* exhibits patternicity by reading meaning into the number 1595544534—and yet, their paths are changed by their unique interpretations. Do you think their paths would have led to the same place if they hadn't come into contact with the numbers? Why or why not? Are there seemingly random events that have changed the course of your own life?

4. In the first story, Kurt seems haunted by anguished voices trapped inside articles of clothing. Despite this, Kurt actually seeks out new

articles of clothing, searching for more voices. Why do you think Kurt seems paradoxically driven to look for something that he wants to hide from himself?

5. Corrine, the main character in the second story, says she's proud to be a "bottom feeder." Judging by her behavior, would you agree that she's comfortable thinking of herself as a bottom feeder?

6. In the third story, when Grace's tattoos begin to offer her glimpses into the lives of her clients, she doesn't seem terrified; instead, she seems to gain a sense of purpose, and even begins to kick her heroin habit. Why do you think this is? What does it say about Grace as a character?

7. Stan, the main character in the final story, is fixated on the image of a catfish from his childhood. What do you think the catfish represents for him?

8. How are the main characters in each of the stories alike? How are they different? Do they change or grow as they interact with each other?

9. Do you think the paths of these characters may cross again at some point in the future? Why or why not?

10. If you asked each of the main characters at the beginning of their stories what they most want in life, what would their answers be? Would their answers be different at the end of their stories?

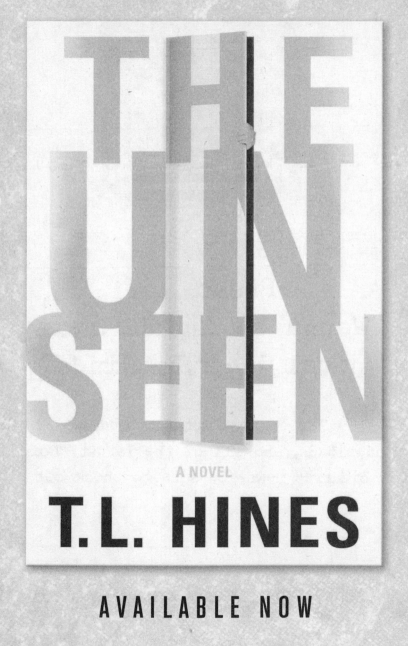

ALSO FROM T.L. HINES

THE
UN
SEEN

A NOVEL

T.L. HINES

AVAILABLE NOW

About the Author

T.L. Hines writes "Noir Bizarre" stories, mixing mysteries with oddities in books such as *The Unseen, Waking Lazarus,* and *The Dead Whisper On. Waking Lazarus* received Library Journal's "25 Best Genre Fiction Books of the Year" award.